THEN THERE WERE NUN

NUN OF YOUR BUSINESS MYSTERIES

DAKOTA CASSIDY

DAKOTA CASSIDY

Then There Were Nun (Book 1 Nun of Your Business Mysteries)

Copyright © 2018 by Dakota Cassidy

ISBN: 9781720113560

Imprint: Independently published

ACKNOWLEDGMENTS

Welcome to the Nun of Your Business Mysteries! I so hope you'll enjoy this first adventure for Trixie Lavender and her pal Coop, an ex-nun and a demon, respectively, just trying to make their way in the world —*together*.

Please note, I currently live in the beautiful state of Oregon, just outside of Portland. And though not a native (New Yorker here!), I've fallen in love over and over again with my new home state every day for the almost five years we've been here. That said, I've created a district (sort of like the Pearl District, for you natives) in a suburb of Portland that is totally fictional, called Cobbler Cove. You may recognize some of the places/streets/eateries I mention, but do keep in mind, I'm also flagrantly instituting my artistic license with the geography of gorgeous Portland to suit my own selfish needs. Any and all names for characters or groups mentioned herein are completely fictitious.

As I've mentioned in my previous cozy mysteries, there is an ongoing mystery surrounding Coop and Trixie that will play out over the course of the series (sorrysorrysorry!), but the central mystery in each story will be all wrapped up in a pretty package with a nice bow by book's end.

That out of the way, welcome to the crazy world Trixie and Coop inhabit. I hope you come to love them as much as I do!

Also, in gratitude to my amazing narrator, Hollie Jackson, who brings all of my indie projects to life in audio. Her voice is one part Mary Poppins, two parts Disney princess. In other words, sweet and sassy. As such, Trixie is written in her honor with much love.

To my editor, Kelli Collins, an owl lover, and the one responsible for suggesting Trixie and Coop's side-kick have an Irish accent. Quigley Livingston is for you!

And last, but never least, to Scott Preston Drummond, for the amazing series title after a fun post on Facebook. You rock!

Dakota Cassidy XXOO

THEN THERE WERE NUN

BY DAKOTA CASSIDY

CHAPTER 1

"So, Sister Trixie Lavender, how do we feel about this space? Open concept, with plenty of sprawling views of the crumbling sidewalk from the leaky picture window and easily room for eight tat chairs.

"Also, one half bathroom for customers, one full for us—which means we'd have to share, but there are worse things. A bedroom right up those sketchy stairs with a small loft, which BTW, I'm calling as mine now. I like to be up high for the best possible views when I survey our pending tattoo empire. A tiny kitchenette, but no big deal. I don't cook anyway, and *you* sure don't, if that horse pucky you called oatmeal is any indication of your culinary skills. Lots of peeling paint and crappy plumbing. All for the low-low price of...er, what was that price again, Fergus McDuff?"

Short and chubby, a balding Fergus McDuff, the

landlord of the current dive I was assessing as a candidate for our tattoo parlor, cringed and visibly shuddered beneath his limp blue suit.

Maybe because Coop had him up against a wall, holding him by the front of his shirt in white-knuckled fists as she waited for him to rethink the price he'd quoted us the moment he realized we were women.

Which was not only an outrageous amount of money for this dank, pile-of-rubble hole in the wall, but not at all the amount quoted to us over the phone. It also looked nothing like the picture from his Facebook page. I know that shouldn't surprise me. He'd probably used some Snapchat filter to brighten it up. But here we were.

A bead of perspiration popped out just above Fergus's thin upper lip.

Coop's dusky auburn hair curtained her face, but his stance remained firm. "Like I said, lady, it's three grand a month—"

Cutting his words off, Coop tightened her grip with a grunt and hauled Fergus higher. His pleading gray eyes darted from her to me and back again in unadulterated fear, but to his credit, he tried really hard not to show it.

Coop licked her lips, a low hum of a growl coming from her throat, her gaze intently focused on poor Fergus. "Can I kill him, Sister Trixie Lavender? Please, please, pleeeease?"

"*Coop*," I warned. She knew better than to ask such a question. "She's just joking, Fergus. Promise."

"But I'm not. Though, I promise I'll clean up afterward. It'll be like it never happened—"

"Two thousand!" Fergus shouted quite jarringly, as though the effort to push the words out pained him. "Wait, wait, wait! I meant to say two thousand a month with *all* utilities!"

That's my demon. Overbearing and intimidating as the day is long. Still, I frowned at her, pulling my knit cap down over my ears. While this behavior worked in our favor, it was still unacceptable.

We'd had a run-in with the law a few months ago back in Ebenezer Falls, Washington, where we'd first tried to set up a tattoo shop. Coop's edgy streak had almost landed her with a murder charge.

Since then (and before we landed in Eb Falls, by the by), we'd been traveling through the Pacific Northwest, making ends meet by selling my portrait sketches to people along the way, waiting until Coop's instincts choose the right place for us to call home.

Cobbler Cove struck just the right chord with her. And that's how we ended up here, with her breathing fire down Fergus McDuff's throat.

Coop, who'd caught on to my displeasure, smirked her beautiful smirk and set Fergus down with a gentle drop, brushing his trembling shoulder with a careful hand to smooth his wrinkled suit.

"That's nice. You're being nice, Fergus McDuff. I like you. Do you like me?"

"Coop?" I called from the other end of the room, going over some rough measurements for a countertop

in my mind. "Playtime's over, young lady. Let Mr. McDuff be, please."

She rolled her bright green eyes at me in petulance and wiped her hands down her burgundy leather pants, disappointment written all over her face that there'd be no killing today.

Coop huffed. "Fine."

I looked at her with my stern ex-nun's expression as a clear reminder to remember her manners. "Coop…"

She pouted before holding out her hand to Fergus, even though he outwardly cringed at the gesture. "It was nice to meet you, Fergus McDuff. I hope I'll see you again sometime soon," she said almost coquettishly, mostly following the guidelines I'd set forth for polite conversation with new acquaintances.

Fergus brushed her hand away, fear still on his face, and that was when I knew it was time for me to step in.

"You do realize she's just joking—about killing you and all, don't you? I would never let her do that," I joked, hoping he'd come along for the ride.

But he only nodded as Coop picked up his tie clip and handed it to him in a gesture of apology.

I smiled at her and nodded my head in approval, dropping my hands into the pockets of my puffy vest. "Okay, Fergus. Sold. Two grand a month and utilities it is. A year lease, right? Have a contract handy?"

Fergus nodded and scurried toward the front of the store to get his briefcase. It was then Coop leaned toward me and sniffed the air, her delicate nostrils flaring.

"This place smells right, Trixie Lavender. Yes, it does. Also, I like the name Peach Street. That sounds like a nice place to live."

I looked into her beautiful eyes—eyes so green and perfectly almond-shaped they made other women sick with jealousy—and smiled, feeling a sense of relief. "Ya think? You've got a good vibe about it then? Like the one you had in Ebenezer Falls before the bottom fell out?"

And you were accused of murder and our store was left in shambles?

I bit the inside of my cheek to keep from bringing up our last escapade in a suburb of Seattle, with an ex-witch turned medium named Stevie Cartwright and her dead spy turned ghost cohort, Winterbottom. It was still too fresh.

Coop rolled her tongue along the inside of her cheek and scanned the dark, mostly barren space with critical eyes. Any mention of Eb Falls, and Coop grew instantly sullen. "I miss Stevie Cartwright. She said she'd be my friend. Always-always."

My face softened into a smile. I missed Stevie and her ghost compatriot, too. Even though I couldn't actually hear Winterbottom—or Win, as she'd called him—Coop could, and from what she'd relayed to me, he sounded delightfully British and madly in love with Stevie.

Certainly an unrequited love, due to their circumstances—him being all the way up there on what they called Plane Limbo (where souls wait to decide if they wish to cross over)—and Stevie here on Earth, but they fit one another like gloves.

Stevie had been one of the best things to ever happen to me; Coop, too. She'd helped us in more ways than just solving a murder and keeping Coop from going to jail. She'd helped heal our hearts. She'd shown us what it meant to be part of a community. She'd helped us learn to trust not just our instincts, but to let the right people into our lives and openly enjoy their presence.

"Trixie? Do you think Stevie meant we'd always be friends?"

I winked at Coop. "She meant what she said, for sure. She always means what she says. If she said she'll always be your friend, you can count on it. And I miss Stevie, too, Coop. Bet she comes to visit us soon."

Coop almost smirked, which was her version of a smile—something we worked on every day. Facial expressions and body language humans most commonly use.

"Will she eat spaghetti with us?" she asked, referring to the last meal we'd shared with Stevie, when she'd invited her friends over and made us a part of not just her community, but her family.

"I bet she'll eat whatever we make. So anyway… We were talking the vibe here? It feels good to you?"

"Yep. I can tattoo here."

"Gosh, I hope so. We need to plant some roots, Coop. We need to begin again Finnegan."

We needed to find a sense of purpose after Washington, and this felt right. This suburb of Portland called the Cobbler Cove District felt right.

Tucking her waist-length hair behind her ear, Coop nodded her agreement with a vague pop of her lips, the wheels in her mind so obviously turning. "So we can grow and be a part of the community. So we can blend."

"Yes, blending is important. Now, about threatening Fergus…"

Her eyes narrowed on Fergus, who'd taken a phone call and busily paced the length of the front of the store. "He was lying, Trixie Lavender. Three grand wasn't what he said on the phone at all. No, it was not. I know what I heard. You said it's bad to lie. I was only following the rules, just like you told me I should if I wanted to stay here with you and other humans."

Bobbing my head to agree, I pinched her lean cheek with affection and smiled. "That's exactly what I said, Coop. *Exactly*. Good on you for finally listening to me after our millionth conversation about manners."

"Do I win a prize?"

I frowned as I leaned against the peeling yellow wall. I never knew where Coop was going in her head sometimes. She took many encounters, words, people, whatever, at face value. Almost the way a small child would—except this sometime-child had an incredible figure and a savage lust for blood if not carefully monitored.

"A prize, Coop?" I asked curiously, tucking my hands in the pockets of my jeans. "Explain your thinking, please."

She gazed at me in all seriousness as she quite visibly concentrated on her words. I watched her sweet, uncluttered mind put her thoughts together.

"Yep. A prize. I saw it the other day on a sign at the grocery store. The millionth shopper wins free groceries for a year. Do I get something for free after our millionth conversation?"

Laughter bubbled from my throat. Coop didn't just bring me endlessly sticky situations, she brought me endless laughter and, yes, even endless joy. She's simple, and I don't mean she's unintelligent.

I mean, sometimes she's so black and white, I find it hard to explain to her the many levels and nuances of appropriate reactions or emotions for any given situation, and that can tax me on occasion. But she's mine, and she'd saved my life, and I wasn't ever going to forget that.

And I do mean *ever*.

She'd tell you I'd saved *hers*, but that's just her innocent take on a situation that had been almost impossible until she'd shown up with her trusty sword.

I gazed up at the water-stained ceiling and thought about how to explain the complexities of mankind. I decided simple was best.

"Trixie? Do I get a prize?" she inquired again, her tone more insistent this time.

"No free groceries. Just my love and eternal grati-tude that you restrained yourself and didn't kill Fergus. He's not a bad man, Coop. And when I say *bad,* I mean the kind of bad who kicks puppies and pulls the wings off moths for sport. He's just trying to make his way in the world and get ahead. Just like everybody else. It might not be nice, but you can't kill him over it. Them's the rules, Demon."

"But he wasn't being fair, Sister Trixie Lavender."

"Remember what we discussed about my name?"

Now she frowned, the lines in her perfectly shaped forehead deepening. "Yes. I forgot—again. You're not a nun anymore and it isn't necessary to call you by your last name. You're just plain Trixie."

Plain Trixie was an understatement. Compared to Coop, Angelina Jolie was plain. My mousy, stick-straight reddish brown (all right, mostly brown) hair and plump thighs were no match for the sleek Coop-ster. But you couldn't be jealous of her for long because she had no idea how stunning she was, and that was because she didn't care.

"Right. I'm just Trixie. Just like Fergus isn't Fergus McDuff. He's just plain old Fergus, if he allows you to call him by his first name, or Mr. McDuff if he prefers the more formal way to address someone. And I'm not a nun anymore. That's also absolutely right."

My heart shivered with a pang of sadness at that, but I'm finally able to say that out loud now and actu-ally feel comfortable doing so.

I wasn't a nun anymore, and I'm truly, deeply at peace with the notion. My faith had become a bone of contention for me long before I'd exited the convent, so it was probably better I'd ended up being kicked out on my ear any ol' way.

In fact, I often wonder if it hadn't *always* been a bone of contention for the entire fifteen years I'd lived there. I'd always questioned some of the rules.

I'd never wanted to enter the convent to begin with —my parents put me there when they could no longer handle my teenage substance abuse. They'd left me in the capable, nurturing hands of my mother's dear friend, Sister Alice Catherine.

But after I'd kicked my drug habit, and decided to take my vows in gratitude for all the nuns of Saint Aloysius By The Sea had done for me, I came to love the thick stone walls, the soft hum and tinkle of wind chimes, and the structure of timely prayer.

They'd saved me from my addiction. In their esteemed honor, I wanted to save people, too. What better way to do so than becoming a nun in dedicated service to the man upstairs?

Though, I can promise you, I didn't want to leave the convent the way I did. A graceful exit would have been my preferred avenue of departure.

Instead, I left by way of possession. Yes. I said *possession*. An ugly, fiery, gaping-black-mouthed, demonic possession. I know that's a lot of adjectives, but it best describes what wormed its way inside me on that awful, horrible night.

"Are you sad now, Trixie? Did I make you sad because you aren't a nun anymore?" Coop asked, very clearly worried she'd displeased me—which did happen from time to time.

For instance, when she threatened to kill anyone who even looked cross-eyed at me—sometimes if they just breathed the wrong way.

I had to remind myself often, it was out of the goodness of her heart she'd nearly severed a careless driver's head when he'd encroached on our pedestrian right of way (the pedestrian always has the right of way in Portland, in case you were wondering). Or lopped off a man's fingers with a nearby butter knife for grazing my backside by accident while we were in a questionable bar.

Still, even while Coop's emotions ruled her actions without any tempered, well-thought-out responses, she was a sparkling diamond in the rough, a veritable sponge, waiting to soak up all available knowledge.

I tugged at a lock of her silky hair, shaking off the memory of that night. "How can I be sad if I have you, Coop DeVille?"

She grimaced—my feisty, compulsive, loveable demon grimaced—which is her second version of a smile (again, she's still practicing smiling. There's not much to smile about in Hell, I suppose) and patted my cheek—just like I'd taught her. "Good."

"So, do you think you're up to the task of some remodeling? This place is kind of a mess."

Actually, it was a disaster. Everything was crumbling. From the bathroom that looked as though it hadn't been cleaned since the last century, to the peeling walls and yellowed linoleum with holes all throughout the store.

Her expression went thoughtful as she cracked her knuckles. "That means painting and using a hammer, right?"

I brushed my hands together and adjusted my scarf. "Yep. That's what that means, Coop."

"Then no. I don't want to do that."

I barked a laugh, scaring Fergus, who was busily rifling through his briefcase, looking for the contract I'm now positive changes with the applicant's gender.

"Tough petunias. We're in this together, Demon-San. That means the good, the bad, and the renovation of this place. If you want to start tattooing again, we can't have customers subjected to this chaos, can we? Who'd feel comfortable getting a tattoo in a mess like this?"

I pointed to the pile of old pizza boxes and crushed beer cans in the corner where I hoped we'd be able to build a cashier's counter.

Coop's sigh was loud enough to ensure I'd hear it as she let her shoulders slump. "You're right, Sis...um, *Trixie*. We have to have a sterile environment to make tattoos. The Oregon laws say so. I read them, you know. On the laptop. I read them *all*."

As I said, Coop's a veritable sponge, which almost makes up for her lack of emotional control.

Almost.

I patted her shoulder as it poked out of her off-the-shoulder T-shirt, the shoulder with a tattoo of an angel in all its magnificently winged glory. A tattoo she'd drawn and inked herself while deep in the bowels of Hell.

"I'm proud of you. I'm going to need all the help I can get so we can get our license to open ASAP. We need to start making some money, Coop. We don't have much left of the money Sister Mary Ignatius gave us, and we definitely can't live on our charm alone."

"So I've been useful?"

"You're more than useful, Coop. You're my right-hand man. Er, woman."

She grinned, and it was when she grinned like this, when her gorgeously crafted face lit up, I grew more certain she understood how dear a friend she was to me. "Good."

"Okay, so let's go sign our lives away—"

"No!" she whisper-yelled, gripping my wrist with the strength of ten men, her face twisted in fear. "Don't do that, Trixie Lavender! You know what happens when you do that. Nothing is as it seems when you do that!"

I forced myself not to wince when I pried her fingers from my wrist. Sometimes, Coop didn't know her own demonic strength. "Easy, Coop. I need my skin," I teased.

In an instant, she dropped her hands to her sides

and shoved them into the pockets of her pants, her expression contrite. "My apologies. But you know I have triggers. That's what you called them, right? When I get upset and anxious, that's a trigger. Signing your life away is one of them. We have to be careful with our words. You said so yourself."

She was right. I'd poorly worded my intent, forgetting her fears about the devil and Hell's shoddy bargains for your soul.

As the rain pounded the roof, I measured my words and tried to make light of the situation. "It's just a saying we use here, Coop. It means we're giving everything we have to Fergus McDuff on a wing and a prayer at this point. But it doesn't mean I'm giving up my soul to the devil. I promise. My soul's staying put."

At least I thought it was. I could be wrong after my showdown with an evil spirit, but it felt like it was still there. I still had empathy for others. I still knew right from wrong—even if all those morals went directly out the window when the evil spirit took over.

Coop inhaled and exhaled before she squared her perfectly proportioned shoulders. "Okay. Then let's go," she paused, frowning, "sign our lives away to Fergus McDuff." Then she smirked, clearly meaning she understood what I'd said.

Our path to Fergus slowed when Coop paused and put a hand on my arm, setting me behind her. There was a commotion of some kind occurring just outside our door on the sidewalk, between Fergus and another man.

A dark-haired man with olive skin stretched tightly over his jaw and sleeve tattoos on both arms yelled down at Fergus, who, after Coop, had probably had enough of being under fire for today. But holy crow, this guy was angry.

He waved those muscular arms—attached to lean hands with long fingers—around in the air as the rain pelted his sleek head. His T-shirt stretched over his muscles as he gestured over his shoulder, and his voice, even muffled, boomed along our tiny street.

I couldn't make out what they were saying, but it didn't look like a very friendly exchange—not judging by the man's face, which, when it wasn't screwed up in anger, was quite handsome.

Yet, Fergus, clearly at his breaking point after his encounter with Coop, reared up in the gentleman's face and yelled right back. But then a taller, leaner, sandy-haired man approached and put a hand on the handsome man's shoulder, encouraging him to turn around.

That gave Fergus the opportunity to push his way past the big man and grab the handle of our door, stepping back inside the store with a bluster of huffs and grunts.

Coop sniffed the air. She can sometimes smell things the rest of us can't. It's hard to explain, but as an example, she smelled that our friend Stevie isn't entirely human. She's a witch. Or she was. Now, since her accident, she only has some residual powers left.

But Coop had smelled her paranormal nature

somehow—which, by definition, is crazy incredible and something I can't dwell on for long, for fear I'll get lost in the madness that demons and Hell and witches and other assorted ghouls are quite real.

"The man outside is not paranormal. He's just normal, as is the other man, and Fergus, too. If you were wondering."

I popped my lips in Coop's direction. "Good to know. I mean, what if he was some crazy hybrid of a vampire who can run around in daylight? Then what? We'd have to keep our veins covered or he might suck us dry."

Coop gave me her most serious expression and sucked in her cheeks. "I already told you, you don't ever have to worry anyone will hurt you. I'll kill them and then they'll be dead."

Ba-dump-bump.

"And I told *you*, no killing." Then I giggled and wrapped an arm around her shoulder, steering her past the debris on the floor and toward a grumpy Fergus, feeling better than I had in weeks. We had a purpose. We had a mission. Above all, we had hope.

We were going to open Inkerbelle's Tattoos and Piercings. I'd pierce and design tattoos, and Coop would handle the rest. We'd hopefully hire a staff of more artists as gifted as Coop. If the universe saw fit, that is.

And then maybe we'd finally have a place to call home. Where I could nest, and Coop could ink to her heart's desire in her tireless effort to protect every single future client from demonic harm with her special brand of magic ink.

During her life under Satan's rule, Coop had tattooed all new entries into Hell. She'd been so good at it, the devil left her in charge of every incoming sinner. But it was a job she'd despised, and she eventually escaped the night she'd saved me.

Lastly, I'd also try to come to terms with my new status in this world—my new freedom to openly share my views on how to get through this life with a solid code of ethics. Oh, and by the way, it has more to do with being the best person you can, rather than putting the fear of scripture quotes and fire and brimstone into non-believers.

I don't care if you believe. I know that sounds crazy coming from an ex-nun once deeply immersed in a convent and yards and yards of scripture. But I don't. You don't have to believe in an unseen entity if you so choose.

But I do care deeply about the world as a whole, and showing, not telling people you can live your life richly, fully, without ever stepping inside the hallowed halls of a church if you decide that's what works for you.

I want anyone who'll listen to know you can indeed have a life worth living—even as a low-level demon escaped from Hell and an ex-communicated nun who suffers from what Coop and I jokingly call demoniphrenia.

Also known as, the occasional possession of an ex-nun cursed by a random evil spirit.

And I was determined to prove that—not only to myself, but to this spirit who had me in its greasy black clutches.

CHAPTER 2

"*S*ister Trixie Lavender?"

I sighed, wiping the sweat from my brow. It was a rainy early June day in Cobbler Cove. And the shop was stuffy and damp, a climate you'd think I'd be used to coming from a convent on the Oregon coast made primarily of stone.

But instead, I was annoyed, and I didn't even try to hide it.

I threw my hands up, my aggravation at DEFCON proportions. Since we'd signed this lease yesterday, anything and everything had gone kaplooey.

I mean gone to utter and total garbage. The stairs to our living quarters had decided to give way, leaving us without a path to the upper landing—which put you right in the kitchen as you entered. Because of the damage, we had to jump from the top stair into the kitchen, which could be funny if you hadn't been a very athletic nun, choosing to read and ponder introspectively rather than run laps.

The bathroom sink—a disgusting mess of rust with some kind of gunk in every corner I don't have enough descriptive words for—had fallen off the wall from the pressure of a water pipe bursting. Spots in the floor were rotting right down to the plywood beneath, and it didn't help that the ceiling was leaking in not two, but four different locations.

We'd spent the night in a cheap motel, plotting and planning our new venture after signing the lease yesterday. Today, we'd come to assess what we were faced with—and what we were faced with was an "as is" situation. Apparently, even as much of a disaster as this place was, it was considered prime real estate, and Fergus McDuff had made it abundantly clear we were renting at our own risk.

Counting to ten, I prayed for patience. I didn't want to snap at Coop, but I'll admit, I had to clench my teeth to keep from doing so. It wasn't her fault everything about this place we were convinced we could turn into a tattoo parlor was beyond a fixer-upper. It made me long for the cute shop we'd had so briefly in Washington, and for our friends Stevie, Belfry, Arkady, and Winterbottom.

"Um, Trixie?" Coop said again.

I looked up to find her with a bucket hooked at her elbow, sponge in hand, and a frown on her exquisitely proportioned face.

"What's up now, Coop?"

"Where did Mr. Knuckles go?"

I almost burst out laughing. Knuckles—or Donald P. Ledbetter, according to his application—was a burly man of, were I to guess, six foot three, easily three hundred portly pounds, and a gentleman of very few words.

When he'd seen us from our grimy picture window, wobbling in our attempt to hang up our new sign, he'd strode into the store, his sleeve tattoos brilliant and intricate, and immediately stuck out a beefy hand to introduce himself.

As he approached me, I remember thinking he looked typically Oregonian, with his ratty but clean T-shirt, three silver studs above his left eyebrow, a nose ring fit for a bull, with graying chestnut-brown hair buzzed at the sides and the longish top brushed casually to the side. His face was round, his eyes wide and clear blue and, above all, friendly.

He reminded me of what a Portland version of Santa Claus would look like. All beards and laid-back T-shirts with peace signs on them.

He'd stomped toward me as though I owed him money and introduced himself as Knuckles, the best tattooist in the Pacific Northwest. Then he'd just stared at me, seemingly unmoved by Coop or her ethereal beauty when she'd come to stand next to me in protective mode. Because you know, he was a stranger, and Coop was ultra wary of all strangers.

I'd stuck my hand out and introduced myself, and after he'd swallowed my fingers in his wide grip, he'd pulled a photo album of his portfolio from under his arm and opened it without speaking a word.

I wasn't ready to hire anyone just yet or even consider renting the spaces. I wasn't even ready to trust we could walk across the floor without falling in, but I found myself popping open the black vinyl album anyway and perusing while Coop looked over my shoulder.

She'd pointed a slender finger at one particular tat of a fully opened rose sprouting from a woman's belly button, so multi-faceted and layered, it had taken my breath away.

Coop's, too, because she'd muttered, "Well done." Which was indeed high praise coming from the Coop-ster. Then she'd paused in thought for a moment. "Do you think that thing on his face requires a lot of conditioner?" she whispered.

I laughed at her, tugging my T-shirt down over my hips. "You mean his beard? I don't know, but he has enough hair on his chin to make a bald man weep," I whispered back.

"I love conditioner. We didn't have that in Hell," she'd informed me in her matter-of-fact way before returning to her work, leaving me alone with Knuckles.

He looked at me with his intense blue eyes and said, "Bathroom? May I?"

"If you could call it that—in the back to the right. But I warn you, it's worse than a Porta Potty at a toxic waste site on a hot July day."

He nodded and waved a meaty hand dismissively at me as though smelly Porta Potties were no sweat and went off to the back to use the bathroom. And that was the last I'd heard from him as I went back to pulling up more flooring.

Now, when I looked at Coop, her hair up in a messy bun, her cheeks heightened by a splotch of crimson, I had to wonder. Where *had* Knuckles gone? And why was he called Knuckles, anyway? Donald was a nice enough name. Did tattoo artists go by pseudonyms? Oh, dear. I had so much to learn...

Pushing the bandana I wore up on my forehead, I frowned. "He asked to use the bathroom. I don't know where he went. Maybe I'd better check."

As I rose, pulling my gloves off, Coop grabbed a hammer and held it up—which meant look out; she'd clobber first, ask questions later. At least it wasn't her sword. I'd managed to convince her the fine people of Cobbler Cove wouldn't appreciate that weapon of shiny menace waved under their noses.

I shook my finger at her. "Coop, I don't think we're going to need a hammer for this. Simmer down, Terminator."

"I'm not a Terminator. That's a specific breed of demon. I only terminated when threatened," she said, letting the hammer swing at her side.

I shook my head. "That's not what I meant. It was a movie…" Then I flapped a hand in the air. "Never mind. Regardless, we don't know if he's a threat yet, Coop."

Still, her eyes narrowed, glittering and brilliant green. "What if he's stealing our things?"

Sighing, I asked, "Like what? Our Hibachi grill and my underwear? Don't be silly, Coop. We don't have much to steal. We haven't even unloaded the car yet, and the rest of the stuff Stevie so kindly sent via UPS won't be here until tomorrow. And you can't hit him in the head with a hammer for it, anyway. You must always ask before you rush to judgment, Coop, unless catching someone in the act, of course. And even then, violence isn't always the answer."

She looked at me pensively, twisting a stray lock of hair around her finger. "Gosh. All these rules. I was only going to hit him in the knees."

As the rain pummeled the roof and slid through the holes in the ceiling, I grimaced. "Put the hammer away, Coop. We'll be fine." Brushing past her, I went down the long, narrow hallway leading to our dink of a filthy bathroom and knocked on the warped door. "Knuckles?"

When no sound came from the bathroom, my heart skipped a beat. "Um, Mr. Ledbetter? Are you okay?"

"I'm here." Knuckles's hoarse whisper came from near the dark exit door at the very end of the hall, his gravelly voice sounding odd.

Coop was behind me in an instant, a protective hand on my shoulder, her steady breathing in my ear and, as seen from the corner of my eye, the hammer held high in the air.

I hated thinking about why Coop was so quick to assume the worst. To always be on guard the way she was had to be exhausting.

But I suppose she'd been in Hell for a very long time. Likely, she'd seen things. Horrible things—things I hoped one day she'd talk to me about. Horrible things I prayed hadn't happened to her personally. But I never asked. Not yet. Not until she was ready.

"Coop," I soothed, feeling slightly hesitant now myself. "Slow that roll. No violence. Remember?"

"I'm just keeping my options open. Stevie said always be prepared. I'm only preparing."

I patted the hand she'd placed on my shoulder and tried to remain calm. "Knuckles, what are you doing back there?"

I still couldn't see him clearly, which reminded me we needed to replace that dangling light bulb above the exit door tout de suite.

I heard him clear his throat, and then I finally saw the outline of his bear-like body just before I heard Coop take a whiff of air.

"I smell something familiar," she whispered in my ear, her voice laced with what I had to guess was fear. A rarity, as Coop is so emotionless—even when she's ecstatic.

I froze and sniffed, too, but I didn't smell anything except for damp air and possibly some mold. Yet, Coop's sense of smell, be it chicken and waffles or an emotion like fear, was fierce, and that scared me.

"Familiar? Familiar from where?"

"Hell." She offered the answer with the kind of nonchalance one offers when asked if they'd like ketchup with their fries.

Yikes.

But I couldn't dillydally with what Hell smelled like right now.

"Knuckles?" I called again, though this time my voice sounded shaky to my ears.

So, here's the score. I'm no chickety-chicken, as Coop sometimes calls me when referring to my trepidation about bridges (and parallel parking, if you must know), but I also don't have the strength of ten linebackers on steroids the way Coop does.

Well, not unless I'm in the height of possession, that is. If you listen to my demon tell the story, then I'm like an entire pro football team gone rabid *and* on steroids.

Either way, Knuckles is a big guy. Enormous. He outweighs me by at least a hundred and fifty pounds.

Yes. I weigh a hundred and fifty pounds, okay? Portland is a Mecca for delicious food. From food trucks to gourmet dining, and sometimes I stress eat, as I did last night at this insanely amazing place called Pine State Biscuits. Oh, angel wings and the Pearly Gates, it had to be one of the most scrumptious meals I've ever had the pleasure of eating. Crispy fried chicken breast smothered in cheese on a soft, doughy biscuit, slathered in sausage gravy...

Anyway, back to Knuckles. Maybe he wasn't so much a teddy bear as a grizzly and Coop was right to be suspicious. Though, he was older than me by at least twenty years. Maybe I could take him if I was spry enough.

"Knuckles?" Coop called out.

"Don't come back here!" Knuckles suddenly shouted, his voice gruff and commanding. "This isn't something nice girls like you two should see."

Aw, grapes of wrath. I wasn't sure how to process that warning. I haven't experienced life outside the convent the way most thirty-two-year-olds have, if you know what I mean. So who the frick-frack knew *what* he was seeing?

A shiver skittered up my spine, much like the one I get just before the evil spirit who shall not be named possesses me.

Hellfire and cabbage. What was Knuckles seeing that ladies like us shouldn't see?

I inched a bit closer with Coop hot on my heels. "Is someone in a state of undress, Knuckles?" I squeaked.

Coop clucked her tongue in aggravation. "What sort of question is that, Sister Trixie Lavender?" Then she scratched her head. "Um, I mean Trixie. Just plain Trixie."

I turned around to face her, flustered, my total calm gone the way of hair scrunchies and Beanie Babies. "I don't know, Coop! He said ladies shouldn't see whatever it is he's seeing. It was the first thing that came to mind as un-seeable goes."

She made a face at me, sucking in her supermodel cheeks before letting the hammer dangle at her side again. "There are a million things that come to mind, and they have nothing to do with your born day suit."

"Birthday," I corrected. "It's birthday suit."

Coop cocked her head, nodding in concession. "That does sound much better."

We must have moved forward while we debated nudity because Knuckles shouted again, "Ladies! Please stay where you are! I insist!"

"Is Knuckle's mansplaining, Trixie? That word's definition always confuses me. But I like it so much. My tongue likes it, too."

"Not quite. It's more like he's trying to protect us, Coop," I said, patting her on the arm.

And I'd had enough protection. We had work to do —heaven above, so much work. So, I rushed forward toward the sound of his voice, just as Coop grabbed at my arm to prevent me from going any farther.

Which was fortunate.

If she hadn't, I would have tripped over the body— possibly slipped in the wide pool of crimson blood seeping along the floor—and landed square on my rear end.

We both gasped as our eyes adjusted to the dark hallway, where Knuckles stood over the lifeless body of none other than Fergus McDuff.

"Blood," Coop muttered as she pulled me away from Fergus's body. "Yup."

Swallowing hard, I clenched my fists together and asked a question to keep from screaming my horror. "Yup, what?"

"Yup. I told you I smelled Hell."

CHAPTER 3

*K*nuckles held a thick hand up as he pulled his cell phone from his pocket. His expression remained as flat and unblinking as it had been when he'd introduced himself.

"We need to call the police," he stated, his deep voice somber.

Coop instantly stiffened, and I can't say as I blame her. This wasn't the first, but the *second* landlord who'd ended up dead in a store we'd rented. Like I said earlier, Coop had been *this close* to landing in jail for the murder of our last landlord, Hank Morrison. There but for the grace of Stevie Cartwright, who'd doggedly pursued justice for Coop and had almost gotten herself killed in the process, she'd have been charged with murder.

But I'd learned a thing or two about solving a murder from our friends Stevie and Win during that mess. Stevie especially loved a good mystery, and because that drama involved us directly, when we were a safe distance from it, I found I loved a good mystery, too.

Since we'd left Stevie and Ebenezer Falls, I'd read more than a dozen of them at night under my covers so as not to bother Livingston (our yappy, opinionated but beloved owl. I'll get to him later), with my flashlight as my guide.

Anyway, I'd learned the police weren't always on your side, and I'm sure that's what Coop's afraid of at this very moment. They'd hauled her off to the police station and questioned her for six solid hours that horrible day.

That alone had been terrifying for someone who'd only been here on Earth a short time and had no last name until Winterbottom's connection had concocted an ID and life history for her. Add a fight to the death with an angry couple of killers then top that with almost seeing our newfound friend killed, too, and Coop had every right to be tense.

Now I put her protectively behind *my* back as I paid close attention to not just Knuckles, but the scene of the crime. During the week we'd spent with Stevie, her assortment of otherworldly friends and eclectic pets, she'd taught me some of the things she looks for when a mystery needed solving.

One of them is to always look at *everything*—every detail of the crime scene—and take pictures if you can get away with it before the police come.

As Knuckles dialed 9-1-1, I turned to Coop. "Listen

to me, Coop," I whispered, my tone urgent. "Have you been studying the birth certificate and ID Win had made for you? You'll need them for the police."

She nodded solemnly, her green eyes flitting from Fergus's body to my face. When given a task, Coop was on it, and she didn't get off it until she'd mastered said task. I expected this task would be handled with nothing less than her ardent studiousness.

"My name is Cooper O'Shea, Coop for short. I come from a small town in Michigan called Sturgis. I'm thirty-two years old and five-feet-ten-inches tall. I weigh one hundred and thirty-five pounds and Stevie says that's why people are jealous of me. I don't understand jealousy unless it pertains to coveting an item. I'm not an item. But I love Stevie, and I believe she speaks the truth always. I live with my best friend, Trixie Lavender, and we own a tattoo shop called Inkerbelle's. My social security number is—"

My hand flipped upward to stop her. "Good girl. I'm so proud of you. Remember that when the police ask you, okay? But *only* answer the questions they ask. Don't volunteer any information. *None.*"

But Coop, normally unruffled, was ruffled. I saw it all over her face as her eyes skittered about the hall, even if outwardly, she appeared emotionless. "I don't like the police, Trixie. They don't like me, either."

This was a fine line I was walking when it came to Coop and authority. I didn't want her to be fearful of every police officer, but I did want her to know her

rights and be cautious because she was indeed innocent and easily led.

"That's not true, Coop. The police just didn't know
you yet. Remember Stevie's friend Dana Nelson? He
liked you just fine, didn't he? He sat right next to you
on spaghetti night at her house before we left."

She did that weird smirk of a smile that left her eyes
squinting and her lips in an awkward tilt upward so
she showed some teeth, and nodded. "Yes. He was very
nice. He gave me his last meatball. I love, love, love
meatballs," she crooned in her odd, almost detached
way.

"Right!" I agreed. "Well, he's a police officer, and he
was just doing his job, Coop. Sometimes that's just the
way the cookie crumbles for guys like him. He didn't
believe you were guilty, but he had to do what his boss
at the police station told him to do."

She frowned, the lines in her gorgeous face wrinkling. "He didn't give me cookies. I like cookies, too.
Did he have cookies?"

"No. It's just an—"

"Expression," she finished for me. "Humans are
stupid with their words. Except Stevie. She's not
stupid. And you. You're not stupid, either. But
Livingston definitely is sometimes."

Blowing out a breath, I forced myself to stay
focused. These next minutes were crucial, according to
Stevie. As Knuckles began to wander while he was on
the phone with 9-1-1, I eyeballed Fergus McDuff's
body, splayed out on the floor at my feet, and remem-

bered the last time we'd done this. I didn't want to get so lost in the chaos this time.

And speaking of Livingston... "Coop, while Knuckles calls the police, would you go check on Livingston for me, please? We don't want another disaster like the last one, where he was left for hours without food, do we?"

Livingston is a demon just like Coop, but he didn't leave Hell unscathed. He's also her dearest friend from Hell. Except, when he escaped with her, because he didn't have a body to inhabit the way Coop did, he needed a vessel. And unlike Coop, he was forced to inhabit the first body he came upon in order to remain here on Earth.

Which happened to be a dead owl on the side of the road.

When he complains, we remind him his fate could have been plenty worse, as far as roadkill goes. He could have landed in the body of an opossum or a skunk or worse, a snake.

Coop's expression was one of distaste when she wrinkled her nose. "Aye, lass," she said, mimicking Livingston's Irish accent to perfection. "We can't have the wee bairn goin' on and on about how we starve him to death and the only ting standin' 'tween him and death's door was the last cupcake he stole right out from under my nose, can we?"

I almost laughed at her accurate description of Livingston's very dramatic take on just about every-thing—especially food—but then I remembered there was a dead man on our store's floor and, even if he wasn't the nicest man on the planet, he didn't deserve to die because he was surly. Respect was owed.

"Yes, that. So please go check and see if he's still sleeping in his cage, would you?"

Coop saluted me like she'd seen a character on *Hogan's Heroes* do, one of her favorite new earthly addictions. "I'm on it."

Left alone with Fergus's body, I sighed and sent up a small prayer for his soul.

Habit? Maybe, no pun intended. But mostly, I liked believing there was someone out there looking out for all of us. Real or imagined, I needed that image in my mind to console me in my darkest hours. Hell certainly exists. I can attest to that. Coop can, too. So why not Heaven?

Someday, I wanted to sit and have a long chat with Coop about its existence. I know she'd be open to answering my questions. I simply wasn't ready for the hardcore truth, and my deep-rooted fear it would vary greatly from the solace I took in what I'd always believed—still mostly believed.

Either way, the dead body didn't frighten me. I'd seen plenty of them in my time as a nun when families sought aid and counseling from the convent. What frightened me was how this had happened—*again*. I was beginning to feel as though we were a real pox on surly landlords.

Rooting around in the back pocket of my jeans, I pulled out my cell, turned on the flashlight app, and began to take pictures as discreetly as I could so as not to catch Knuckles's attention. I didn't want him to think me some sort of murder groupie.

As I snapped away, sometimes quite haphazardly, and I listened to the low hum of Knuckles's voice on the phone, I gave a critical look to Fergus and the surrounding area near his body.

He'd clearly been hit on the head, judging by the size of the blood pooled underneath his skull. In fact, what little hair he possessed had begun to dry and mat in spots from the blood, meaning this had happened before we'd arrived at the store. But how long before?

Which begged the question, why had he been at the store when we weren't, in the first place? We'd tied up everything yesterday and he'd left us with this mess. Had it happened while we were at the motel last night? While we had dinner? Early this morning while we were showering and preparing for our day?

I didn't know how to judge times of death, but I'd certainly text Stevie and ask. Though, I was betting it had happened last night. He was still wearing the same blue suit he had on when we'd met him here at the store, and to be frank, he looked rather stiff.

I took as many pictures as I could, just the way Stevie had when Hank Morrison had been killed, all the while wondering who would want Fergus McDuff dead?

That's when I noticed the angry red scratch marks on Fergus's neck, right under his second chin and along the column of his throat.

Leaning in a bit closer, I realized they weren't scratch marks at all. They looked intentional. He certainly hadn't had those marks on his neck yesterday. I'm positive of that much.

Still, how odd. Was this some kind of serial killer's work? Didn't serial killers all have some kind of calling card? Could that be what the marks represented? And what the fiddle-faddle *was* that mark? But I didn't have time to examine further. The police were going to be here any second, and it wouldn't do to be caught hovering around a corpse.

I shivered at that word, not as curious now as I was frightened.

Then, in a rush of recollection, I remembered the good-looking man Fergus had argued with yesterday just outside the store and made a mental note to tell the police about him. Who was he, and was he the man responsible for this? He'd sure been angry yesterday— so angry, that other man had pulled him away from his conversation.

As Knuckles's voice grew closer again, I pushed my phone into my back pocket. I had no business getting involved in this. Stevie had Win, and he was an ex-spy. He knew what he was doing. I was an ex-nun, for pity's sake, and about as far away from a spy as one can get. I truly needed to stop playing Nancy Drew and pay closer attention to this pickle we were in.

And were we ever in a pickle. How could we hope to renovate a store if it had turned into a crime scene? When this happened back in Ebenezer Falls, they'd locked us out of our freshly rented space. We couldn't afford to have this happen again.

Then guilt washed over me in a tidal wave of remorse. I shouldn't be thinking of anything other than this poor man's death, and shame on me for doing everything but.

Knuckles came into view, taking my mind off my worries, his enormous body lumbering its way to the back of the store with the phone pressed to his ear.

In the distance, I heard official voices and took a deep breath, bracing myself for what was to come.

And all the while, as I braced, I tried to think about anything but Fergus's body, and the fifty bafrillion questions I had about how it had gotten there.

~

"And you are, love?" the woman, maybe in her early forties, with tousled graying-at-the-roots blonde hair and very round glasses, asked in a clear British accent, reminding me distinctly of the ladies from *Absolutely Fabulous* and my dearly departed Nanna, who was British born and raised and loved that show.

Also reminding me, at this very inopportune moment, how much I missed having Nanna in my life.

The woman been one of the first officials on the scene; standing against the backdrop of the amazing mountains Portland had to offer as she leaned on one of the police cars parked at the crumbling curb.

We stood outside the store on the cracked sidewalk while the police and forensics guys crawled all over the inside like ants on a hill, putting things in bags and swishing big brushes over tiny surfaces.

The weather had turned from rainy to sunny, and now the breeze was warm and inviting, making me wish I was walking along the Hawthorne Bridge instead of answering questions about my dead landlord.

I hated that I felt that way, but that's just my truth. We'd had a lot of murder in our lives lately, and it wasn't a bellyful of laughs by a long shot.

They'd separated Coop and me, and as hard as I tried to keep one eye and an ear on what the other detectives were asking my far-too-honest demon, I had trouble doing as much because the police lady kept blocking my view of her.

"Um, miss. Your name, if you would please?"

"My name's Trixie Lavender." I tried not to squirm as I said it, but gosh my hands were clammy and my mouth was dry.

She peered down at me over her owl-like glasses, her sparkling blue eyes a complete contradiction to the tired lines forming around her mouth. "Is that your stripper name, pet? You know, like the memes my mates post all over my Facebook page? The month you were born and the road you lived on when you were a lass equals your stripper name?"

All I could do was stare blankly at her. I'm new to this social media thing. Sure, the convent had a Facebook page, but they definitely didn't let me loose on it. I'm certain due to fear I'd spew some of my misgivings about the Bible.

Also, I do know what a meme is. Stevie showed me a bunch on social media, and I'm really getting the hang of having an online presence, for both the store and my own personal page. I don't remember anything about strippers, but I promise you, that won't be for long. I intend to find out what my stripper name is posthaste.

So I thought about what the lady said, and answered, "That would make me November Convent."

"You lived on Convent Road?"

"No. I lived *in* a convent. Sorry, I must have misunderstood you. I thought it was my birth month and the place I lived."

Her penciled-in eyebrow rose. "You lived in a convent did you say, love?"

"I did. I was a nun." And that was all I said. Hopefully, the part about my being a nun would make her think twice about the possibility I'd lie.

Stevie had said to always lead with that whenever I felt like someone doubted me—it was what she called my holy ammunition.

The lady snickered a little, tapping her pen on her small notepad. "So I guess it's *Sister* Trixie then?"

"Nope. It's just Trixie. As I said, I'm not a nun anymore."

She waved a hand in the soft breeze and smiled.

"Neither here nor there. I was only having a laugh about your stripper name, of course."

So I laughed, because it seemed like the right thing to do. "Then it was very funny."

Then she cast apologetic eyes my way. "Apologies. It's just your name is quite unusual. Is Trixie your real name?"

I cupped my hands over my eyes to block out the bright sun that had decided to make an appearance. "That's my real name."

She stuck out her hand. Her nails, though short, were polished in a bright red. "Detective Tansy Primrose."

"Is that *your* stripper name?"

She threw her head back and laughed—like, really laughed, flashing white, not-quite-even teeth while producing lines around her mouth. "Touché, love. That's my Welsh mother's romantic nature rearing its flowery head. Do you have any idea how hard it 'tis to be taken seriously by a bunch of men at the station when your name is Tansy Primrose?"

"Probably the same as it is when your name is Trixie Lavender."

"Touché again," she said on a wink, and Detective Tansy, being so jovial, made me wonder if this was a technique Stevie had talked about. The one where you buddy up to a suspect in order to glean information from them. "So, this Fergus McDuff, he's your landlord, correct?"

"Was."

She jabbed a finger in the air, the motion batting away a fly. "*Was*. Right-o. Any ideas about what might have happened to our poor Fergus McDuff?"

In the effort to never give more than is asked, I peered up at her very pleasant face. "He was killed."

Detective Primrose laughed again, the sound tinkling and light. "I don't know if you're pulling my leg or pulling my leg, but *now* who's having a laugh, love? Though now," she leaned down to me, her mouth half-tilted upward, "I must be very serious and play detective to keep my insurance benefits and my superiors content. I can't cock this up or I'll lose my job and be shipped right back to jolly old England with my tail 'tween my legs. Understood?"

I didn't say anything, but I nodded vigorously.

"Righty then. First, I don't see the immediate need to take you downtown, Trixie, because your alibi for last night checks out, and Mr. McDuff does appear plenty fermented. That's good for your defense, innit? Plus, your wee stature makes you come off harmless and unassuming, but make no mistake, I will shuffle you right off to Buffalo if you give me the roundabout. So, if you feel like sitting in a putrid room vaguely smelling of a London trash bin with nothing but a table and a two-way mirror, say aye."

My stomach lurched. It was all fun and games until the sassy British detective got serious. "I vote nay. I most certainly do not feel like sitting in a putrid room with a table and a two-way mirror."

Her head bobbed up and down, a smile back on her

face. "Indeedy. As long as you answer my questions and don't give me a speck of trouble."

"Deal."

"So, did you see anything? Anyone suspicious?"

"Do you mean did I see someone kill Fergus?"

She eyed me for a moment, assessing me from head to toe with sharp eyes. "Aha. I see how this is. You're a cut-to-the-chase kind of girl. I like that. Admire it even. And yes, that's exactly what I mean. This *is* a murder investigation."

"Has is already been ruled a homicide?" Was that a stupid question to ask?

"Well, love. I don't know about you, but there's a bloke in there with his head smashed six ways to Sunday. I think it's safe to say he was murdered without too many repercussions from my higher-ups."

"Primrose?" a gruff, deep voice shouted. Not an unpleasant sound in my ears, mind you.

Detective Primrose whipped around at the sound of the voice and broke into a smile—a wide smile, once more revealing her very white teeth surrounded by red lipstick that matched her fingernail polish.

"*Higgs?* What in the name of all the king's horses are you doing here in Cobbler Cove?" she asked, clearly pleased by his presence. Dare I say giddy, judging by the twinkle in her eyes.

The incredibly good-looking man swooped her up in a big hug and swung her around while I watched before setting her down and grinning at her, his generous smile revealing grooves on either side of his mouth. "I got tired of living like an Eskimo in Minneapolis, so I left. Great place, Portland, huh?"

Detective Primrose patted him on his broad shoulder and grinned even wider, then smoothed a hand over her navy-blue blazer. "You bet your daffodils. Anything's better than homicide in Brooklyn, I can tell you true. Hades beats homicide in Brooklyn. That's where I went when I left Minneapolis, by the way. Just transferred here a couple of months ago. But look at us now, bloke. Small world, init?"

He chuckled, low and husky, just like his voice. "No kidding. Good seeing you. We should grab dinner or something. If Marvin will allow it, of course."

She laughed and made a face, her fair skin glowing under the buttery ball of sun. "Marvin Schmarvin. As if he has a say in whom I choose to dine with. Old coot."

Higgs gave a light squeeze to her shoulder. "An old coot who's the love of your crazy life. Who are you trying to kid?"

Pulling her notepad to her chest, she sighed, breathy and with longing. "You're right. He's *my* old coot, and now that I have my claws in him, I'm not letting him go."

"So you investigating this mess?" he asked, his dark eyes finally landing on me, very obvious curiosity in them.

"You betcha," she said in a pretty good American accent. "I was just having a chin-wag with Miss Lavender about whether she saw anyone or heard anything that might have been suspicious, wasn't I?"

Swallowing hard, I nodded and wiped my hands on my thighs, suddenly self-conscious about my ratty T-shirt and dirty sneakers.

"You betcha," I responded, making her grin.

"So, where were we, Miss Lavender?"

I inched closer to the detective. I didn't mean to, it just happened. Out of fear. Higgs's stare made me uncomfortable. "You asked if I saw anyone who might have murdered Fergus, I believe."

"Riiight, right, right. Sorry, I let myself get distracted by this handsome sod. We used to work together ages ago, didn't we, Higglesworth?"

Higglesworth? What an interesting name for such a manly-man. I'd have gone the opposite end of the spectrum and expected his name to be something along the lines of Spike or...or Lumberjack. But Higglesworth reminded me of a butler to a superhero. Like Batman's Alfred.

"We did indeed, Detective Primrose. In the frozen tundra," he joked. His words breaking my reverie as he folded his arms over his broad chest and stared down at me.

If my hands were sweaty before, now they were positively dripping.

"Now off with you, mate. You're distracting me from doing my job." The detective turned back toward me then, her pen at the ready once more. "So, Miss Lavender, did you see anyone who might have hurt Mr. McDuff?"

It was now or never. I summoned my inner Stevie

in order to get through this. Stevie was a clever lady, and she'd never cower the way I wanted to cower. I wanted to go back to the cheap motel we were temporarily staying in, grab my favorite blanket, and hide under it until my stomach stopped jumping around like a cat on a hot tin roof.

But I asked myself, WWSD—what would Stevie do? She'd give the police as much real information as she had, and she wouldn't bat an eye for doing so. She was no chicken, and in her honor, I wasn't going to besmirch her good name and all she'd taught me by batting my eye, either.

I say that as though I ever dreamed I'd end up in a situation almost identical to the one we'd left behind us in Ebenezer Falls, but here I was once more.

Standing but a few hundred feet away from a dead body.

Squaring my shoulders, I looked Detective Tansy Primrose right in her cheerful eyes and said, "I did see something. I saw your friend—Higgs, I think you called him—arguing with Fergus McDuff yesterday afternoon."

CHAPTER 4

I leaned into her so she knew I was serious. "And it was quite heated. There were arms flying around, and hand gestures, and then another man came and pulled your friend Higgs away."

Higgs's eyes flashed hot at me, but he didn't speak a word. Which of course almost made me squirm. But then I thought about Stevie and, I'm proud to say, I didn't flinch under his scrutiny.

Okay, I admit, I was still standing close to Detective Primrose, and she did have a gun which helped in the non-flinching department, but that's neither here nor there. The point is, I didn't flinch.

Rock solid was I.

Also, we'd argued with Fergus, too. Now under normal circumstances, the one where Coop had never been accused of murdering our last landlord, I'd tell the detective. I pride myself on my honesty.

But that wouldn't work in our favor today, and I

47

admit, I was a little afraid to tell her. Besides, the good detective would find out soon enough with a simple Google search. And another thing? I knew we didn't kill Fergus. We had a rock solid alibi I'd dare anyone to refute.

Detective Primrose eyed me hard, but I couldn't read whether her gaze said she was surprised or mildly annoyed. "Let me be clear. You're saying Higgs had an argument with Mr. McDuff?"

The tone in her voice suggested my statement bordered on preposterous, almost definitely because he had something to do with law enforcement at one point or another and they'd worked together.

But my statement was true. So I reaffirmed without hesitation. "That's exactly what I'm saying. So, maybe your friend *Higgs* murdered my landlord?"

After I said those words, a small cluster of noise broke out from the officers on the scene. Higgs gave me the evil eye—a very attractive evil eye, if you must know, with long, thick lashes and a color reminiscent of dark chocolate. Dove dark chocolate, by the way— my weakness.

And who could blame him? I'd just told the detective this dark-haired devil she appeared quite fond of could be one of her suspects in a murder investigation.

Clearly, he'd been connected to the police. I'd lay odds, judging by the look of him, all brawny and fit, he hadn't worked in the mailroom.

Detective Primrose gasped, her eyes going wide behind her round glasses at my words, taking a step back while all the officers and some stragglers along the sidewalk came to eavesdrop.

Some of the officers were quite vocal about my statement (and it was a rather disgruntled type of vocal. Definitely not a supportive one), but Higgs, after his initial reaction, grinned—wide and amused.

And it was a nice grin, as warm as the day, as bright as the sun, leaving two deep grooves on either side of his lips.

He cupped his mouth with both hands, revealing a small tattoo on the inside of his wrist I couldn't quite make out. "Guys, simmer down. It's okay," he yelled to the other officers then turned back to us. "She's right. I did argue with Fergus. He just couldn't seem to accept the concept that I run a homeless shelter, and there inevitably will be homeless people lining up along the sidewalk for a place to sleep for the night. He called it loitering and bad for business. I disagreed. And it was, in fact, heated. Jay came and intervened."

Detective Primrose appeared to know who this Jay was, and now she also knew I was telling the truth.

I fought the temptation to stick my tongue out at all of them in childish fashion as if to say, "See?"

All the police officers' faces went from angry to understanding in an instant as they clapped this large man on the back and returned to keeping the crowd gathering in the street at bay.

"Now," he said with a great deal of authority when he looked to the detective with sharp eyes. "Had Miss Lavender cared to ask, she would have known that

Fergus McDuff had real trouble renting this store out or, for that matter, keeping a tenant. Not only is it a disaster in there, it's also considered a dicey area because of the shelter—even though my lot of regs are pussycats and haven't been given so much as a ticket for loitering.

"Fergus has seen plenty of people come and go here, and I guess he was worried you ladies would do the same once you found out what you'd gotten yourselves into. He behaved as though he wanted me to hide my bunch somewhere you wouldn't see them in order to keep you here. I simply came to tell him that wasn't going to happen. Jay did what he always does when it comes to Fergus—kept me from serving him a knuckle sandwich."

Was there egg on my face? Metaphorically, I'm certain there was. He ran a homeless shelter, for the love of rice and cheese. Boy, did I feel like a chump.

But then a little voice inside my head (StevieStevie-Stevie) reminded me killers could be nice guys and run homeless shelters, too. She said sometimes the least suspicious suspect is the one you should keep your eye on.

So I made another mental note to keep my eye squarely on him because certainly, a man friendly with a detective was the least likely suspect, right? Yet, I found myself silently commending him for his community service—for protecting people who couldn't protect themselves. We had that much in common.

But I didn't have to like it.

Detective Primrose clucked her tongue, her eyes squinting against the sun's new position in the sky. "Leave it to Jay to keep your head planted on those big shoulders."

"Couldn't run the shelter without him," Higgs remarked with a deep tone of sincerity.

Detective Primrose turned to me, cupping her chin. "Seems like a reasonable explanation, don't you agree, Miss Lavender?"

But I, taught to be skeptical by my mentor Stevie, wasn't going to concede his innocence so easily.

I toed a pothole in the sidewalk and shrugged before I said, "Reasonable? Yes. True? Only time will tell."

Higgs merely smiled brighter, rocking back on his heels as he hooked his fingers into the pockets of his jeans, relaxed and easy. "I knew I should have brought a casserole."

I frowned, itching my forehead, now damp with a light sweat. "A what?"

"A casserole," he repeated slowly. "It breaks the ice when your neighbor thinks you're a murderer."

Detective Primrose covered her mouth with the back of her hand and snorted before straightening and giving him an overexaggerated stern look I was convinced was for my benefit.

She waved a jovial hand at him and grinned. "Oh, posh. You bugger off, Higgs. She's merely doing her civic duty. She doesn't know you from a hole in the wall."

He nodded at Detective Primrose, his long-ish hair falling over his forehead. "You're right. I was just kidding. My sense of humor sometimes gets the best of me, and I can't resist a good poke. My apologies, Miss Lavender. Let's start again, yes?" He stuck out a hand with shortly clipped nails and offered it to me. "I'm Cross Higglesworth—Higgs, because it's just a heck of a lot easier. I run the homeless shelter two doors down from your shop. Pleasure to meet you."

Cross...

I wondered why he didn't go by his first name. Maybe he hated it as much as I hated mine.

I'm named after my maternal grandmother, Beatrix, who, as I said, was British and came from Cardiff. My mother wanted to name me after her, but my dad wasn't crazy about the name Beatrix. He claimed it sounded too old for someone so tiny. So they'd compromised with Trixie. Which, growing up, hadn't been easy, either—you can believe that's the truth.

Anyway, as Cross Higglesworth smiled down at me quite pleasantly, and the scent of his cologne threaded through my nostrils (also not unpleasant), I decided it was best to keep things distant but friendly. I mean, he was friends with a detective from the Portland PD and all the officers behaved as though they knew him. Odds were, I was safe-ish in this window of time.

Sticking out my hand, I finally took his and, for a

brief moment, when our fingers connected, we both paused.

And I don't know why…

But I was the first to withdraw, jamming my digits into the pocket of my jeans, my cheeks burning hot for no darn reason at all. "You already know my name, but good to meet you, too, Mr. Higglesworth."

"Just call me Higgs. I'm sure we'll be seeing a lot of each other once you settle in. No need for formalities."

I fought a shiver, but I'm not sure what I was shivering about. It was easily eighty degrees, so it wasn't the warm weather. Maybe it was the fact that I'd be seeing him around the neighborhood and he could be the one responsible for Fergus's death. That left me feeling uncomfortable, to say the least, but I couldn't let him see that. Never show your cards, Stevie had said.

Rocking back on my heels, I peered at him tentatively. "Then Higgs it is."

He nodded before turning back to Detective Primrose. "Need anything else from me, Tansy?"

She winked and smiled, tucking her pen back into her blazer pocket. "Not at the moment. I think all's well, Higgs. But expect to see my gorgeous face before I head back to the precinct."

I held up a finger. "Hold on a minute. You're just going to take him at his word? You're not going to thoroughly question him?"

Detective Primrose never missed a beat as she began to head toward her vehicle. "Not with you present, Miss Lavender. That's not how it works."

"But shouldn't you be putting him in cuffs and taking him downtown for questioning?"

She stopped midway to her car and turned to look at me, her blonde hair ruffling in the warm breeze, her eyes amused. "Have you been watching a bit of *Law & Order*?"

What if I had?

"Why do you want to know?" Gosh, I felt naked—like she'd been peering through the window of the motel room while I binged on Netflix and Ice T.

"Because that's usually what people ask when they watch too many copper shows, but it doesn't work that way. I have to have probable cause to bring him and his cheekiness down to the station."

"But I gave you probable cause. He fought with Fergus. Isn't it probable he could have killed him, too? They were pretty angry."

"From what I'm gathering, it appears *everyone* had a row with Mr. McDuff. I need a stronger probable cause than a heated argument. For instance, did you hear what they said to one another?"

Okay. No. I didn't hear what they'd said. "No…" I answered rather sheepishly.

"Precisely. You didn't hear death threats or even threats of bodily harm. Listen, Miss Lavender, I promise you, I'll question Mr. Higglesworth—all within the law, when I'm done talking to a few other people."

Now I was suspicious of the detective's relationship with him. "Was he a police officer?"

Detective Primrose paused again and stared at me, her open, pleasant face going dark for only a moment. "I'll let Mr. Higglesworth tell you. Until then, please let me do my job."

With that, she turned on her heel, waving to her partner, a Detective Ramsey, to signal they should take their leave.

"But wait!" I called to her, blocking the glare of the sun with my hand cupped over my eyes. "What about the store? We're staying in a motel, but our time there's limited and soon we'll have nowhere to go. Plus, we have things to unpack."

That sounded so petty, in light of the fact that a dead man was, well…dead, right on the floor.

Her lips went thin as she popped open the drivers-side door of the car. "That will have to wait, Miss Lavender. Your store's a crime scene now. Until this is cleared up, and forensics has done its job, it's a no-go." Then she smiled, bright and cheerful. "But welcome to Cobbler Cove. Pleased as rum punch to have you."

My shoulders sagged in defeat. I, in no way, wanted to take away from Fergus's horrible death, but for the love of popsicles, we couldn't afford to delay opening any more than necessary, and there was still so much to do.

"You could always stay at the shelter. I have a couple of beds open for tonight, what with the weather fore-cast saying it's going to be warm the next few days," Higgs commented from behind me.

My spine went stiff as I turned to face him. "No thank you."

He chuckled, warm and husky. "What if I promise not to murder you?"

Okay. He wasn't going to let this go, and to be fair, I probably wouldn't let it go if someone called me a murderer, either. But still...

"Do murderers always keep their promises?"

"All the murderers I know do."

I almost laughed, but seeing Coop, the worry on her face clear, I refrained.

"Trixie?" Clearly done with the questions from one of the other police officers, Coop loped across the sidewalk to stand next to me, her eyes thoroughly scanning Higgs from head to toe as her nostrils flared.

Coop was *scenting* him and his emotions—or something like that. I didn't question this odd habit of hers.

Instead, I let her sniff.

Her hand went to my shoulder in protective mode as she loomed behind me. "Everything all right?"

Higgs didn't let me answer. Instead, he thrust his hand at Coop and said, "Cross Higglesworth, your neighbor from just down the block. I own Peach Street Shelter, or as some jokingly call it, The Guy-MCA because it's for men only. You are?"

The Guy-MCA? Somebody had a sense of humor.

Coop rolled her tongue in her cheek and lifted her chin, her green eyes glittering as she shook his hand. "Cooper O'Shea. But everyone calls me Coop, Cross Higglesworth."

"Everyone calls him Higgs," I mentioned as I sucked in my cheeks, and didn't even bother to remind my demon she didn't have to use his full name. Suddenly, I was very tired. At this very moment, I didn't have it in me to correct her.

But Coop and her odd greeting didn't appear to faze him at all. "Yep. Your friend's right. Just call me Higgs. Nice to meet you." Then he turned to me, his dark eyes twinkling with amusement. "Now, if you're done accusing me of murder for today, Miss Lavender, I'm going to go back to work," he teased. And it wasn't at all with a malicious tone. Not even a hint.

"You accused him of murder?" Coop asked, wide-eyed, tucking her hair behind her ears.

Higgs smiled. "She sure as heck did. But it's okay. It's not exactly how I'd planned the perfect meet and greet with my new neighbors, but I've been accused of worse."

Worse than murder? What was worse than murder?

I wrinkled my nose and fought making a face at him. "I didn't accuse him of murder, Coop. I just mentioned the argument he had with Fergus to the detective—the very *heated* argument," I found myself replying defensively.

"Potato-potahtoe," he joked amicably. "And now, I really do have to go. The next time we meet, I hope it'll be under better circumstances." Then Higgs threw a hand up and sauntered off down the sidewalk, his strong legs eating up the pavement as he turned into the space two doors down and disappeared.

"He thinks you're pretty," Coop commented in that dry way she had of observing everything with a black-and-white lens.

I fought my surprise and the flush of my cheeks. Which was silly. Why the heck was I blushing? Who wanted a murder suspect to find them attractive?

"Just my luck," I mumbled.

Her brows knitted together. "Luck? Is this another metaphor—or maybe it's an analogy. I can't get those straight. So please explain."

I walked toward the door of the shop and leaned back against the brick façade, under the shade of the ratty awning needing replacing, and sighed.

"Lucky as in, the first man I meet since leaving the convent who thinks I'm pretty could be the man responsible for killing Fergus."

"Do you want to meet a man, Trixie?" she asked, leaning back next to me and putting her hands behind her.

That made me pause. I hadn't really given meeting men much thought. I was too busy trying to keep Coop from killing anything that moved and fighting off the evil that had lodged itself inside me.

I forget sometimes that I'm free to date if I so choose, now that I'm no longer a nun. But I haven't been on a date since I was a teenager in high school, and to be quite frank, I don't remember much about that time in my life because of my addictions. However, I'd been a nun for thirteen years, the idea of a relationship with anyone other than the man upstairs would take some getting used to. The thought made my stomach feel topsy-turvy.

But I couldn't think about dating now anyway. There was a dead man in our store. The second one in a matter of months. We were definitely a pox upon our landlords.

"Trixie?"

"No. I don't think I want to meet a man, Coop. Not right now, anyway. I want to fix this dump up and start earning a living. That's what I want. We need to make some money—and soon. That flea-infested motel is ridiculously expensive for the kind of accommodations they provide. We'll only last so long before we run out of cash and have to dip into what we planned to use for Inkerbelle's inventory."

"But you can't do that until the police clear the store, right?" asked Knuckles, obviously done being questioned, too, his serene face red from the sun as he approached us.

I gave him a look of genuine apology. I liked this big, burly man with his tattoos and piercings. He had kind eyes. "It seems so, Knuckles. I'm sorry, but I think for now, we're in a hiring freeze."

I hated that I was going to have to send him away, because his work was brilliant, but who knew how long this investigation could take on top of all the renovations? Tattoo shops were everywhere in Portland. He'd be snatched up in no time flat, and we'd be sadder for the snatching.

"That's okay. I can wait. So can my clients," he said,

pulling out a camouflage handkerchief from the back pocket of his jeans and tying it around his head.

"*You have clients?*" Boy, could we use some of those. The way things were going for us as of late, we'd probably be better off putting a chair outside and tattooing in the middle of the street.

"Yep. Just been lookin' for the right place to bring 'em."

I almost laughed out loud as I thumbed over my shoulder at the store. "And you thought here—*this dump*—was the right place?"

His nod was solemn when he shrugged his wide shoulders. "Yep. Feels right. Can't say why. Just does. Somethin' told me to stop here today. So I did. I always go where the old gut takes me. It's never been wrong before." He lifted his eyes upward at the brick needing a power wash and grunted again. "Doesn't look like much, I suppose, but she's a pretty girl who doesn't know she's pretty yet, that's all. We can fix her up when the police clear out. You'll see."

His words held such conviction, they made me want to believe.

I peered up at him, watching the sun glint off his piercings, unsure what to think, but my heart warmed to him for his kind words—they made me think of that word "community" and what Stevie had impressed upon us.

Still, I sighed. "It could be a while before we're able to set up shop, let alone take in clients, Knuckles."

"That's okay, too," he responded, crossing his burly

arms over his wide chest and leaning back against the building on the other side of me—almost as if in solidarity.

And there the three of us stood while police came in and out of the store, strewing yellow crime scene tape everywhere, and other officers held back the crowd of busybodies as the sun shined and the sounds of Cobbler Cove swirled about us.

Inhaling, I tried to absorb everything that had happened today and where to go from here, but my mind was a blank.

"So what's next, Trixie?" Coop asked, craning her neck to look at me with intense eyes.

But I had no answer. I was at a loss. I'd spent so much of our time since leaving the convent juggling plates, trying to keep everything in the air so we could move forward, I'd used up all the tricks in my hat.

Rubbing my eyes with the heels of my hands, I shook my head. "I... I'm not sure what's next, Coop."

Knuckles grunted, his stomach jiggling. "I am."

I turned my head to look at him. "You're what?"

"Sure what to do next."

"What should we do next, Knuckles?"

He turned and smiled down at me with warm eyes, a twinkle in them just like Santa Claus. "Solve a murder, of course, m'dears."

My heart clenched in my chest. There but for the kindness of strangers...

CHAPTER 5

"*Y*ou *live here?*" I asked on a squeak—and I *know* I squeaked—which is horrendously rude, but I was astonished and awed all at once. "I mean, this is all yours?"

"Yep," Knuckles responded, sweeping a broad hand in a gesture that said we should enter his not-so-humble abode via a maroon door with stained-glass panels. "Welcome. Happy to have you."

I looked around at the entryway to his house, the floors flanked in bleached hardwood all the way through the open concept space, where each room blended into the next. It was beautiful—stunning, in fact. So stunning, my mouth fell open.

The walls were done in creamy pale beige with wood-framed pictures of people and their tattoos, people I'm going to assume Knuckles had tattooed personally, seeing as he was in some of the pictures.

And then there was the canvas art, splashes of green and blue with no particular design, but a perfect accent to his moss-green kitchen cabinets and gray and off-white furniture.

There were the plants and flowers—everywhere, too. Blue and pink hydrangeas in terra cotta vases, three or four fichus trees, and an entire corner by the dining room's wide French doors dedicated to various potted greenery I couldn't identify off the top of my head.

In a word, it was gorgeous.

"It smells nice in here," Coop commented, setting Livingston's cage down. He was under strict orders to keep his little beak shut while we were at Knuckles's house. We had enough trouble. We didn't need more if someone found out we had a sass-talking owl with an Irish accent to boot.

"Eucalyptus," Knuckles said plainly as he scooped up Livingston's cage and set it on the deep gray-and-white marbled countertop of his kitchen island. "I love eucalyptus." Then he drove a finger into our ornery owl's space and said, "Hey, little guy."

Coop was at his side in two seconds flat, fearing what I feared.

That Livingston would bite his finger off.

He can be a cranky little bugger given just an inch. We were always on guard with him because if he had the chance, he'd take advantage of the fact that we couldn't reprimand him the way one would a toddler (which was how we approached his behavior) without looking as though we were out of our gourds.

I shot Livingston a look that said *do it and die*, and to his credit, he settled on his perch quite nicely, but the swivel of his head said he was annoyed (surprise-surprise!).

"Does he need mice or something?" Knuckles asked, his forehead furrowing.

Livingston's feathers ruffled in discontent, and groaned. "Ack! That's disgus—"

"That's delightful of you!" I chirped over our bird, casting him a stern nun's frown before putting a hand on Knuckles's shoulder and nudging him away from the cage, hopefully distracting him from Livingston altogether. "But he's eaten for the day. We're good, Knuckles. Thank you, though."

Knuckles smiled for the second time since I'd met him earlier this morning and pointed to the white ceramic kettle on his shiny silver chef's stovetop with the red knobs. "How about some tea? Grew the herbs myself."

Tea? Why had I expected he'd offer us some Jack or maybe even moonshine?

Because I was stereotyping and it was rude.

"Don't go to any trouble. Please," I said on a smile. "We don't want to be in your way. You've already been too kind."

And he had. It was Knuckles who'd suggested we go back to his place to try to figure this thing out so we could move into the store. For the time being, he'd been cleared of any wrongdoing due to the fact that Fergus's body was hours old and I'd told Detective Primrose that Knuckles had only shown up this morning to apply for a position.

Also, he had an alibi for yesterday right into this morning.

So, as we'd followed him over in our hot mess of a Caddy that there but for the grace of God was still running, we wondered out loud where a man like Knuckles would live.

Coop figured it was in the back of some dive biker bar, and I'd guessed maybe a small apartment with peeling paint and a rusty showerhead.

When we'd pulled onto Knuckles's street, lined with beautiful green trees and manicured front lawns, tiny as they were, and had seen the houses, all mostly Craftsman style, we'd been convinced he lived with his mother. Maybe even his grandmother, if long life spans and having children early ran in his family—and some cats. Because Coop said all the TV shows she watched with men who lived with their parents at Knuckles's age (which was almost sixty, according to his application, by the by) had cats—lots of cats.

Thus, we'd gone with caution. Coop can scent a lot of things, but according to her, she can't always tell if someone's intentions are good. Though, she'd declared her general first impressions were much like mine, in Knuckles's case.

His eyes were kind, and that was enough for me. I didn't worry so much about his size if he did in fact have ill intentions. Coop could take him. I'd seen her in action on several occasions and for someone so pretty and finely boned, she could be a frightening warrior if the opportunity presented itself.

But when we'd pulled up to Knuckles's beautiful steel blue/gray and white house with a generous front porch and copper hanging lanterns swaying from the ceiling in the late-afternoon breeze, we were both flabbergasted. Add in the amazing guesthouse, a miniature replica of the main house, in his backyard, and I was floored.

That'd teach us to make assumptions, eh?

"This is very unexpected, Trixie Lavender," Coop whispered as Knuckles set about making the tea he'd offered.

"Yeah. But what a lovely surprise, yes?"

She nodded, tucking her hair behind her ears. "It is. It's almost as nice as Stevie's house, don't you think?"

Stevie lived in a mini-mansion high on a cliff overlooking Puget Sound, or as she'd dubbed it, Mayhem Manor. An old Victorian she'd renovated with Win's help, and it was amazingly beautiful and we both had fond memories of the comfy beds and Egyptian cotton sheets—a far cry from the shoddy, cheap-by-comparison motel we were in now.

"If not as big, but yes. It's beautiful. Maybe there's a Mrs. Knuckles?"

"Nope. Just me," Knuckles said from behind me, his gruff voice making me jump.

My face went red, my palms sweaty. "I'm sorry, Knuckles. That was rude. You have immaculate taste. We had no business speculating."

He held up two mugs of steaming tea and hitched his square jaw toward the plank-wood dining table with the soft beige tufted chairs surrounding it. "Don't sweat it. I get that all the time because of the flowers and plants. Everyone always thinks I either live with my parents or I have a wife. Oh, and cats. A passel of cats. But really I only have two."

I fought a giggle as I followed him into the dining room and he removed a glass vase of freshly cut lilacs from the table. He had us pegged, for sure. Still, I didn't want to be like everyone else. I wanted to live my life without assumption—without stereotyping. How could I live it any other way if I expected people to accept an ex-nun possessed by an evil spirit and her demon friend?

Reaching a hand out, I patted his brawny arm in another form of apology. "Regardless, it was rude of us to assume you weren't capable of such a beautiful home. Especially seeing as your tattoos are so amazing and detailed. You've obviously done very well for yourself, Knuckles. Good on you."

Coop's eyes went to the pictures of him with his clients and she nodded as she took a seat. "Definitely amazing."

High praise coming from a skilled artist like my

Coop. High praise indeed. In all the time we'd spent browsing the Internet, looking at shops and other artists' work, she'd mostly only grunted, with the occasional nod of approval. But to hear her use the word *amazing* was positively gushing for someone as unenthusiastic about almost everything the way Coop was.

And that brought me to one of my bigger fears. Our history. I figured I needed to get this all out of the way before we became any more involved with Donald P. Ledbetter. You could put whatever you wanted on a piece of paper, like names and social security numbers, but we had zero experience in real-world tattoos.

I couldn't very well explain that Coop used to be the devil's head tattoo artist, could I?

I cleared my throat and looked Knuckles directly in the eye. "Which brings me to this again. Why would you choose Inkerbelle's? We're definitely not established. The space is a wreck. We have nothing to show in the way of a resume but the tattoos on Coop—"

"Hold the phone, Nellie! Who inked that on you, Coop?"

Coop gave him her direct stare. "Me."

"You inked that yourself?" he asked with wonder in his gruff tone, eyeing the intricate unicorn tattoo on the front of Coop's left shoulder in all its beautiful colors, peeking out beneath her spaghetti-strap top.

Oh, dear. Had I revealed something I shouldn't? Was it unusual to do your own tattoos? Did demons have some magical high tolerance for pain a human wouldn't?

But Coop nodded after taking a sip of her tea. "Yep. I did." And that was all she said.

"How did you do that all by yourself?"

I bit my tongue because I didn't know how she'd done it either. I just took for granted she'd done some magical demon thing and poof—tattoo.

But Coop just looked at him dead on, relaxed as ever. "I used a mirror and I'm ambidextrous."

He half-smiled, his nose ring shifting when his lips rose. "*Wow*. Impressive."

I kept my sigh of relief on the inside and said, "Anyway, it's obvious you've had bigger fish to fry, Knuckles. We need you far more than you need us. So let's lay all our cards on the table before we go any further. Why us?"

Knuckles shrugged, pulling off the handkerchief he'd put on his head earlier before looking down into his mug of herbal tea. "Like I said, and I'm tellin' you true, can't explain it. Just know it's right. Yep, your place is a dump. Nope, I don't need to rent a space or work for anyone if I don't want to. I've done all right for myself. I *choose* to work because tattooing is what I love. Well, that and my flowers and cats. But I don't want the hassle of owning my own shop.

"I've been looking around for a few months now, and when I saw your Facebook page, hit me like a ton o' bricks. I just knew. I know it sounds weird, but that's the truth. I got a good feeling about you gals. I'd like very much to work at Inkerbelle's. And after hearing

Coop did her own tat, I'd *really* like to work with you ladies."

I grinned at him, my heart full. Even Coop managed to move her facial muscles just a hair in the direction of a smile. "Then I won't ask again, I'll just be grateful the universe sent you to us."

He patted my hand with his much bigger one and smiled. "Fair enough. Now can I ask *you* a question?"

I tried not to stiffen, but I knew what was coming, and I wanted to be as direct as I possibly could without making a liar out of myself. I know he heard Detective Primrose ask me about being a nun. Were I Knuckles, I'd want to know why I'd left the convent, too.

"You absolutely can."

His pause was thoughtful, as though he were measuring his words so he wouldn't offend me. Blowing out a breath, he straightened in his chair. "What made you decide to leave the convent and take up tattooing? Kinda unusual for a nun, don't ya think?"

"It's definitely unusual, but I didn't really choose tattoos. They sort of chose me, I guess. When Coop and I met, I commented on the beauty of her tattoo and she liked some of my sketches. The rest just sort of happened."

Out of necessity, mind you, but how we'd come to our endeavor was mostly true. Once the mess at the convent had simmered down and I was out on my keister with Coop stuck to me like glue, we just started brainstorming, and it all fell into place.

Either way, I thought he'd be satisfied with my

answer, even though I hadn't really answered his question at all. But he said as much when he asked, "So you still haven't told me. Why did you leave the convent?"

Listen, sometimes the truth really is stranger than fiction. I figured if I led with the truth, I wouldn't have to lie-lie—which I hated doing, and I knew Knuckles would think I was merely joking. So, short of being dropped off at the nearest psych ward for evaluation, I let 'er rip.

Keeping my face as serious as I could, I asked, "If I told you it was because I was possessed by an evil spirit who made me do horrible things—like moon my fellow nuns and steal a centuries-old relic once allegedly owned by the archangel Gabriel—all while trying to eat my soul, would you believe me?"

That was mostly the truth. I'd left out the part where my most cherished mentor and priest, Father O'Leary, was the one who'd asked me to get the relic in the first place. And I'd blindly done his bidding without thinking twice, even though his request was incredibly out of character.

But that was neither here nor there.

Coop hissed a breath, but she remained silent, her posture stiff as a board as her hand curled around the mug of tea.

Knuckles, on the other hand?

Knuckles burst out laughing, throwing his head back and literally howling. In fact, he laughed so hard, he had to bend over as he shook his head. "Noooo!" he squealed on a series of snorts that sounded hilarious coming from a man so large. "I wouldn't believe that."

I grinned and squeezed his hand even as his shoulders still shook and he wiped tears from his eyes with his thumb. "Then suffice it to say, I had a crisis of faith, and I happened to meet Coop at the right time and place when I needed a change in my life, and..." I spread my arms wide. "Here we are."

Inhaling deeply, he blew raspberries from his lips to shake off his fits of giggles then bounced his graying head in response. "Good enough. And you're funny. Really funny. All the nuns I've ever met were cross and very serious, but not you, eh, gal?"

I chuckled. Yeah. Funny.

Coop eyeballed me over his head and I could tell she was breathing a mental sigh of relief.

Next up, diversion, something I'd become very good at.

Rubbing my hands together, I looked at them both and smiled. "Then let's solve a crime, huh?"

~

Three hours and an Uber Eats delivery of some amazing Thai food later, and we were all not only yawning, but at a standstill.

I'd done what Stevie had done when we were trying to figure out who'd killed our landlord in Washington. I'd printed all the pictures of the crime scene and spread them out on Knuckles's dining room table. I'd even texted Stevie to get some tips from her on how to go about this crime-solving thing and what to do next.

As a result, we'd come to some small-ish conclusions.

We had no idea what we were doing—Stevie really had made it look much easier than it was—and we were probably out of our heads to even attempt to solve this without help from a skilled expert. Still, we persevered.

I pointed to the picture of Fergus's head and the wide pool of blood beneath, tapping it with my nail. "Obviously, Fergus was clobbered over the head. We don't have an official cause of death, but I feel secure in saying it was probably blunt force trauma. Nothing left behind one can see with the naked eye."

Except a lot of debris. There definitely was plenty of that spread around Fergus's body, and I wanted to kick myself for not at least taking closer pictures of it. A stray piece of newspaper or a crushed soda can could hold key evidence.

Knuckles leaned back in his chair and let his hand rest of his burgeoning belly. "Blunt force trauma. That's a pretty technical term."

"Blame it on *Monk*." I didn't solely watch *Law & Order*, thank you very much. I spread my mystery-loving binge watching around.

He grinned and pointed to the back of Fergus's head, where you could just see the edges of the gash in the picture. "Okay, so blunt force trauma. With what? Who nailed him over the head like that? Because

73

wowee and a hootenanny, that's some gash in his noggin. That means someone was madder n' a hornet, right?"

My finger shot up in the air as I gave that thought. "Good point! It definitely suggests someone was angry with him or at the very least there was passion involved. So maybe he has a wife or a girlfriend he angered? But anger also points to that Higgs man. He had an argument with Fergus yesterday right outside the store."

"The guy who runs the shelter? Cross Higglesworth?" he asked, frowning.

"That's the one."

He clucked his tongue. "Oh, I dunno." I heard the doubt in Knuckles's tone—oddly, it sounded like Detective Primrose's brand of skepticism. "He's a pretty good guy from what I hear on the street. He's always out bringing blankets to the folks under the Hawthorne—hot food, too. Offering them a place to stay. Helping them get jobs."

Could this Higgs do no wrong? Not only did everyone know him, everyone liked him. He was a real rock star around Cobbler Cove.

I looked at Knuckles's broad face thoughtfully. "So you know him personally?"

"Nope. I know *of* him. He's legend in the community. I've seen him at some of the places I do community service. In fact, he was at the Children's Center last year when I played Santa. He helped decorate the tree and read a bedtime story to the kids at the pajama party afterward."

If Higgs was the killer, I was going to have a hard time convincing anyone this saint was guilty even if I found hardcore evidence to the contrary.

Yet, I found myself warmed by Knuckles's own confession of community service. In fact, it made me smile. "How long have you lived here, Knuckles?"

"In Oregon? About half my life. I was raised in Bend, moved to LA to do celebrity tats when I was in my mid-twenties, moved back a year or so ago because I couldn't spend another second under that infernal sun. All that bright light gets old after a while. Discovered I missed the heck outta the rain. So after my wife Candice died, I packed up Biscuits and Noodles in their carriers, kissed my granddaughter and my little girl goodbye—who's your age, by the way—put my house up for sale, got in my car and drove home to my folks—who are still spry and active as ever in their eighties. Figured it out from there."

"You have a daughter and a granddaughter?"

He grinned as broadly as I'd ever seen him, the wrinkles by his sharp eyes deepening. "Yep. My Gwyneth and my little petunia, Starla. I fly back and forth to see 'em twice a month on the weekends. Miss 'em like crazy, though. Gwen's the one who suggested I should move back here. She knew how much I missed Candice and tattooing. So she told me to go find my smile again."

Then he pointed to yet more pictures of himself

with a tall, thin beauty with hair as dark as coal and a tiny girl of maybe three or so with dark curly hair and a killer smile on her chubby cheeks.

As I stared at the pictures once more, I asked, "And Biscuits and Noodles are?"

"I like biscuits and noodles," Coop proclaimed, patting her non-existent belly and making me chuckle softly.

He grinned at Coop, his eyes wrinkling at the corners. "I do, too. That's where I found them. At a place in LA that sells the some of the best biscuits and noodles. Anyway, they're my cats," he said proudly, pointing to a picture on the whitewashed buffet positioned behind the dining room table.

Eyeing the picture in the silver frame, I smiled at the two cats, sitting side by side on a rather elaborate cat condo. One the color of midnight, and the other a calico. "They're beautiful. Where are they?"

He hitched his jaw over his shoulder. "In the other room. Takes 'em a while to get used to new people. They'll come out when they're ready. Until then, got any more ideas about who killed Fergus?"

"Trixie Lavender!" Coop popped up from her chair, her eyes closer to flashing excitement than I'd seen thus far. "The man outside the store yesterday. Remember him? You were going to give him your leftovers from lunch but he was gone when we came back."

My eyes opened wide. "Omygosh, that's right!"

There'd been a homeless man parked right outside the shop as we were all leaving, with Fergus just ahead of us. He'd asked for money, but I'm more inclined to offer a hot meal due to the fact that money can be used for things that won't nourish your body, if you know what I mean, but I would have given him my leftovers had he been there when we'd returned.

As I remembered his hand when he'd stuck it out toward me, not nearly as weathered as I would have expected from someone who lived on the streets—especially after this past winter—I remembered the coat he was wearing. Far too warm for the weather we were having, despite the rain yesterday and early this morning.

It was a navy pea coat, tattered, spots of grease along the lapel with a tear right above the first button. Beneath, he wore a dirty white thermal shirt covered in dark stains, and shorts—he'd been wearing red basketball shorts. He'd had a green backpack slung over his arm and a hat like Gilligan wore on the show. His attire added up to an odd combination of outerwear, but he might not be too difficult to find if we were going to pursue this to the question phase of things.

Maybe he'd been there when Higgs and Fergus argued and he'd heard something we didn't—or something Higgs didn't want to confess?

Coop voiced my thoughts. "Bet he won't be too hard to find with that hat he had on. Should we go look for him—maybe under the bridge? Do you want me to hunt him? Maybe he heard something when Fergus McDuff argued with the man who runs the homeless shelter?"

I gave her the warning look; the one that said there'd be no hunting today because when Coop said hunt, she literally meant track, locate, accost her prey.

"No. Instead, I'm going to text Detective Primrose this information. I'd forgotten all about him, Coop. Good detecting. Soon you're going to be as good at this as Stevie."

"Who exactly is Stevie?" Knuckles asked then cleared his throat. "If you don't mind me asking. If it's private, no sweat."

Coop came very close to what one could call animated when she answered him. "Stevie is my friend. She said we'd always be friends. Always-always."

Knuckles cocked his head momentarily before he smiled warmly at Coop. A gesture I felt sure meant he didn't quite understand her almost emotionless words or her odd way of addressing people, but he did understand her fierce loyalty, and that made not only my heart swell, but my beginning affection for him grow.

If we were to work with other people, rent out spaces at Inkerbelle's or whatever, they needed to understand Coop's brisk nature and her idiosyncrasies.

"That's really cool, Coop. There's nothin' like a good friend. Nothin'."

Grinning at him, I pulled the laptop closer. "Stevie is someone who was very good to us back in a place called Ebenezer Falls. She's an amazing human being," I expounded without revealing too much just yet.

"So are we going to talk to the homeless guy?" he asked, folding his hands together.

A shiver ran up my spine. The last time we'd become embroiled in a murder investigation, we'd almost ended up dead after a tussle with the killers. This time, we weren't suspects, but the urgency of settling this weighed heavy on me due to the store's opening.

As in, we needed to open it ASAP.

"We'll see. But for now, look at this." I pointed to Fergus's neck and the scratch marks. "That looks intentional, don't you guys think? Like someone carved it into his skin on purpose."

Knuckles, big guy that he was, shivered. "Pretty intense, but I think you're right." Then he ran his hand over the bushy hair on his chin. "You know *what* it looks like, don't you?"

"A hashtag or a tic-tac-toe board," I muttered.

I'd been so caught up in taking pictures of Fergus that, while I'd noted the marks and remembered wondering if this was some sort of serial killer calling card, what the scratches resembled only just now registered.

Knuckles dropped his palm down on the table, making the plastic container of pho bounce. "Yep. That's it, for sure."

Coop leaned over and looked at the picture, squinting as she tucked her hair behind her ear. "It looks like it was done in a rush, too."

I cocked my head. Certainly whoever had killed Fergus wouldn't want to hang around, but I wondered what led Coop to make that observation. "Why do you say that?"

She tapped the picture and pursed her lips. "Look at the lines. They're all symmetrical but the last one." She dragged a finger over the final line intersecting the two vertical ones. "It's shorter and wobblier."

"Okay. An interesting point," I muttered as I stared at the picture. A point I don't think I'd have caught if not for her. I grabbed my laptop to scroll through the pictures to see if we had a better one of Fergus's neck. "So what do you think it means? Is it some kind of sign? Have there been other murders with this symbol carved into the victims? Because it definitely looks intentional. We're new to Cobbler Cove, Knuckles. Hear about any serial killers on the loose around here?"

He grimaced and scratched his ear. "Not that I know of."

Helpful tattoo artist is helpful. I sighed as I googled the word hashtag, but not much came up except for the definition and something having to do with the show *Psych* called the Hashtag Killer.

"Stevie was really good at this," Coop commented, pushing around some noodles on her plate with her chopsticks.

"But Stevie isn't here, Coop."

"So this Stevie... What's she good at besides being your friend?" Knuckles inquired, his eyebrow raised in question.

Coop gave him one of her deadpan looks. "Finding murderers."

Oh, holy ham and cheese. Now we were going to

have to explain this wasn't our first rodeo with a dead landlord.

"So you've done this before? Solved a murder?" His tone said he was intrigued, his eyes said "maybe I've made a mistake."

A chill raced up my spine and spread over my arms. We needed Knuckles on our side, not terrified to be in the same room with us. I gave Coop my "stop talking" look and decided to answer his question head on.

Were he so inclined, he could easily look us up on the Internet and find out what we'd been involved in back in Eb Falls. This question had come up a little sooner than I'd anticipated. Of course, I'd eventually have shared it with him, but now it was go big or go home.

"Well, we didn't really solve a murder. I guess Stevie didn't either, truthfully. She sort of fell into the answer to the puzzle. But she's solved other crimes." I held up a hand. "I'm getting off track. Forgive me. Yes. We've been part of a murder investigation, and in order to save ourselves from prison, we had to find out whodunit."

His look was as blank as the pages of my sketch-book lately.

"Wanna know who the murder victim was?"

"Is it going to be like your story about why you left the convent?"

I fought a snort and sat up straight. "Sort of. But outlandish in a different, maybe more ironic way."

His head bobbed up and down. "Then yep. I want to know."

"Okay, but remember, you wanted to know…"

His lips tilted upward a little as he folded the tops on the cartons of food. "I do. Was it somebody famous? Or a politician, maybe?"

"Nope. It was our landlord."

CHAPTER 6

"Well, at least he didn't boot us out on our butt-ox."

I burst out laughing as we drove back to the motel, the sun only just now beginning to set at almost nine in the evening. One of the million things I loved about summer.

I crossed my eyes at her and giggled. "It's *buttocks*, Coop. All one word. And really, buttocks?"

She shifted in her seat to face me, the fading sun kissing her model-like cheekbones, her brow creased. "Isn't that the right word?"

"It's definitely the right word. It's a little formal. You could just say butt. Or backside, even."

"Or arse!" Livingston said on a rumbly chuckle, clearly pleased with himself for his contribution to our conversation.

I made a face and wrinkled my nose in distaste. "Are you still learning new words, Coop?"

"I am. I study Webster's Dictionary online every day. I'm up to the letter P. Today I learned *palpebrate*."

"Wow. Sounds like something you catch in a public pool," I joked, pulling onto the highway.

"How do you catch a public pool?" Coop pondered, her interest clearly genuine.

My favorite owl rasped an annoyed sigh. "Ya can't, goose. And it means eyelids, or rather that ya have eyelids, lass," Livingston provided.

I eyed him from my rearview mirror. "Are you learning the dictionary with Coop, too, buddy?"

"Hah. Not on purpose, mind ya. I'm forced to hear her drone on and on while she studies, stuffed in this cage the way I am. Sometimes I pick up a ting or two in the learnin'. None of it worth a hornswaggle, mind ya. I'm not allowed to talk to anyone, as per your orders. Remember?"

Coop turned around and stuck her finger in Livingston's cage, something she did quite often. "You're not allowed because humans will be afraid of you. There are no talking owls in the history of owls ever, Quigley Livingston. We'd stick out like a sore finger—"

"Thumb. Stick out like a sore thumb," I corrected.

"Yes. That. And you should pay closer attention to the words I'm learning, my feathered friend. It's important we learn all things human."

He hooted in response (and if you listened closely enough, you'd hear the sarcasm in it, the way I did). "Have ya heard a single soul use the word palpebrate in a sentence since we've been here with the infernal humans, Coopie?"

"No, but it can't hurt to expand your mind, Livingston. Knowledge is a good thing. It's useful. I want to be useful."

"But must ya learn it all in one day, lass?"

Coop turned back around, but she didn't answer. Instead, she stared straight ahead and folded her arms over her chest.

"Are you afraid you're going to miss something, Coop?" I knew my demon pretty well by now. Coop was mostly an open book, and one of her biggest fears was being shipped back to Hell—in a handbasket—a phrase she'd begun to use the moment she'd heard it on some show she'd been watching.

"Maybe," was all she offered from tightly compressed lips.

Coop didn't like to show any kind of fear, big or little. It left her feeling vulnerable, not to mention weak in front of her superiors in Hell. Her words.

"Coop... Talk to me. Remember what I said about keeping everything bottled up?" I nudged, shooting her a glance of sympathy, my heart aching for the uncertainties she kept deep within.

"Then yes. I want to learn everything so if I have to go back to Hell someday, I'll have knowledge on my side."

"For all the good knowin' what the fiddle-dee-fee palpebrate means. Ya won't have to worry 'bout your eyelids because Satan will surely burn 'em off after ya betrayed him by escapin'—and he'll take me wit ya."

"Livingston!" I admonished, glaring at him in the rearview mirror. "No one's going back to Hell. Not as long as I'm around, okay? Now knock off all the doom and gloom, both of you, and let's focus on this murder."

Livingston shifted in his cage, his gray speckled wings flexing and rustling against the bars. "What's there to focus on, lass? Did ya suddenly become Sherlock Holmes? Nice bloke, by the way."

"You knew Sherlock Holmes?" I paused with a frown. "Wait, is he in Hell?"

"'Course I did. Fine chap he was."

"Livingston is pulling the wool over your head, Trixie. Sir Arthur Conan Doyle wrote the *fictional* character Sherlock Holmes. Livingston knew the pretend Sherlock Holmes. That one came from Queens, New York, and he was quite cruel. *And* he picked his nose. He was not a fine chap at all."

I narrowed my eyes at Livingston and squeezed the steering wheel. "He's pulling the wool *over my eyes*, Coop. And no, Livingston. I'm not Sherlock Holmes. I'm just trying to hurry things along so we can get into the store. The sooner we get into the store, the sooner we open shop. We need to open soon."

"Do you think Knuckles is still going to want to work for us, now that he knows this is the second landlord we've killed?"

I rolled my eyes. "We didn't kill either one of them, Coop. Don't say that out loud."

"But what if he *thinks* we did. What if, deep down, he thinks we're murderers?" The worry in her voice was something new.

I wasn't sure if humanizing her, so to speak, teaching her how to have empathy and morals and all the things a kind human should have, was actually a good thing, because along with those emotions came doubt and fear.

So I set out to soothe her with a gentler word. "I think he was just a little rattled..."

Poor Knuckles. Just when I'd thought he was at peace with who we were, we lambasted him with another surprise. I think that ended up being the icing on his acceptance cake. After we told him our previous landlord was dead, too, he grew very quiet. That made me sad. We never even had the chance to meet his cats...

And that's not to say he wasn't a complete gentleman, but his silence left me feeling uncomfortable. In light of the fact that I couldn't do anything but tell him the truth or he'd find out anyway, I had to allow him the time to digest—or not. It was his choice.

So we took our leave, and now we were going to pop by the store to see if the police tape was still surrounding the door.

Foolish? Probably. It had only been a few hours and likely we'd find it as we'd left it, but maybe luck was on our side today.

Coop's face went a bit sour when she wrinkled her nose. "Rattled? Does that mean afraid, Trixie? I would never want Knuckles to be afraid of us. I like him so-so much. He's an outstanding tattooist—a true artist. Did you see those pictures on his wall?"

"You mean the ones with the celebrities and their tattoos?"

"Yes!" she said with about as much passion as I'd ever heard in her voice. "He's amazing. I don't want him to be afraid we'll kill him. I'd never kill him. I want to learn from him. I want to be his friend. Just like Stevie's."

I gnawed on my lower lip before I said, "I don't think afraid defines what was happening with Knuckles, Coop. It was just a lot of revelation for one day. That's all. Sometimes, folks need to let things digest. They need to process the words—absorb them. Let's not worry about it for now. He said he'd call us, and he seems like a man of his word."

Or he could blow us off forever—and who could blame the poor guy?

"I hope what you say is true, Trixie Lavender."

I grinned at her, fighting to keep my optimism. "I hope what I say is true, too, Cooper O'Shea."

"Hey!" Livingston squawked. "You two hens are cluckin' over Pinky while I'm starvin'. I haven't had anythin' since breakfast when ya threw that stale biscuit at me."

"His name is *Knuckles*, Livingston," Coop corrected. "Don't be rude. It's unkind and unnecessary."

"Quack, quack, quack," Livingston replied in a dry

tone. "That's all I hear is ya quackin' at me while I'm starvin' to death."

Chuckling, I sighed. "I got your back, Livingston. I'm going to drop you guys off at the motel. Coop, you sneak Mouthy McMouth in and I'll go and see what's up at the store. Okay?"

The motel didn't allow pets, so we had to be very careful bringing Livingston in and out. It did force him to be quieter, which was a blessing in disguise sometimes.

Coop frowned as we pulled up to the motel, its exterior sporting splotches of mold along the siding and brick foundation, very common in Oregon with all the rain. She peered out the window. "It's getting dark. Should you go alone? I don't mind going with you."

I pulled into a parking space and flapped a hand at her as Coop climbed out and opened the back door, throwing a garbage bag over Livingston's cage in order to carry him into the motel. "Nah. I'll be fine. There are plenty of people all over the place. It's not that late. Get Mr. Feed-Me-Now-Or-Suffer-My-Wrath fed and settled for the night, and I'll be back before you know it."

With a curt nod, she hauled Livingston's cage from the backseat and sauntered toward the motel with purposeful strides, making me smile. Coop didn't do anything halfway. If you asked her to do something, she did it with gusto.

I decided to walk to the store, it was only a hop, skip and a jump away, and besides, it was a nice night.

The sky was clear, the stars were even out, twinkling bright in the black silk falling over Cobbler Cove. I loved it here. I loved the people and their easygoing ways. I loved the mountains and the water so close by.

I loved the kooky personalities, like the man who drove a van covered in gargoyles. I loved the smells of the food trucks and the heat of the day rising from the pavement to escape into the fresh air of evening.

Despite the problems we were having, I clung to my optimism. The police and forensics would likely clear out in a couple of days. I mean, how long did it take to sweep a crime scene? Maybe we'd be set back a week at most. That wasn't an eternity, right?

Squaring my shoulders, I almost skipped the rest of the way—until I caught sight of the store and groaned, panic flooding my veins.

No, no, no!

Dashing across the street, I just barely missed running into the front end of an old Volkswagen van that honked at me with piercing anguish.

"Sorry!" I bellowed as I skirted the front bumper and beat feet to the store, stopping short in front of a huge pile of boxes. *So* many boxes.

Well, our inventory had arrived.

A day early, at a place covered in crime scene tape, but whatever, right?

Clenching my fists, I gritted my teeth to keep from screaming my frustration at the way the universe was treating us these days. Every time we got back up, something else knocked us down.

I did a quick sweep of the store with my eyes, looking to see if anything had been disturbed, but all appeared well.

Except for that noise.

I paused and cocked an ear. What *was* that noise? A scuffing of some kind. As though someone was digging through something.

I followed it blindly, not giving much thought to the fact that I was heading behind our building and toward the dumpsters in the alleyway.

"Hello?" I called, not really thinking anyone would answer back.

And then I heard it again. *Scratch, rustle, scratch.* I narrowed my eyes and got a good glance at my surroundings.

There was no way out of the alleyway, no pass-through behind the buildings. Just a brick wall with but a mere two inches between the building and the brick —meaning, whoever or whatever it was had to get past *me* to make an exit.

Now, listen. I'm not used to being in peril. I mean, I virtually spent half my life in a convent. Peril, at least until I became possessed, didn't really come into play, so I wasn't always aware of its existence or how to sense it. Sometimes, fools really do rush in. In fact, once I'd saved a kitten in the sewer by the convent gates by climbing into it without thinking twice about how I was going to get the heck out.

Do you have any idea how much it rains in Oregon and how often cars passed the convent? A lot. Thankfully, Sister Alice Ambrosia happened upon me during one of her commune-with-nature walks, and helped both the kitten and me to safety. But not before I'd spent almost six hours in a stinky, damp drain, screaming for help.

Anyway, this time, the shiver racing along my arms and up my spine *did* make me think "peril," which should have made me turn around and hit the bricks.

Did I?

No. I foolishly, albeit briefly, thought an animal might be in trouble with all the scratching and rustling around. Which is why I went deeper into the alleyway, beyond where the streetlamp's thin rays glowed and toward the dumpster.

"Hello?" I whispered, inching forward, peering into the darkness.

Just as I hit the lip of the dumpster, someone exploded from inside, virtually dropping down on top of me, shooting up loose debris and the ripest smell I've ever smelled.

In those brief seconds, while I fell to the ground and hit my knees so hard, I almost bit my tongue in half, I wondered, what would Stevie do?

After she was done screaming in pain, that is. Which, I did. I'm not Superman, folks. It hurt like a son of a gun.

Anyway, Stevie'd try to catch whoever had fallen from the sky and grill them about why they were rooting around in a dumpster behind her store, that's what. She'd also take in as much as she could beyond what was right in front of her. She'd said scent was just as important as sight.

So I did the same as I fell forward, trying to clutch the perpetrator's ankles, my fingers clamping on to a boot. I'm sure it was a boot because I caught the top of it between my fingers—and definitely made of a suede-ish material.

And I sniffed the air as deeply as I could. Garlic. I smelled garlic. Sure, I know that could have been from any restaurant up and down the street, or even the dumpster itself, but when whoever it was had landed on my head, I'd gotten a huge whiff of garlic, and I smelled it right now as I struggled to latch onto anything I could to keep this person from getting away.

Clinging to the perp's ankle, I grit my teeth and tried to pull him toward me while my knees stung, my fingernails tore and my heart raced. But I kept my eyes open and tried to take in as much as I could see—naturally, that happened to be mostly nothing. I saw the shadow of an outline of someone who was pretty long and had jeans on, but that was it.

But just as I screamed out, "Stop! I just want to talk to you!" the person escaped, yanking their ankle from my aching grip and rising up to race off out of the alleyway.

And I lay there stunned, covered in wet dirt and gravel.

Forcing myself upward on a heaving breath, I fell toward the dumpster, my hip catching the corner of the metal as I steadied myself. Bracing my hands on my thighs, I backed up against it and breathed in, all the while wondering if this had something to do with Fergus McDuff's murder or was it just someone dumpster diving.

Though, in the latter case, I had to wonder why they'd make such a big deal about it by running off. And if it wasn't someone homeless, what could they possibly be digging for?

Rather than do the smart thing and head back to the lighted areas, I looked at the face of the building and remembered the window upstairs, facing the alleyway. Maybe they'd been trying to get up there via the fire escape?

Hmmm.

I had so many questions and very little to go on. But I was determined to at least try. As my head whirled and my knees stung, I gathered my wits—only to remember the boxes.

The boxes!

All alone on a sidewalk where anyone could cart them off. That lit a fire under my behind, making me run around the side of the building to confront my next hurdle despite the ache in my knees and my bleeding fingernail.

Seeing the boxes still safe, I closed my eyes and took deep breaths, one after the other, praying for patience to see me through this ordeal. And I'll be honest, I fought a tear or two. The hot liquid threatening to seep from my eyes left me angry.

Where the heck were we going to put all these

boxes? There were easily thirty or forty of them in all sizes. There was no room in my car, and lugging them to the motel would be almost impossible. It would take all night. I was going to have to sleep on top of them so no one would steal our stuff.

Blowing out a breath, I squared my shoulders. Okay, enough feeling sorry for myself.

Weaving my way through the maze of cardboard boxes almost as tall as me, I was just about to attack my task when someone hacked a phlegmy cough, making me jump.

Did the person from the dumpster want a round two?

My eyes fought to find the spot the cough was coming from when the shadowy figure of a man jumped up from behind the last stack of boxes, his thin frame weaving to and fro. "Who goes there?" he shouted, his voice gravelly and worn. "Identify yourself, intruder! This is my land, thief, and I will not have you pilfering my fields without a fight. Dost thou wish to dual here in the deep of night? Show me your sword and let us fight like men!"

First, I don't know if I was more insulted about the idea that he thought I was a man, or that he wanted to fight me for some boxes. But I recognized this for what it was. A homeless man staking his claim. Staking it in a very colorful way, but staking it nonetheless.

Thus, I took a gentle approach as I inched my way closer to him to get a clearer view while keeping my tone friendly. "Aw, c'mon now. You don't want to dual with me, do you? *Me?* I'm harmless as a newborn kitten. Plus, I don't have a sword. Come and stand under the streetlight and you'll see I'm incapable of harming anyone. I'll meet you there, okay?" I coaxed as soothingly as possible.

I took a couple of steps out of the intricate path of boxes and into the light and held up both my hands, hoping he'd reveal himself. "See? It's just me. Do I look like a girl who'd pilfer your fields? I'm no pilferer. Honest."

He huffed as he came into view, clinging to a cart from a supermarket with one hand, a scruffy army blanket wrapped around his shoulders.

He adjusted his gold Viking hat with his free hand and peered at me with suspicious eyes. "Who art thou, and what dost thou want?" he groused then coughed again, the residual effects making his shoulders shake as he wheezed an inward breath.

"My name is Trixie Lavender, and I come in peace, my liege." I curtsied, hoping the term "liege" came from the proper era. I'm a little lost when it comes to medieval-speak (at least I think that's what he was shooting for), but then, he wore a plastic Viking hat. So I'm not sure he knew the proper era, either. In fact, let me be blunt. History wasn't my thing. I don't know anything about eras except my own, and even that has some blank spots.

"Speak!" He shouted the demand, pulling the blanket tighter. "State your reasons for trespassing or it's off with your head!"

Keeping my tone even, I proceeded carefully, as though there were nothing unusual about our interaction. "I'm getting ready to move into the store here." I hitched my bloody index finger over my shoulder at the door covered in crime scene tape. "And these are my boxes of things for my tattoo parlor. But I don't mind if you sit by them at all. In fact, please make yourself comfortable, sire." I pulled one of the boxes down and patted it to indicate he could sit with me, cursing my aching knees as I did.

As he came closer—warily, mind you—I saw the dirt streaking his gnarled face, and his wrists were so thin, I could wrap one hand around both of them. Rather than assess him further, I went about my business.

Yet, he didn't appear at all interested in the shop or tattoos—only the boxes, which made for good shelter, I suppose.

Hopping up on the box, I began to chat—the goal being to get him to trust I wouldn't take anything from him or, worse, harm him. "And how shall I address you, kind sir?" I asked finally, letting my legs swing while I pretended to look at my nails in indifference—even though they surely needed looking at after my incident in the alleyway.

Now he became bashful, his tired eyes downcast as he rubbed his nose with the side of his hand, his reply quite 2018. "I'm Solomon."

"Nice to meet you, Solomon."

And then he did a one-eighty as though he'd

forgotten to stay in character, and bellowed, "That's Solomon, King of Hawthorne to you, peasant!"

He announced his title in such a way that I expected trumpets to blare.

Instantly, I sat up straight and gave him my full attention. "Of course, your majesty. What brings you out on an eve as fine as this?"

He shrugged his shoulders, the greasy tangles of his hair poking out from beneath his Viking hat blowing in the cool night air. "I was just looking for a place to take a nap."

Peering at him from the corner of my eye, I nodded, guessing our time travel game was over. "Well then, Solomon. You're welcome to take a nap on my boxes any day of the week."

"Really?"

I smiled as he inched ever closer to the box I'd pulled down for him to sit on. "Really-really." Pausing for a moment, I decided to inquire about his general well being. "Might I ask, have you supped this day, sire?"

I couldn't smell any alcohol on him, and I usually have a good nose for these things, but I also couldn't tell if he was a drug user. His arms were essentially covered by his blanket and his feet were dressed in some tattered, matted fuzzy slippers.

"Maybe… Why do you care?" He gripped the rusty handle of the cart, filled with black bags and two stained pillows.

So he wouldn't bolt, I shrugged as if indifferent. "I

was just making conversation, that's all. You don't have to tell me if you don't want to."

He rolled his tongue around the interior of his mouth, and it was then I saw he had only a few teeth. "You a social worker?"

A homeless soul's biggest nightmare, I suspect. Looking up at the stars, I pretended to gaze at them. "Nope. I told you, Solomon, I'm leasing this shop. It's going to be a tattoo shop called Inkerbelle's. My friend Coop is the tattoo artist and I do some sketching. Mostly, I'll just be managing things. If you're around here sometime, I'll introduce you to her if you want. I think you'll like her."

Now he lifted his chin, giving me a full view of his craggy face and wrinkling neck. He was too thin, and his cough worried me. "I don't like people."

Sighing, I smiled at him. "Sometimes I don't either, Solomon. But sometimes they're not so bad. You just have to give them a chance and find out which way they're gonna go."

Suddenly, he made a confession. I was certain I hadn't earned his trust yet, but for whatever reason, he'd lost sight of his medieval play and decided to switch topics. "You know who I don't like?"

"Who don't you like, Solomon?"

He stuck a knobby finger featuring a cracked nail out at me and pointed with aimless abandon. "I don't like that mad guy. He was really mad."

My ears went hot, but I wasn't sure why. This likely gentle soul talked like an actor from the Medieval

Times. To give any credence to what he said could be just this shy of madness. But what if he knew something he'd been too afraid to share? It could all be street melodrama, there was plenty of that to go around even among the homeless. They had bullies and social butterflies just like every community did. Sometimes it was like a Telenovela with the shenanigans.

Still, I asked, "Who's the mad guy? Do you know his name, Solomon?"

Shaking his head, Solomon flicked his hand and hiked the blanket over his shoulder. "He's been here. He's been right here. Right here, all the time. Nobody listens, nobody listens to Solomon," he repeated, almost like a parrot. "Nobody believes Solomon. Nope, nope, nope. Nobody believes him."

His words were starting to pick up speed, worrying me. He was becoming agitated, and the last thing I wanted to do was upset him. But I had to proceed, even if it was with caution.

"Hey, Solomon?" I asked, using a quiet tone. "Do you like soup?"

He stopped all motion, the flicking twitch of his hand slowing as he held it in midair, applying his fingers. "What kind?"

I tilted my head so he could see my face. So he'd see I was genuinely interested—and make no mistake. I was.

"My specialty is chicken noodle with teeny-tiny ground chicken meatballs. Sounds crazy, right? But it's really good. I'm not much of a cook, but it was my mother's recipe."

"I like soup."

"Then promise me this, when the store's finally open, you'll drop by for a bowl, okay? I make it all the time for our lunch. I'm happy to share."

That stopped him cold for a second, and it was then he finally looked at me. Really, truly looked at me—lucid and aware, making my heart tighten.

"Will the mad guy be there?"

"I don't know who the mad guy is, Solomon. I'd like to think I won't have any mad guys here, but I can't know for sure unless you tell me who he is."

"He gives me the goose bumps. Scares me right out of my pants. He was here last night. I saw him. He was mad. Mad, mad, mad."

Who was the mad bad guy, and why was he scaring Solomon? And did this involve Fergus McDuff's murder? That was the real question.

"I promise I won't let any mad guys come around if you come for soup. But," I nudged, "it sure would help if you told me who the mad guy is. Or even if you just tell me what he looks like. Then there'd be no mad guys period. You can trust that."

Leaning into his cart, he began to grip the handle so hard, his dirty, weathered knuckles went white. "He has a tattoo. Maybe he'll get more at your shop. I don't like the mad guy. Solomon doesn't like the mad guy and the mad guy doesn't like laundry."

Laundry? Somehow, I guessed there were several

things going on in Solomon's head and he'd mixed them up.

But clearly, the mad guy frightened Solomon enough to make him speak about himself in third person, and I didn't want him frightened. "Nobody likes a mad guy, Solomon. But he's not here now, is he?"

Now his eyes—a hazy blue if I wasn't mistaken, when they flashed under the streetlamp—went wide as he scanned the sidewalk and the surrounding street. "Not now, but he'll be back! Yes, yes, yes. He comes back. He always comes back! He's everywhere!"

Sliding off the box, I winced when my feet hit the concrete. My knees needed an aspirin and a warm cloth to soothe them. Yet, I wanted to handle this as carefully as I could, but still glean some information from him.

"Well, he's not back now, Solomon. Why don't you sit with me a spell? I have to figure out what to do with these boxes, and I have nowhere to go until I do."

Just when I thought he was going to join me, he began to back away. "But he might come back right while we're sitting here. He does bad things. That's the mad guy. Bad and mad!"

"What if I promise to protect you from the bad mad guy?"

He shook his head so violently, the Viking hat he wore almost fell to the ground. "Nobody can protect me. He's too big. He's too scary. He has powers! Special powers! Laundry powers!" Solomon yelped, his thin frame wobbling with the force of his words.

This was going south fast, and I knew it. So I made an executive decision to push just a little bit, but with a gentle hand.

Taking a chance, I reached out and placed my palm on his arm, hoping to reconnect him with the world around him. "Solomon? Do you know what happened here last night?"

He coughed, the phlegm-filled hack echoing around my head, but it appeared to slow his roll just a little. Running a finger over his throat to mimic a knife, he said, "He's dead."

Just my hand on his arm had me worried. He was warm enough even through the army blanket to fry an egg. He needed medical attention. But first, I had to keep him calm before I could convince him to see a doctor.

"Do you know *who* died, Solomon?" I asked, wishing I'd brought my purse so I could at least offer him some tissues.

"Yep, yep, yep I do. Old Fergus McDuff bought the big one last night. He was mean to me and the people of my kingdom. Mean, stupid, mean!"

"Is *he* the mad bad guy you're talking about?"

Solomon shook my hand off and began to shrink away from me. "No! But he knows him. He knows him. They tell secrets. Ugly secrets!"

"Who tells ugly secrets, Saul?"

At the sound of the new voice, one not unfamiliar

to me, Solomon didn't just back away, he plowed backward, pushing his shopping cart so hard, I thought it might tip over. Solomon's eyes were as wide as if he'd seen a ghost.

"You—*you* stay away from me, you rapscallion! I'm not going with you. No I'm not!"

"It's okay, Saul," the voice said, emerging from the darkness. "Everything's fine. You know I'd never make you do anything you didn't want to do."

"No it is not either, you…you…*meaniepants*! Nothing is fine. You leave me alone!" Solomon bellowed, turning to break into a running start as he gave his cart a hard shove to get it moving, the wheels clacking against the pavement sounding his escape.

And that left me alone with the voice, and not much else.

Unless you count the boxes.

I still had the mountain of boxes.

Mercy.

CHAPTER 7

I closed my eyes and inhaled. Just when I was finally getting somewhere with Solomon, who was also apparently Saul, I'd been foiled.

Argh.

"How's it going?"

I popped open my eyes instantly at the sound of the now familiar husky voice tinged with that hint of amusement. Cross Higglesworth stared right at me, his dark eyes smiling, his mouth in an upward tilt as he made his way through the maze of my inventory to where I stood.

I backed away, swallowing hard, almost knocking over one of the stacks of boxes. Could he be who Solomon was talking about—or maybe even the person in the dumpster?

I sniffed the air, but I didn't pick up the scent of garlic. Instead, I smelled a freshly scented cologne. So he probably wasn't the person from the dumpster.

And if Higgs ran a shelter, he'd surely crossed paths with Solomon. He had called him Saul, meaning he obviously knew him.

Thus, I folded my arms across my chest, and in a random moment, noted the greasy spot of pho on my T-shirt. Still, I stared Higgs dead in the eyes anyway. I was all about the motto "show no fear"—even if my knees were wobbling and my pulse raced like a Formula 1 race car.

"Well, well. If it isn't the snitch," he said, his tone teasing and light.

Hah. Hah.

In my resolve for bravado, I chose sarcasm as my weapon and lobbed his words back at him. "Well, well. If it isn't the *murder* suspect."

Higgs chuckled, deep and rumbling, tucking his thumbs into the belt loops of his jeans, his stance casual and relaxed. "Me? A suspect? I'm not a suspect. No one ever said I was a suspect."

I jabbed a finger in the air. "But the question is, *should* you be?"

He thumped his chest in the vicinity of his heart. "That cuts me deep, Trixie Lavender. I wouldn't hurt a fly."

My eyes narrowed and my fists clenched. "But would you hurt a human? In particular, a human named Fergus McDuff?"

He laughed again, and this time it was attractively warm. Which, I'll tell you, I didn't like one little bit. Also, he didn't answer, he skipped right over my question and moved on to Solomon.

Leaning against a stack of the boxes, he crossed his feet at his ankles. "So I see you met Saul—or King Solomon, to his minions under the Hawthorne Bridge. It depends on what day it is. Some days he's Captain Swarthy, pirate of the *Bearded Lady*."

I fought a smile. I liked Solomon more and more, and if it weren't for the fact that I hadn't yet mentally cleared Higgs of murder, I'd like him, too—for the service he did for the community. That is if, in fact, Solomon wasn't running away from him, meaning Higgs was the mad bad guy who had laundry, or did laundry, or something along those lines...

"I did meet him. He was camped out here on these boxes. Boy, did he take off when he saw you, huh?"

"Saul's a good guy, you know," he said as though he needed to defend him. Which I found a little admirable, and yes, I hated that, too. "He's just a little mixed up in his head, and terrified of the social workers who canvas in their efforts to help the homeless. He's sort of lumped me in with them as being part of the larger conspiracy to lock him away forever."

"And are you a bad guy?" More specifically, a *mad bad guy*?

But he didn't answer my question directly. "He thinks they're going to lock him up and throw away the key. Which they might, I suppose. He obviously has issues requiring medical attention. I don't have much background on him, but he'd never hurt anyone, in case you're wondering. He's more afraid of you than you could ever be of him. You have my word."

Higgs appeared to worry I'd consider Solomon a problem, and I guessed it was because his life revolved around helping the homeless. His effort to reassure me and vouch for Solomon might have been well received if not for that little niggle in the back of my head, screaming he could be a killer.

So I waved him off, the motion reminding me there was still blood on my fingernails. "He wasn't a problem at all, and I certainly wasn't afraid. The whole medieval speak was fun for a minute or three. But he did have a cough that concerned me. Sounded like bronchitis. I'm guessing he's afraid of doctors, too?"

Higgs's eyes went dark with concern. "Argh, matey! He'd sooner die of the scurvy than see one of those quacks. His words, not mine. Anything having to do with the medical field is a strict no-no for Saul. I'm also a no-no for Saul. That's why he ran away. For some reason, he thinks accepting a bed and a hot meal means I can lock him up and throw away the key. He sees me as an authority figure with the power to put him on lockdown rather than a helper."

I liked that he used the word *helper*. I'd read Mr. Rogers once said his mother had told him if there were ever a scary situation, he should always look for the "helpers." You'll always find people helping, and it had stuck with me ever since.

So I wondered if Solomon hadn't run away because he was afraid of Higgs? Or was this just a cover-up story to keep suspicion at bay? Or did Solomon have something to be afraid of concerning Higgs?

"Your impression of a pirate is pretty aces," I commented.

He grinned. "Ya think? I've been practicing in the hopes Saul will let me be a part of his band of merry men."

"Wasn't that Robin Hood? I don't think Robin Hood had any pirates, and pirates don't have a band of merry men."

"Hey," he said, reaching for my injured fingers. "What happened? Let me take a look."

I shooed his hand away and drove mine into the pocket of my jeans. "I just had a little accident and tore a couple of nails. No big deal."

"And is that why you're covered in dirt?"

Either that wasn't him in the dumpster or he was a really good actor, and I couldn't use that excuse for everything he did. I decided that hadn't been him in the dumpster. There hadn't been enough time for him to go back and clean up afterward.

I looked down at my jeans, streaked with dirt. "Mud wrestling. I figured I'd better take on a second job to pay the rent until we can get into the store and start tattooing. Somebody's gotta pay the bills, right?"

He nodded, his smile back on his face. "Ahhh. I prefer Jell-O. Green, mind you, because I'm a lime-a-holic, but to each his own."

I fought a giggle but managed to remain silent,

despite his eyes, which felt like they were seeing right through me.

Higgs paused a moment and peered into the darkness, his eyes clouding over in seriousness. "So Saul has a cough, you say?"

I remembered the hacking sound and cringed a bit. "A pretty rough one. And his skin was warm. I felt it right through the blanket on his arm."

Higgs blinked, clearly surprised. "Wait. He *let* you touch him?"

"Only for a second or two, but yes, and I'd bet he has a fever. That, coupled with the cough, says he should really see a doctor. Do you know where he stays at night?"

I planned to go and see if I could find him after I figured out where to put these infernal boxes.

And during my search, I fully intended to go over every word of my conversation with Solomon. He knew something about what had happened to Fergus. I knew it.

Higgs was on his cell phone, texting someone before I'd even finished my sentence. "I'm letting one of my staff know. They'll send someone to look for him and hopefully convince him to see someone. So confirm for me again, Saul *let* you touch him?"

I guess that was super unusual… "I swear he did. It was very brief. Is that unusual?"

Higgs sighed. "I suspect a touch of autism. Not confirmed, mind you. He won't let anyone near him for long enough to find out, so that's not an official diagnosis. But Saul's not fond of anyone touching him, *ever*. So color me impressed that he let you. He must feel comfortable with you."

My chest tightened. Poor Solomon. "Had I known, I never would have attempted it, and I'll be far more careful in the future."

"You plan on communing with the homeless a lot?"

My chin shot up in the air. "I plan on doing tons of community service, thank you very much. That means communing with all those in need—including, but not exclusive to, the homeless."

"I keep forgetting you're a nun. Though, based on the bits of the conversation I heard, you were very nice to Saul. Very kind."

He'd heard the conversation? Did that mean he knew Solomon was possibly ratting on him? Maybe he was the mad bad guy and this was all a ruse?

"Ex-nun, and I'd do it if I were a ditch digger."

I think I saw admiration in his eyes, and for a moment, my heart wiggled in my chest. But I crushed that movement like an annoying fly. It wouldn't do for me to preen if Higgs were the killer.

Cocking his head, his shiny hair catching the street-lamp in all its gleaming, rich color, Higgs asked, "So, what are you doing out here so late anyway, Sister Trixie Lavender? Don't you have to wait for the police to clear the store?" He pointed at the yellow crime scene tape sprawled across Inkerbelle's dirty glass door.

I didn't answer him. Instead, I used Stevie's trick to

avoid his inquiry. I answered a question with a question. "What are *you* doing here?"

His eyebrow rose, dark and skeptical. "Did someone teach you to answer a question with a question?"

I peered into the darkness and noted there wasn't anyone else around. That made me lift my chin to show him I was no scaredy cat. So if he was planning on murdering this girl, he was in for a fight.

"No one taught me that. I thought it up all on my own."

Higgs scratched his head and scanned my eyes for a moment before he appeared to shake it off. "What do you say we start again? What brings you to the store so late at night when you can't even get into the store until the police clear it, Sister Trixie? Is it these boxes? Are they yours? I don't have my contacts in, so I can't tell."

I leaned against a stack of boxes, refusing to be riled by him calling me *sister*. He knew I wasn't a nun anymore. It was a blatant tactic meant to stir my pot. "What brings you down to my end of the street so late at night? Don't you have a homeless shelter to run?"

"Well, duh. I was doing what all good murder suspects do. I was looking for my next victim, silly."

He said it with such amusement in his voice, I almost laughed out loud. But to my credit, I didn't. I wasn't ready to believe he had nothing to do with this. I didn't have gut feelings on this the way Stevie claimed she had whenever she found herself embroiled in a murder investigation (and apparently, that was quite often). At least not yet, anyway. So I had to stay on my toes and consider all angles.

Instead, I countered, "That's what I figured. Everyone who's looking for their next victim comes to the scene of a crime to hunt their prey. I hear in murderer circles, it's the trendy thing to do."

He gave me a lopsided grin, the dark night enhancing his very white teeth. "You know, for a nun, you're kinda funny."

"I'm an *ex*-nun, and for a murder suspect, you're *not* so funny."

"Murder isn't exactly a humorous business."

"You know, for a guy who could go to jail for *murder*, you don't look terribly worried."

"That's what makes me so good at my murdery job. I don't sweat the small stuff." Then he paused and looked at the boxes. "So, is this all yours?"

My eyes narrowed and my stance shifted. "Maybe..."

"It's sort of a yes-or-no question. Either they're yours or not."

"What if they are?"

He clucked his tongue at me in admonishment, his eyes roaming over the stacks of boxes I'd enmeshed myself in. "Now you're just being combative for combativeness' sake, and it's hurting my feelings. As your neighbor, I'm just trying to be helpful. So, once more, for the cheap seats, are they yours? Because if they are, you'll want to get them somewhere safe. It's not terribly dangerous here at night, but unopened boxes are just a little too much temptation for almost anyone. Just ask this alleged murderer. If you hadn't come along, I don't know if I could have continued to withstand the temptation to see what's inside them."

Now I did laugh. He was really willing to go the extra mile with my accusation, and he certainly wasn't taking it very seriously.

I held up my hands like two white flags. I could be wary and distantly friendly at the same time. In fact, if I were at the very least cordial, maybe he'd slip up and say something he shouldn't about killing Fergus and we'd solve this mess and be done.

And in truth, if I let my character assessment of Higgs be my guide, he had a decent enough vibe about him. Or maybe he was simply a good actor. But maybe not…

Cheese and rice, I was bad at this. I waffled more than a waffle maker.

Which was what made me decide to make a little peace but continue to stay wary. "Okay, okay. Listen, I saw what I saw yesterday. I can't change that. I *won't* change that. I told the detective the truth, which is my obligation as a concerned citizen with a dead guy in her newly leased store. That said, I just want to get into the store and start handling the mess. I mean, have you seen it? It looks like Hiroshima in there minus the mushroom cloud. In fact, as of right now, I don't even know what's going to happen to our lease because Fergus is dead. That could mean his holdings and real estate will go into probate and we'll be out on our ear."

THEN THERE WERE NUN

Just like they had at the last store we'd leased. Golly, that would be the crummiest of crummy crumbs.

"Oh...I guess you didn't know or maybe he didn't tell you? Fergus doesn't own the building, Trixie. He just does the dirty work, like collecting rent and code enforcement—stuff like that. The building is owned by Crowley McDuff. His brother. So he'd be the guy to talk to about where you stand with the lease."

My eyes widened in surprise. How had that piece of information slipped past us? "I had no idea. Fergus made it appear as though he owned the space."

Which, in turn, instantly made me wonder if he'd raised the rent so he could skim off the top, and if so, had he done that to other tenants? Tenants who might be angry and want to murder him?

How did Stevie handle all these questions? No sooner was one answered than another one cropped up.

Higgs's jaw, already razor sharp, tightened and he planted his hands on his hips. "You know why that is, don't you? That's because Fergus McDuff was a jerk. Ask any of his other tenants and they'll tell you the same."

Uh-huh. Though, Solomon had backed that statement up.

Crossing my arms over my chest, I wondered aloud, "Should you be telling *me*, the snitch? It doesn't look good for your defense."

"I'm just speaking the truth. And the truth is, I didn't kill Fergus McDuff, and truer still, he really was a jerk. I didn't wish him dead, but how he lived his life was a testament to his character. He was cruel to a lot of the guys who come to the shelter. He didn't like the lines of guys waiting to get a bed at night. Claimed it detracted from any businesses moving into the spaces he took care of for his brother. But my guys are good guys, just a little lost—and okay, maybe some a little more lost than others. They're not all saints, but they're not monsters, either. They just need a break. Maybe a little redemption. A hot meal and a purpose. A reason to get up in the morning."

As Higgs spoke, his voice filled with liquid warmth when he talked about the men at his shelter, and his eyes burned bright into the dark of the evening. I knew passion for a cause, and this was a man with passion. Deeply rooted passion. That much, I couldn't deny.

I also couldn't deny I had the same passion for the homeless, the downtrodden, animals, the elderly.

I'm pretty sure I wasn't supposed to feel any sort of connection to Higgs if he turned out to be the guy who did it, but I did. Just a thread of connection, mind you, but a connection nonetheless.

So I softened, but only a smidge. "Well, thanks for the information about who owns this shipwreck. It'll be good to have in the coming days while we try to figure this out. I'll make it my mission to find Crowley McDuff."

Higgs smiled, hitching his razor-stubbled jaw at the boxes. "So, they *are* yours then. Need help loading them up somewhere? Happy to oblige. You know, neighbor to neighbor. Or should I say, murder suspect to snitch?" he teased.

"So you're admitting you're a suspect?"

"I admit nothing, fair maiden. And I'm really not a suspect. She questioned me just like she did you. I could call Tansy so you can confirm, if you'd like? While I do that, would you like help with the boxes?

Did he have to be so neighborly? So accommodating? He was making it difficult to keep him at the top of my suspect list—and my list was small. I couldn't afford to lose a suspect.

"Actually, I was planning on building a box fort and sleeping here tonight."

He looked up at the sky, littered with stars and a milky-white moon. "Well, if you had to pick a night, tonight's one of the better ones. At least it's not raining."

I nodded. "All I need is a pillow and a blanket."

Turning to begin counting how many boxes there were, I frowned. My sheet of inventory was in the store, of course. So there was no way to compare what we'd received and what we hadn't.

Higgs tapped me on the shoulder. "Seriously, I'm happy to help—"

"Higgs?" a male voice emerged from the darkness, smoky and friendly. As the outline of a man appeared, I instantly recognized him. This was Higgs's friend, Jay. At least I think that's what Detective Primrose called him. He slapped his buddy on the shoulder from behind. "What's goin' on, pal?"

Higgs turned to his tall, lean, sandy-blond-haired friend and motioned to me. "Jay Craig, meet Sister Trixie Lavender. Our new neighbor."

I wasn't sure if he was continually mocking me by calling me sister, or if he kept forgetting, but I chose to ignore him anyway.

I put a bright smile on as I looked up at Jay's handsome, lean face. "It's just Trixie these days, and nice to meet you, Jay." I stuck my hand out and let him envelop it in his cool palm. "Sorry it's under such weird circumstances."

He ran a hand over his Kelly-green polo shirt and bounced his head up and down in sympathy. "You mean murder?" he asked, then cringed. "Saw you out here talking to the police earlier today. Good to meet you. Sure sorry about your store. This has to be tough on you and your friend."

"It's definitely been tough, but we're nothing if not survivors. We'll figure it out," I said, totally faking how I really felt, and trying to hide my panic over several thousand dollars in inventory sitting on a sidewalk, just waiting to be pilfered. We didn't have much money left, and we surely couldn't afford to replace any of this if someone stole it.

Jay motioned his thumb at the boxes then fisted his hands together. "These yours?"

I drove my hands into the pockets of my jeans and sighed. "Yep. They weren't supposed to be here until tomorrow, and I requested a signature upon delivery, but I guess you know what they say about good help these days."

"Need help getting them somewhere?" he offered, his voice cheerful and pleasant as it rumbled in my ear. I liked it. It filled me with a nice steady vibe I don't think I've ever felt from a man before. But it reminded me a lot of the way Sister Alice Ambrosia's voice had affected me.

I used to love our group discussions on scripture, not so much because I believed every word of it (as I've said, I was quite contrary and often found myself in hot water for asking too many questions), but because I loved the sound of her voice humming through my ears. It was soft and gentle with syrupy-sweet undertones, like Winnie The Pooh's, but soothing and kind like Mr. Rogers'.

"Trixie? Can I help you get these inside?" Jay asked again, interrupting my thoughts.

"That's very kind of you, but I have nowhere to put them. We can't go into the store until the Portland PD clears it. They won't fit in my car, and carrying them over to the motel at this time of night doesn't seem prudent. It's late, and ten trips up and down that rickety elevator might break it—or wake half the clientele."

"Then why don't you bring them to the shelter?" Jay suggested, his boyish grin made handsomer by the lock of sandy-blond hair falling over his forehead. "You can lock 'em up, right Higgs? Maybe in the storage closet by your office? They should be fine there."

"Oh, no. I couldn't impose like that."

Because if Higgs turned out to be a murderer, I could end up in his storage closet in plastic bags right alongside my inventory.

"I was going to offer, but we're still working on getting past my murdering ways," Higgs interjected in his amused voice.

Jay's brows smooshed together when he cocked his head. "Say again?"

Planting my hands on my hips, I decided to take control of this ongoing joke. "What your friend is trying to say is, I accused him of murder—sort of. I told his friend, Detective Primrose, that I saw him arguing with Mr. McDuff yesterday just before someone, who I can now identify as you, came and pulled him away. I didn't accuse him of murder in those exact words, but when asked if I knew anyone who'd had any issues with Fergus, your buddy and their disagreement—a heated one, by the way—came to mind."

Jay began to laugh as he latched on to a box and hoisted it up to his chest, the sound pleasant and rich. "Higgs? Murder Fergus? That's pretty funny."

Ah. Another fan of Cross Higglesworth. But I reminded myself, it stood to reason. He was Higgs's BFF, after all. I'd stick up for Coop. I *did* stick up for Coop.

"Did he tell you what he used to do before he ran the shelter?" Jay asked.

My ears perked up as I reached for a box. "He

didn't." I'd surmised, of course, but there'd been no official word.

"Jay, I'm pretty sure Trixie doesn't want to hear about what I used to—"

"He was an undercover cop in Minneapolis. Deep cover. Gangs. Hardcore gangs. Tough gig, no doubt."

Did you hear that *womp-womp-womp*? That's the sound of my trombone of disappointment. This new information put a pin in my bubble. It surely didn't mean Higgs couldn't have killed Fergus. There were plenty of murderous police officers on the books.

But it probably made it less likely.

My stomach sank and my fists clenched.

Higgs watched me intently, his eyes clouding over for a moment. I suspect he was looking for a reaction, as though I might gush at his feet and beg his forgiveness for ever considering he'd kill someone. But he was mistaken. I was a little less skeptical than before, but not enough to make me totally rule him out.

Brushing my hands together, I reached for a box and stared down Higgs. "So I guess this means you won't steal my stuff then? Seeing as you're a former *officer of the law*?"

He shrugged his shoulders. "Depends on what the stuff is inside those boxes. If it's anything covered in chocolate, a kitchen utensil, something we sorely need at the shelter, or a bunch of ribeye steaks, all bets are off."

Then he grinned that infuriating grin again.

And my stomach did that weird spiky jumping thing.

Which I promptly ignored while I silently gathered a box and headed down the sidewalk to Mr. Charisma's shelter.

CHAPTER 8

"Coop? What in all saints are you doing?" I asked from the edge of my bed in our motel room as her dusky red hair swished about her waist in effortless abandon, shining like a glorious sheet of silk.

If I were a lesser mortal, I'd hate her guts that I'd been stuck with this mousy brown hair and average face. Let me tell you, it was no picnic sharing a mirror with such a babe.

Coop pulled one side of her mouth upward with two fingers and stared hard into the mirror. "Practicing."

"Practicing what, my friend?"

"Smilin'," Livingston croaked from his perch on the back of the torn chair by the round table. "She tinks it's important so she can blend in like ya told her she should. So she's been in there while ya been off gettin' our breakfast, yankin' at her pretty face like it's Silly Putty. The numpty."

Ahhh. Coop tried so hard. Yet another reason to love her more madly than I already did. I didn't want to discourage her, but I didn't want her to feel as though she'd failed if she couldn't pull it off.

"You know, Coop, it's super cool to sort of have what they call resting bitch face."

She whipped around so quickly, I jumped, her fingers still holding one side of her mouth up. Her eyes flashed her usual reprimand when I broke one of our rules. "That's potty language, Trixie Lavender. You said we must always take care not to use foul language. You're not following the rules."

The rules. We had plenty—they went hand in hand with my calendar for marking off days since my last possession. I'd lain many out for Coop, to help her acclimate to living with humans. I'd forgotten the majority of them because there were so many to institute when you started from scratch, but not Coop. She had a memory like an elephant.

I hopped off the bed and went to the table, opening the Styrofoam carton filled with a luscious Western omelet. One of Coop's favorites since we'd come to Cobbler Cove and found this little hole in the wall just down a block or so from the motel.

"That I did. The goal being not to offend. But sometimes the expression is what it is. 'Resting mean face' doesn't really have the same effect, don't you agree?" I asked, holding out a plastic fork.

Her arms dropped to her sides in defeat, the graceful

limbs encased in a red, loosely fitting T-shirt flopping against her hips. "Whyyy can't I smile, Trixie? I've done it only two or three times before, and I liked how it felt on my face. That means I must be capable of smiling. I so want to be like everyone else, and everyone else smiles. You smile all the time and it makes me feel happy. I want to make people feel happy, too."

I sighed in sympathy and patted the chair at the table, indicating she should sit and eat before I took my own chair, pulling my container of fluffy scrambled eggs in front of me. "I think when you do smile, it's a truly genuine gesture, my friend. Maybe that means you only pull out all the stops when you really mean it. You're the real deal, Coop DeVille."

She pushed a forkful of omelet into her mouth and shook her head. "That is untrue. I've had many happy moments since I left Hell and met you. People will think I'm angry all the time if I have resting mean face. I'm *not* mean. Look," she said, pointing to her face. "I'm happy right now. See?"

I gazed at her near perfection and sighed. Her expression was as blank as a fresh canvas, awaiting the stroke of a paintbrush—frozen in aloofness. But in truth? If I looked like her, I don't suppose I'd care if I couldn't smile.

I'd resting mean face all day long.

Besides, "mean" didn't define my girl Coop in the least. Determined, fiercely protective? Yes. But never intentionally cruel. She loved all creatures great and small until you crossed her. That's when she became extreme.

"Aw, c'mon, Coop. No one thinks you're mean. Maybe it'll just take some time to learn how to show emotions you're not used to. Maybe it just has to happen naturally. So why don't we think of something else to keep us occupied until it does happen?"

"Okay, then tell me what happened to your fingernails and your knees—and your jeans? They're caked in mud. You said we should always present ourselves to the outside world with a tidy appearance. Your jeans were not tidy when you came back last night. You looked like you'd been in the pit wrestling tenth-level demon alligators."

Wait. What? "There are *demon alligators*?"

"And piranhas, too. It's very messy. My jeans used to look like that, too. Were you wrestling tenth-level demon alligators last night, Trixie?"

Her words left me at a loss, something I didn't have the energy to address right now.

"No alligators, demon or otherwise. Just a little accident while I was hoisting boxes. I'm fine."

Looking down at the tips of my fingers, still red and sore after clipping my nails short, and my knees, bruised to high Heaven, I winced. But I didn't want to divulge what had happened just yet. It would only put her and her sword on guard.

And there was still Higgs and his undercover work in gangs to process. That was also marinating in my head.

"I told you, Trixie Lavender. I would have helped you if you'd just texted me. I'm stronger than those two men plus ten more."

"Which is probably why it's not a good idea to share that with everyone just yet. That's going to take some explaining. So next subject. What else is on our agenda?"

Swigging from a carton of orange juice, Coop pointed to her phone. "The list of inventory's in my to-do notes. I saved it. We should go to Cross Higglesworth's place of employment and compare them. I'll send it to you in a text."

Sipping at my richly brewed coffee, silky and luscious, I toyed with a piece of bacon, letting the jolt of caffeine surge through my veins. Last night, Jay and Higgs had helped me load box after box onto a dolly and drag them down to the shelter, all the while making easygoing conversation.

I'd relaxed with Jay there, and we'd made simple enough work getting everything off the street and into the storage closet. I tried to keep my curiosity at bay until we had our killer, but I definitely wanted to do some volunteer work at the shelter—or a shelter some-where nearby, if we eventually found out Higgs was involved in this mess.

So it was with great interest upon entering Peach Street Shelter that I'd taken quick glimpses around the rec room with its worn pool table and a pinball machine, where some younger men sat on plastic lawn chairs, talking with one another.

We made several passes through the tatty but sparkling-clean kitchen with older mix-and-match appliances. The concrete floor was swept clean as a whistle; the countertops were a serviceable stainless steel, holding a variety of pots and pans and an enormous willow basket of fresh fruits and vegetables.

The entire atmosphere was warm and homey. There were pictures on the wall of the long hallway leading to the storage closet at the back of Higgs's office, a variety of faces, all smiling, and in one way or another showing off their uniforms for work. Jobs I'd bet Higgs had been instrumental in helping these men find.

My heart had tightened in my chest when I'd seen them. Add to that the fact he'd been an undercover police officer and his stats made for a pretty decent guy.

But those words Stevie had once whispered, that everyone was a suspect until proven otherwise, stood out.

"Do you like Cross Higglesworth better today, Trixie? Now that you know he was a police officer of the law?"

Or an undercover agent in a gang...

"Oh, she likes him all roight, she does," Livingston chirped. "Shoulda seen her face last night when she came back from her adventure. All glowin' and moony-eyed, she was."

I leaned over and stroked Livingston's head rather than put my hands around his little neck and squeeze his snarky retorts right out of him. "I was no such thing. I was, however, happy to have a place to put our things for the moment."

"I don't believe you would put our things at his place of employment if you didn't at least think he was an innocent man." Coop shoveled more omelet into her mouth then burped.

I wrinkled my nose in distaste. "Manners, please, Coop."

She gave me her infamous direct stare and wiped her mouth with the paper napkin. "Excuse me."

"And I put our things at his place because we don't really have anywhere else to put them. Plus, Jay was there, and I felt mostly comfortable with him." Mostly.

"You don't really believe Cross Higgl…er, Higgs killed anyone. I can tell, Trixie. You can't hide the truth from me," Coop accused in her playful tone, which, of course, wasn't playful at all. But I'd learned to read her body language, and she was teasing me.

"I don't know what I believe. But I do know this—today, we need to find Solomon, my new friend, and then talk to Crowley McDuff about the store, and maybe we can get him to spill his guts."

Coop reached for her sword in the corner next to the table, a glint in her eye. "I can make his guts spill, Trixie. Just ask."

I let my head fall back on my shoulders and prayed for patience. *Heaven above...* Sometimes, there was so much to teach my Coop, I didn't know where to begin —it overwhelmed me.

Livingston flapped his wings. "She doesn't mean literally, lass. Put that ting down before ya slice off me toes," he ordered, but his voice held love. Some days, when Livingston realized I was reaching my limit, he lent a hand with Coop...er, make that a wing. "She means metaphorically speakin', and I know that confounds ya, my babe in the woods, but ya can't go 'round lookin' to kill everythin' that moves. We'll end up in the hoosegow eatin' two-week-old bread with slimy beans and usin' the facilities in front of every pryin-eyed Tom, Dick, and Harry."

I didn't have a lot of backstory on Livingston, either. I had tried to look him up online, but he must have died long before the Internet. I didn't know how long he'd been in Hell, or even why. I only knew he was Coop's BFF, and he hadn't been "created" by Satan like her, and she wouldn't have allowed him to stay here if he were truly evil.

Which begged the question, how had he landed in Hell to begin with? I wondered if it hadn't been a bargain for his soul with the devil gone awry. Despite how difficult he could be about his likes and dislikes—especially when it came to food—he loved Coop.

Alas, for now, we had bigger fish to fry. But in due time, I'd ask...

"Who are Tom, Dick and Harry, Trixie?"

Now Livingston let his head fall to his chest, before he lifted *his* eyes to the ceiling. "Oh, dear Lord in Heaven, won't ya help a bird out?"

"Hey. Forget Heaven. What do you know about the hoosegow, pal?" I asked facetiously—well, sort of.

Livingston swiveled his head, his wide eyes, glassy and unblinking. "That's for me to know and you to find out, lass. Someday, we'll have a nice wag about it, and you'll need to be sittin' down when we do—maybe with a pint."

I giggled, closing the container of my eggs. "I don't like beer. Anyway, back to the guts thing. Livingston is right. I don't mean spill his guts as in, eviscerate him, Coop. I mean, get him to tell us what he can about who might have wanted to kill Fergus. It's just another one of those expressions."

She set her sword down and leaned back in the plastic vinyl chair, her lips almost forming a full-blown pout. "I'm in a constant state of confusion between your metaphors and expressions and analogies, but please don't even get me started on oxymorons. Will I ever learn the subtleties of being human?"

"I know, Coop, and of course you will. It just takes time. I had thirty-two years to learn. You've only had a little under a year. That's why we're here. To help you understand and to learn."

Cupping her chin in her hands, she rested her elbows on the scarred veneer table. "How do you *feel* today, Trixie?"

"Me?" I asked, surprised by her question. "I'm good, I guess. I want to get this mess cleared up so we can start tattooing, but otherwise, I'm okay. Why?"

I wasn't sure if she was asking because I'd taught

her it was polite to be interested in the people around her, or if she really wanted to know.

Again, she looked right through me and peered into my soul with that dead gaze. This was her worried expression. "You talked in your sleep last night, Sister Trixie Lavender. I worry you're having nightmares, and we know what nightmares lead to."

My stomach turned and my hands went ice cold. I didn't remember having any dreams at all. In fact, I was so tired, I'd gotten into my bed with the ugly, outdated paisley bedspread and passed out.

"What did I say?" I asked, almost afraid.

"You were talking about the relic and Father O'Leary. You kept calling his name."

"'Tis true, lass. You did cry out."

My eyes went to the far side of the room where a painting hung, ships in a stormy harbor somewhere. I missed Father O'Leary. He'd been my confidant, my mentor, one of the most influential people in my life for a very long time.

I was sick over the fact that not even *he'd* believed my story about what had happened the night I was possessed. I couldn't believe he didn't remember any of it. But I suppose it's only fair, when you consider the idea that I don't remember what happens when *I'm* possessed, either.

However, I do remember the aftermath, when I wake up on a floor or in some corner with Coop on top of me, holding me down like an unhinged, snarling tiger. Why didn't he at least remember *something* like that? Surely our experiences were similar? What had happened to him after the spirit left his body? And was it the same spirit that had hopped into mine?

But maybe that was why I was dreaming about him —due to all the upheaval as of late. But did dreaming about him mean I was headed for another round with whatever possessed me? Was it stress that led to my allowing this *thing* into my body? I couldn't go on ignoring its existence forever. Especially if whatever this was took control in a public place.

I cringed. Heaven's gates and angel wings, that would be dreadful. So far that hadn't happened, but it certainly could, right?

"I don't remember having any dreams," I replied woodenly, and I truly didn't. But I suppose if I did, I wouldn't want to recount them.

Coop looked down at her phone, using her thumb to scroll, and nodded. "Our calendar says it's been over three months since your last possession. That's the longest time between possessions so far."

Swallowing, I took a deep breath. I wasn't going to focus on that or I'd go mad. "Good to know," I said with a stiffness to my voice even I heard as I rose from my chair and cleared my place at the table. "Okay, let's get this show on the road. We need to find out how to get in touch with Crowley McDuff and chat him up. Then, for my peace of mind, I'd like to find Solomon. Even if he won't answer any questions, I'd like to see if I can get him to a doctor. Livingston? We're going to have to leave you covered for today, buddy, and I'm sorry. But we'll put the Do Not Disturb sign up as double insurance and so you can sleep all day without the intrusion of the maids."

He rasped a sigh and hopped from the back of the chair to the top of his antique white cage on the floor, where he waited for me to open the door. "Of course ya do. I wouldn't have it any other way. What ever would I do if I didn't have a garbage bag suffocatin' me half to death all bloomin' day long? It just wouldn't be another day in paradise."

I laughed as I gathered my purse and my phone, catching one last glimpse of myself in the mirror to ensure I looked decent enough. I didn't have much in the way of clothes. Since leaving the convent, I'd picked up some jeans and T-shirts and a dress or two.

If nothing else, I looked clean in my white cotton capris and melon-colored top. Running the brush through my hair, I fluffed it around my shoulders and smoothed the blue streak I'd defiantly dyed myself after leaving the convent for good.

"Promise you'll be quiet, Livingston. We can't afford to arouse any suspicion. The motel doesn't allow pets, and we might need to be here a little while longer. Deal?"

"I am not a pet, kitten."

Coop hauled his cage up, the finely toned muscles in her upper arms flexing, and closed the door, giving him her sternest gaze. "Listen to Trixie and acknowledge her, please."

As he settled on the perch, he sighed. "Fine, fine. I'll be quiet as a church mouse."

Leaning down, I wedged a finger into the cage and Livingston rubbed his head against it. "You do know I love you, right? That I'm only doing this for your own good? For all of us?"

"Isn't that what all kidnappers say to their hostages, lass?" he teased with a purr, his round, glassy eyes closing in contentment.

"No. That's what all good friends say—in an effort to keep them from being a government science experiment, mind you—to their friends when they can talk and are trapped in an owl's body. And still with all your fussing, I love you. So stay quiet, please. You feel me, winged one?"

His feathers rustled as he nestled into his favorite position. "Love-schmove, lass. Now off with ya. I have rest I'm needin'."

Chuckling, I turned to head for the door with Coop in tow. As we stood in the landing hallway with nothing but a railing overlooking the parking lot, I stopped. First, I smelled the fresh air, crisp and cool as most mornings are in Cobbler Cove until the sun took over and the day warmed. Then I inhaled, loving the warmth of the shafts of sunshine, letting them settle in my bones.

"You want to review what we've figured out so far about Fergus's death?"

While I hadn't shared my encounter with Dumpster Diver, I did tell her all about Solomon and the "bad mad guy" and that Higgs had once been an undercover cop, something I couldn't stop thinking about last night while we unloaded my boxes, but she hadn't given me much input about it.

"You mean we should review *nothing*?" she asked innocently, putting her hands on her hips, waiting for my answer.

I scoffed at her suggestion we had nothing. "We don't have nothing, Coop. We have some leads." We did. Sort of. Not big ones, but some…

"If Stevie were here, she'd have more leads."

I frowned. Sometimes Coop really hit hard with her direct nature even if that was probably true. But fair was fair.

"I call foul. I'm new at this, and if you'll remember correctly, Stevie kind of fell into the answer to the last landlord death, but I did help her." I had. I'd googled things. That was helping.

"But she solved a lot of murders before that one. She has a track record. Ask Crispin Alistair Winterbottom."

"I'd love to, but I can't hear him, remember?" I teased. "Only you and Stevie can hear him because he's a ghost. Now, do you want to cast blame and point fingers, or do you want to review?"

"Miss Lavender?" A man dressed in a dapper gray tweed suit, complete with a vest and shiny black shoes, approached us from behind Coop, who, at the sound of his voice, whirled around, ready to pounce.

I latched onto her arm, always afraid she was going

to eat her way through a new person's esophagus before they had the chance to explain who they were. "Ask first, Coop," I whispered in her ear, feeling the tension in her arm. "You know the rules."

"Who are you?" she crowed, making him stop dead in his tracks. His head, mostly bald but for the smattering of white hair sprinkled around the sides of his skull, gleamed under the bright sun, now out in full force.

He held up a hand, as though he sensed Coop's tension. "My name is Crowley McDuff. Are you Cooper O'Shea?"

She puffed her chest out and lifted her chin, her hair blowing in the breeze and directly into my face like a glorious piece of silk. "That's my name. I live in Cobbler Cove, Oregon, and my social security number is—"

"I'm Trixie Lavender, Mr. McDuff. How can I help you?" I stepped in front of Coop, who still didn't understand when was the right time to give her stats, and spat her hair from my mouth. Holding out my hand, I let him take it. Very curious about why he'd come to see us.

His skin was papery and warm, and his eyes, very like Fergus's, danced with a smile, which were very unlike Fergus's. "It's so nice to meet you. I'm so glad I found you. That nice fella down the way from your place said you were here. The big one with all that dark hair."

Higgs?

When I didn't answer, he explained, running a hand over his head. "As you can see, I don't have much of my own. So I'm a little envious, I suppose."

"Right. Because you're bald, and Cross Higglesworth is not," Coop said in her matter-of-fact way.

"Coop!" I hissed, poking her in the ribs.

But Mr. McDuff held up a hand and smiled, appearing not at all offended. Man, he was nothing like Fergus. "No, no. It's quite all right. She's correct. I *am* bald. Not to worry on that front. Anyway, pardon me for bothering you ladies, but might I speak to you both? Maybe we could have a cup of coffee? My treat."

Both Coop and I stared at him, and I knew she was thinking what I was thinking. How could this man, this pleasant man, be related to crabby old Fergus?

"I don't drink coffee," Coop responded, emotion-less. "I drink orange juice, apple juice, sometimes ice tea but only if it's infused with ginger and green tea leaves. Never soda because it rots your teeth."

Oh, dear. Patting her arm, I looked directly into Crowley McDuff's eyes. "But I do, Mr. McDuff. I'd love to have a cup of coffee with you, and please accept my condolences on your brother's passing."

He cleared his throat, tucking his hand into the lapel of his jacket. "You mean his untimely demise? The one he probably deserved?"

My eyes flew open wide. I didn't know what to say. But his words... If we followed Stevie's rulebook, didn't that make him a suspect?

But Crowley wisped a hand over my arm. "Come, ladies. Let's have some coffee down the street and we'll talk, yes? I know a cozy little place." He gestured with his hand to allow us to proceed ahead of him.

As Coop and I made our way down the long hallway and toward the stairs, she whispered, "Was I rude, Trixie? Hellfire. I don't want to be perceived as rude. I'm nice. I mean, I feel nice anyway." She pinched her arms to *show* me she felt nice. "See? Nice. Yet you chastised me."

I smiled in sympathy and patted her shoulder as we headed down the stairs, my heart aching for Coop's insecurities.

"We'll talk about it later, okay? For right now, you're very nice, Coop. A very nice girl. Don't worry about it. But let's go see what Mr. McDuff has to say, okay? He seems very willing to chat with us, and we could use some help here. Maybe he knows something about what happened to Fergus."

When we hit the bottom of the stairs, I let Crowley take the lead and we followed him across the pitted parking lot to a small café down the way called Betty's, where he held the door for us. We chose a booth, with Coop and I seated together across from Crowley McDuff.

The café was kitschy, with funny, cheesy pictures like the one where the bulldog is playing poker, and even a velvet Elvis painting. The floors were brown-painted concrete, and the booths were a light blue vinyl. A familiar genre of coffee shop music played, languid and with lots of guitar, and the delicious scent of freshly brewed coffee mingled with hazelnut swirled around my nose.

The cheerful waitress (most everyone's pretty cheerful here in Cobbler Cove) brought us menus and water before remarking, "You're the girls who just moved into that dump across the street you're gonna turn into a tattoo parlor, aren't you? Where that cranky SOB was murdered? Welcome to Cobbler Cove, you two! Coffee's on me. I'm Delores, by the way. Betty was my great grandmother." She grinned down at us, her dark ponytail curling at the ends, in her cute retro red apron with white polka dots and ruffles.

I winced, but decided it was best to share who Crowley was in the effort to thwart more hurtful conversation. "This is the murdered man's *brother*, and that dump is his," I stressed, which made Delores bite her lower lip. "This is Crowley McDuff."

But Crowley was quick to reassure her by doing what he'd done with us. He waved a dismissive hand, smiling with his kind eyes, and said, "It's fine, Delores. I knew my brother and all his faults. He was unpleasant at best. Unkind at worst. Please do carry on. Cobbler Cove has been good to me for many years, and I hope it will be good to the two of you after such a harsh introduction. Get to know one another. It makes my heart happy."

I smiled up at her. "I'm Trixie, and this is Coop. How'd you know who we were?"

Delores planted a jaunty hand on her hip and

tapped her pencil against her ruby-red lips. "I might as well start our friendship off right, because I know we'll be friends. There isn't a soul up and down this street who didn't see your gorgeous friend here. She's made all of us rethink a visit to the nearest plastic surgeon, if you know what I mean."

"I don't know what that means," Coop whispered to me, tugging on my arm. "Who performs surgery on plastic, Trixie, and why?"

And that's why it's impossible to hate Coop and her ethereal beauty. "I'll explain later. She means you're beautiful, Coop. It's a compliment."

Delores scoffed. "I'm not sure beautiful's the word. It's bigger—better than that. I just can't find one that fits, so 'near perfect' will have to do," she said on a cackle, nudging Coop's arm.

"Thank you very much, Delores. Those are very nice words." Coop reached out for her hand and grabbed it, pumping it up and down.

Delores raised one dark pencil-thin eyebrow, but if she found Coop strange, she kept it to herself and smiled a bright smile. "Anyway, we all heard about what happened, and the mess that's left you ladies in. Oh, and my condolences to you, Mr. McDuff. Anyway, if you girls need anything at all, just holler. I'm happy to help. We all are."

And with that, she took our orders and swished off behind the festively bright red counter, leaving us with Crowley, who toyed with the black-and-white checkered napkin on the paper placemat.

I folded my arms together and asked, "So, Mr. McDuff, what can we do for you?"

"Please, call me Crowley." As the sun shone in through the windows, revealing his wrinkled but tanned face, I saw the hesitance in his eyes.

I grinned. I don't know what it is about Crowley, but I liked him. "Done. How can we help?"

"I hate to do this after everything you ladies have been through yesterday, but I'm afraid I have some bad news."

Coop's eyes narrowed and her posture went stiff.

Me, on the other hand? I could barely breathe. "And that is?"

"I'm selling the building, Trixie."

CHAPTER 9

I'm pretty sure my mouth fell open, but Crowley reached across the table and patted my hand. "After this mess with Fergus... It's time. I hope you understand my position. I'm not getting any younger, and with Fergus gone, I'm too tired to handle things on my own."

This was the second space we'd lost in just a few months. So now what? Oh, universe, what do you want from me? What have I done that I can't seem to rectify? I tried to swallow, but there was a big lump of fear between words and my vocal chords.

So Crowley continued. "I've let things alone for many years because Fergus needed to have a job on the books—"

"On the books?" I squeaked.

What did that mean? Not that it mattered. We were going to have nothing in just a few short seconds. So it wouldn't matter if we found the killer or not. Deflated didn't cover how I was feeling. Defeated came close, though.

As my mind raced with possible alternatives, he cleared his throat and gazed at me. "Well, yes. Fergus was an ex-convict. I suppose I thought everyone knew that—or at least talked about it. He did time for armed robbery twenty-some years ago. When he was released, he needed a job, and I gave him one. I felt like it was my obligation. It's what I always did where Fergus was concerned. I saved him time after time—for our mother, of course, and then it just became a way of life. He's been managing my buildings ever since. But I sold off most of them except yours and one other. Now, with him gone, it's time to call it a day and take the missus somewhere warm. It's rainy and cold in Cobbler Cove during the winter months—we're ready to try the alternative."

As Delores brought our coffee and Coop's orange juice, I struggled with what to say next. "I didn't know Fergus had been in jail," I said lamely as those infamous red spots on my cheeks burned bright.

"Oh, indeed. Fergus was…" He sighed in resignation, running his weathered fingers over the handle of the bright red coffee mug. "Make no mistake, I knew who my brother was. He was crass and cruel, but he got the job done. It's only just this past day, after spending some time in the police station with Detective Primrose, that I've learned *how* crass and cruel. He wasn't just managing my buildings. He'd been hiking up prices without my knowledge and loaning money to people with ridiculous interest rates and, well…I suppose you know what loan sharks do when you don't pay up…"

Ahhh. So Fergus was a dirtier bird than we'd thought originally. If he was hiking up rent along with this loan shark accusation, that could mean any number of suspects.

"I'm sorry, Crowley. Truly. How sad to find this out at such a delicate time." I didn't know what else to say. *Gee, sucks that your brother was a total creep. Hope you feel better soon?*

"Tenfold, I apologize if he was as awful to you as I'm hearing he was to my other tenants. But what upsets me the most? How ugly he was to the homeless men. I can't bear how dreadfully he behaved. Had I known…"

As I tried to catch my breath, I nodded, pressing a hand to my chest to slow my heart. "He wasn't cruel to us, Crowley. He just tried to take us for more than he'd originally advertised the store for on Facebook. But we talked him back down to a reasonable price. Though, now…"

Crowley ran a finger under the starched white collar of his shirt. "Now you're worried someone will buy the place and hike that price right back up or turn it into a condo. You don't have to worry. It's protected by the city of Portland against that. But I'll tell you what I'll do. I'll make sure whoever I sell to will rent to you for the same price Fergus promised you ladies. I can't promise what will happen after a year's lease, but for the moment, I'll make certain it's fair."

Tears stung my eyes and relief raced through my veins—but we still had to find a killer if we wanted to get into the store. "Thank you, Crowley. You have no idea how much that means to us. Right, Coop?"

Coop, who was blowing bubbles in her orange juice with her straw (an endless source of fascination for her), simply nodded.

"But we do still have the problem of getting you ladies *into* the store. I can't do a thing about that until the police clear it for evidence."

I fought the urge to chew on my fingernail, a bad habit of mine. "Did they say how long it might take?"

He blew out a breath, running a hand over the smooth top of his head. "They didn't. They were too busy listing Fergus's infractions. One after the other, I tell you."

Now I reached across the table and placed my palm over his. "I'm so sorry, Crowley. I don't mean to be insensitive, but do you have any idea who might have done this?"

Now his laugh was sardonic as it bubbled from his throat—definitely not a sound he appeared comfortable with.

"Unfortunately, I think the list of names is too long for me to remember at this point. There were plenty of people lining up, wishing Fergus would, at the very least, go away. I'm sure a few of them would have liked to see him dead. I don't like that he was so despised. I did everything I could to help him find acceptance, but Fergus never cared for the rules of society. He didn't care that no one liked him. He was always a loner, and nothing I did could change that. Unless there was a scam to be pulled off. Then he didn't mind a friend or two. It's what landed him in jail."

How funny Crowley had mentioned Fergus doing time. I'd googled him and come up mostly dry but for his Facebook page, where he almost never posted unless it was for a rental space opening up. But I guess, twenty-some years ago, the Internet wasn't the wealth of information it is today.

Yet, that made me think. "You said he was in prison. Did he still consort with anyone from his arrest? The armed robbery—did he have help?"

"He did. Yes, yes. From Slick Yablonski. But Slick's dead now. Did his time and was run over by a bus two days after he got out of the slammer."

I blanched. "How awful."

Crowley shook his head, his eyebrows mashing together. "Not awful. There were plenty of things Slick did that he *didn't* get caught for. He had karma on his back, I'm sure. In fact, I'd bet that bus was going to take him to his next criminal stunt. He wasn't a nice man. No more than Fergus was."

Yikes. Crowley was certainly unafraid to tell it like it is, and that was refreshing. At least he knew how awful Fergus could be.

Yet, I still wasn't sure how to go about these questions. I know Stevie probably went in for the kill from the word go, but I felt like maybe I should tread lightly, being a novice.

So I cupped my chin in my hand and gave him a thoughtful look. "Can you think of anyone he argued with recently, or maybe if someone threatened him?"

He leaned back in the booth and looked at me dead on. "You're not asking these questions because you're getting involved in police business, are you, Trixie? After everything the two of you have been through, I'd hate to see you hurt."

"Yes. That's exactly why she's asking them," Coop answered, finally looking up from her orange juice.

But I shot him a sympathetic glance. "That's not entirely true. I'm only asking because we really need to get the ball rolling and move into the store, Crowley. We've been out of work for a long time. We need an income. If we had something—some lead or whatever —that maybe connects some dots, we could pass it on to the police and maybe they'd catch whoever did this. Then we wouldn't have to wait for them to clear Inker-belle's. I've got boxes and boxes of inventory, waiting to be unpacked. Not to mention, the store's a wreck…"

Maybe I'd overstepped, but it was true. We had a lot of work ahead of us. Surely he knew that.

Now his eyes went sympathetic, the orbs going soft and melty. "I can't tell you how sorry I am the store's in such dreadful condition, or that Fergus had the gall to ask for more than the going price for such a mess. I peeked in the windows today and couldn't believe my eyes. And that's all my fault. I let too much go by the wayside in favor of too many cruises with the missus. I knew Fergus could be harsh, but I didn't know he was threatening people. In fact, I'm finding hardly anyone knew I owned the properties. Fergus had them believing *he* did," he blustered, his cheeks going red.

"That's true. I didn't know until last night, when someone told me that you owned the building."

He winked at me. "Ah, but it's something else I plan to make note of. I'm happy to give you the next month free of rent. You can use the money to spruce things up, yes? And if I sell it before you're able to get back in, I'll have that put in the contract."

"And I always have a hand available to help paint, if you need it," chirped Delores, who'd suddenly reappeared, her smile bright. "Happy to help a fellow business owner. We gotta stick together."

My heart beamed. This was community. This was kindness. This was what I was trying to teach Coop.

A tear threatened to escape my eye, but I pinched my hand to tamp it down. "That's so kind—thank you, both of you. I can't tell you how much this means to us. We've been in a bit of upheaval lately, and hearing this makes everything so much better. *Everything.*"

The jostle of the bell over the door just behind our booth jingled, making me look up to find none other than Higgs and Jay sauntering in, with smiles directed at me.

I'm still not sure how I feel about Higgs. I definitely like Jay. He doesn't make me throw up my guard in quite the way Higgs does. He's easy. Easy to talk to, easy to be in silence with. Just easy.

Higgs made me question everything and everyone —even myself.

Still, he smiled the moment he saw me sitting at the table, his brilliantly white teeth perfect in the backdrop of his olive complexion but for the chip in his right front tooth, which only added to his charm.

"Ladies. Fine morning, yes? And Crowley? How are you, old man? I haven't seen you in ages." He gave Crowley a hearty handshake and patted him on the back.

"Higgs! So good to see you. Listen, let me apologize for Fergus—"

"Bah! No need," Higgs said, cutting him off. "I know you wouldn't condone his treatment of my guys. It's not your fault. Forget it."

Crowley shook his head, remorse in his eyes. "I was just apologizing to the ladies here for his behavior. Might as well throw you into the mix. Apparently, Fergus tried to hike up the rent on them. I'm so ashamed, Higgs. Had I known, I would have put a stop to it, but I was lazy, off in the Riviera with the missus."

I patted his hand again. "It's all right. What's done is done. All we can do is move on from here. That said…" I turned to Higgs and Jay. "Did you find Solomon, Higgs?"

His face went from light to dark in mere seconds, his eyes deep with concern. "I haven't, and I've been everywhere—all his favorite haunts. I had people canvassing the area all last night into the early morning hours, too. But he's disappeared into thin air."

My heart beat a little faster. That cough had been so awful. He needed medical attention. "Does he disappear often?"

That wasn't unusual. Many of the homeless I'd encountered really only wanted peace in their lives, with little to no interference from outsiders. But if this wasn't a habit, that left me concerned.

Higgs shrugged as he looked out the large picture window. "Not usually for very long. Not for hours on end. Solomon's a character. He likes people more than he lets on. When he didn't show up for breakfast today, after we'd been out looking for him all night… Let's just say it isn't like him to miss scrambled eggs and watermelon—two of his favorites."

"You're worried, aren't you?" I asked, now just as worried.

"I am."

Maybe I should have confided in Higgs and told him what Solomon shared with me about the bad mad guy? I didn't know if some of it was just his out-of-touch ranting, much like his medieval speak, or if it was mixed in with some reality. But what if he meant Higgs was the bad guy and I was putting him in danger?

He *had* run away when Higgs showed up last night.

Jay slapped his friend on the back, interrupting my thoughts. "We'll find him. Don't worry. We'll go out again after breakfast, yeah?" he soothed, his gentle voice a balm on my frazzled nerves.

Higgs only nodded. "Yes. After breakfast. Anyway, it

was nice seeing you, ladies. Oh, and, Coop, this is Jay Craig. My buddy and partner in the shelter."

Coop, who'd sat very silent, turned, her gaze landing on Jay who, unlike Higgs, definitely noted her beauty. You could always tell by the way their eyes widened in surprise, and then they looked away just as quickly so as not to gawk.

He stuck out a hand, his expression as kind as it had been last night. "Nice to meet you, Coop."

"You, too, Jay Craig," she said, then winced, which I'm assuming was her attempt at a smile.

Again, there but for the grace of something I couldn't identify, he didn't make an observation about her use of his entire name, just smiled, sticking his hands into the pocket of his chinos. "Pleasure. Have a good day." Then he headed off to find a booth.

Higgs backed away from our booth, rocking on the soles of his tennis shoes. "I'd better go, too. But if you want to scout for Solomon later, Trixie, I'd be happy for the help."

"You bet," I murmured before he turned and went off in Jay's direction. I turned back to Crowley, forgetting where I'd left off in my feeble line of questioning. Geez, I felt inadequate.

But he began pushing his way out of the booth, his phone in hand. "It's the missus. Promised I'd take her to the store. So I must be on my way. But I wanted to be sure we understood each other, ladies. So, do we have an understanding?"

I rose, reaching out a hand to him to shake. "We do.

And thank you again. Your kindness means everything to us. And if you wouldn't mind, could you send me the names of people who rent from you?"

"Are you going to poke around somewhere you shouldn't, Trixie? I don't want to worry for your safety."

"Well," I admitted with a smile. "Poke is a strong word, but I promise to stay out of trouble. *Promise.*"

"I'll write it up and text it to you then. Does that work?"

"It does, and thanks again. You've been so generous."

He waved a hand and smiled. "It's nothing. I'll be in touch."

"And if you think of anything—anything about who might have done this—you'll let us know?"

Now he winked. "I'll let the police know first. But yes, I'll contact you. Take care, ladies," he said before whisking out the door, the bell's ring lingering in the air.

I blew out a breath as I moved to sit opposite Coop, now that Crowley was gone. "So, we still have nothing."

She cocked her head. "Do you think Crowley might have done it?"

My eyes widened as I sipped the last of my coffee, a hearty brew of hazelnut and vanilla French roast. "Wow. I guess I didn't even think it. Even taking into consideration the stuff he said about his brother. He definitely saw Fergus for what he was. But no. I guess I didn't consider him a suspect. Any particular reason you do?"

Coop shrugged, her eyes locking with mine. "I don't, I suppose. But Stevie said we were to take everyone into consideration. Even our own mothers."

I grinned, pushing my cup aside. "Well, my mother is no longer with us, and you don't have one. So at least we can rule two people out, right?"

Coop barked the fakest laugh I'd ever heard come out of her mouth, throwing her head back with abandon, and exposing the slender length of her throat.

I blinked. "*What* was that about?"

"I'm practicing laughing. I saw it on a rerun of *Dynasty*. Joan Collins laughs like that. Did you like that sound? Was it pleasant to your ears?"

Coop was always surprising me.

"Why would you ask?"

"I heard you say you loved the sound of laughter. I was trying to accommodate."

Now *I* laughed, letting my head loll forward on my neck. "Well, thanks, Coop. Job well done. You're getting there. And you weren't really rude to Crowley about the state of his hair, or lack thereof, but pointing out something so obvious *is* a little tactless."

"Roger that."

Roger that? I think it might be time to limit Coop's binge watching.

She tapped the table with a finger. "Now, shall we focus on looking for more suspects and what we have so far, which, FYI, is mostly nothing?"

I let my head rest in my hands. We did have nothing. A big fat zero. "Well, if we can find Solomon, maybe we can get him to spill who this bad mad guy is. That could be a lead, right?"

"Do you want me to bring the sword when we look for him?" she asked, the veins in her arms popping out as she made a fist. "I'll hold it to his throat until he squeals like a—"

"Coop!" I almost shouted as people began to give us strange stares. "*No.* No sword. Solomon's fragile and sick. We don't need to threaten him for information. Sometimes just a kind word or some understanding goes a long way."

"I don't understand understanding."

"I know, Coop. Let's forget about that now and think about what's next. So far, all we have is a bad mad guy who has special powers and does some laundry. I still don't understand how laundry comes into play. Now we know Fergus did time in the pokey and he was a loan shark, which does open up a bunch of possibilities, but not until we know who rents from Crowley. Then we have Higgs, who definitely had an argument with Fergus, but sure is loved by one and all, and he's an ex-undercover police officer. Not that it eliminates him, but it's less likely. And next is Jay. I haven't really talked about Fergus with him, but he did witness the argument between him and Higgs. He does share a partnership with Higgs at the shelter. It's in his best interest to keep Fergus off their backs, right?"

Coop nodded, and pushed her empty glass away,

holding up the silver napkin holder. She looked into it, widening and narrowing her eyes while she tugged at her cheek with her free hand. "It *is* in his best interest. But do you think he's capable of murder, Trixie Lavender? He appears so docile and calm. And then we have to ask ourselves, the shelter isn't a maker of big sums of money, correct? It thrives on donations from kind people."

"Okay. Where are you going with this?"

"Why would anyone kill Fergus because of the shelter? He wasn't taking money from them. He was just being very unkind to the homeless men. What motive does Jay or Higgs have for murdering him other than he was very unkind?"

My mouth fell open. Point for my demon. I held up my hand in front of her. "Give me some, Coop."

She set the napkin holder down. "Give you some what?"

"Skin, baby. Gimme some skin." I pointed to my hand, indicating she should high-five me.

She gasped. "I most certainly will not give you my skin, Sister Trixie Lavender! That's so—"

Sirens whirred in the air, the sound pealing through the quiet of Betty's like a screeching chain saw cutting through the silence of the woods.

Both Coop and I looked out the window to see two police cars and a black sedan, like the one Detective Primrose drove, screech to a halt beside Betty's.

Two men dressed in dark suits burst through the café door, with Detective Primrose hot on their heels.

"Slow down, you baboons! Stop rushing around as though you've found bloody Jack The Ripper! I have heels on today, you heathens," she complained, skidding to a halt behind the tallest of the two men.

"That's the detective who questioned me," Coop whispered, shrinking in her seat.

I grabbed her hand to soothe her as Detective Primrose pushed them aside and threaded her way through the tables, her blonde hair vivid against the red walls of the café.

The two men behind her almost bumped into her back when she stopped short at Higgs's table, making her angry. She whirled around and held up a hand with a very stern gaze on her face. "Back up, Eager Beavers. I said I'd handle this, didn't I? Now go play like nice boys over in the corner and wait until Mummy's done."

They both gave her a sheepish glance before skulking their way to the far corner, where they leaned into the wall, dwarfing the pictures behind them. And then Detective Primrose reached out a hand to Higgs, patting him on the back.

"I think you know I hate to do this, right, love?" she asked, her voice gravelly and chock full of emotion.

Higgs swiveled his upper body in his chair and looked up at her, his handsome face full of suspicion. "Do what, Tansy?"

Then she did something so peculiar. She reached for his arm, his forearm covered in that intricate sleeve tattoo, and she pointed to a spot on the underside of his wrist. "This, Higgs. This tattoo."

My eyes widened. They weren't so far away I couldn't see there was something there. I just didn't know exactly what. The colors were a blur.

"What about my tattoos?"

"No, no, bloke. Not plural as in tattoos. *This* tattoo." She pointed again to something I couldn't see before she let his arm go. Then she closed her eyes and swallowed hard. I watched her throat work up and down, before she popped them open and stared down at him, her jaw tight. "Cross Higglesworth, you're under arrest for the murder of Fergus McDuff—"

But he jumped up and backed away, cutting off her words. "You can't be serious, Tansy. *You know me*. You know I'd never kill anyone without—" He stopped then, his eyes going hard and his lips going thin.

He'd never kill anyone without what? A reason?

I sat there flabbergasted as Tansy and Higgs stared one another down and the two detectives let their hands rest in the vicinity of their guns.

But it was Coop who shocked us all when she exploded out of the booth, climbing over the back of it, her long legs hurdling the backrest as though it were nothing, her feet slapping the concrete floor with a loud clap.

And yelling.

Coop was yelling. *Yell-ing*.

"Unhand him now! Cross Higglesworth is not a murderer!"

CHAPTER 10

*T*hings got a little hinky after that. Okay, a lot hinky. Is hinky the right word here? I don't know. I *do* know it went from intense to complete anarchy in two shakes flat.

Coop threw a punch at one of the police officers, thwarted only by my big mouth when I screamed at her and the detective's quick reflexes.

One of the detectives grabbed Coop by the arm and swung her around, pushing her up against the wall so hard, I swear I heard a bone crack.

Thankfully and blessed mother, she didn't fight back. The last time she'd done that, in Ebenezer Falls when she'd felt as though Stevie was threatened, the detective had landed on the floor across the room and ended up with a broken nose.

I rushed over, ducking under the detective's arm, ignoring everything but her, and whispered, "Coop! Are you okay? Are you hurt?"

Her nostrils flared, but it was the only sign she felt anything at all other than the tic in her jaw, which was clenched tight. "He can't hurt me, Trixie," she responded. "I'm sorry. I lost my temper. I know that's unacceptable. You told me to fight with my words, not my fists."

Gripping her free hand, I urged, "It's okay. We'll talk about it later, but please, *don't fight*. Please. I'm begging you. Do what they say and it will be all right. I'll make sure it's all right," I whispered fiercely.

Her breathing was labored and shallow, her nostrils flaring, but she gave me a stiff nod. "Cross didn't do this, Trixie. Mark my words. I know what my gut is used for now, and it's just like Stevie said. I know he didn't do it in my gut."

Then, apparently because I wasn't listening to the detective holding Coop squawking in my ear, the other one approached, the scent of his heavy, cheap cologne stinging my nose he was so close. He yanked me away from Coop with a hard jerk of my arm.

"Lady, I'm tellin' ya, back up! You're interfering with a police matter. Step back!" He barked the order, and I did as I was told because I'd been here before.

But I wanted to sock him in his smug face. Yes, I did, and I didn't feel at all bad about that.

Yet, I knew enough to know I'd land in jail right along with her, and we needed someone who was free to handle her release. All the while, I wondered what the heck had inspired Coop to make such a bold statement (I still had trouble believing she'd yelled, using real emotion. That was usually reserved for when she was angry, and even then, it was a war cry), and what the tattoo on Higgs's wrist had to do with everything.

But Higgs didn't fight, either. In fact, now he held out his hands and let Detective Primrose cuff him quite peacefully while Jay watched in clear horror.

That everyone was calm did nothing for a frantic Jay. He rocked back and forth from foot to foot, blocking the detective from taking Higgs out the door while the smattering of patrons in the café looked on in silent fear.

"Tansy!" he yelled, his eyes wide, his hands flying in the air. "This is crazy! You know it's crazy. You've been friends for years. How could you do this?"

But she looked him directly in the eye, her stare hard. "Jay. I have to ask you to step aside, please. Do not interfere with police business," she said, unflinching, her British accent especially distinct.

"Tansy!" he cried once more. "This is madness. Higgs is no killer. How could you even consider—"

"Jay!" Higgs barked. "Stop. Let her take me in. She'll see this is crazy. But for now, she's just doing her job. Let it be." His words were stiff and stilted, but his eyes flashed hot and angry.

Jay didn't appear to want to back off, so I put my hand on his arm and forced him to look at me. "Who better than Higgs to know how this should go, Jay? *Listen* to him. I'll grab my car and we'll go together to the police station, okay?"

Gosh, I remember so clearly those words when

Stevie spoke them to me after Coop had been arrested. She'd sat endless hours with me at the police station, and she'd found us a lawyer.

I wanted to pay it forward, mostly because Coop believed.

But Jay remained rigidly in place, so I took a firmer stance, clutching his wrist and forcing him to look at me. "Jay! Stop this nonsense *now*. They're taking him in no matter what you say. It can either be peaceful, or you can join him, and quite frankly, we need each other for support. The both of you locked up does no one at the shelter any good. Now let them go. We'll follow right behind. I promise."

As though a haze cleared, Jay's eyes went from dark and stormy to focused. He inhaled and took a step back. "You're right." And then he looked to Higgs. "I'm right behind you, buddy. I'll call Pensky and we'll get this cleared up ASAP."

Higgs nodded as he let Detective Primrose lead him out, but he stopped when he saw Coop. "Can't you at least let her go, Tanz? She just got a little caught up."

But Detective Primrose shook her head, her eyes somber. "I can't. You know I can't, mate. She tried to assault an officer."

"It's okay, Higgs," I said to him, almost reaching out to touch his arm, but snatching my hand back before I found myself in handcuffs, too. My stomach gurgled in upheaval, but I knew I had to keep a level head. "We'll be fine. You just take care of you. I'll make sure Coop's all right."

Out of the blue, because Coop had a gut feeling, my thoughts on Higgs did a complete one-eighty. When Coop said something, when she was adamant the way she'd been when she'd yelled, I took it to heart. It wasn't often Coop felt that way about much other than myself and Livingston, and this time, I was going to trust her.

I prayed I was doing the right thing as I watched them lead both Coop and Higgs out to separate patrol cars.

Just over the tops of the police cars lining the street, as I dug in my pocket for the keys to our worn Caddy, trying to keep my trembling fingers from losing my grip on them, I caught sight of a group of the men Higgs and Jay must house, hanging around, their weary faces full of fear, but no sign of Solomon.

Though I did see the man wearing the hat like Gilligan, and made another mental note to try to talk to him about whether he'd seen anything the day Fergus had been murdered. Maybe he'd know where Solomon was.

Gosh, on top of everything else, I couldn't get Solomon out of my mind for worrying about him.

But now wasn't the time. I had a demon to keep out of jail.

~

I handed Jay some scalding-hot coffee from the dispenser and experienced more déjà vu. Not long ago, Stevie had offered me coffee and chips while we waited for Coop to be questioned in the murder of our prior landlord.

He took it, his hand shaking ever so slightly. "Thanks, Trixie. Thanks for sticking around. You don't have to now that Coop's free to go. Pensky's here. He'll fix this."

Pensky was their attorney friend. Lisle Pensky. A short, chubby man with a double-breasted suit, a pinky ring, and more hair than a troll doll, but pleasant enough overall with his heavy New York accent and his fancy clothes.

Coop had somehow managed to get off with very little hassle and a big, fat warning from Detective Primrose, making me breathe a sigh of relief. We couldn't afford an attorney—especially not like the one Stevie had hired for Coop. Maybe Higgs had said something to someone. I didn't know how well he knew the officers here in Portland, or if he'd worked with them at one time. But maybe he had some influence. Whatever it was, Coop was free.

Now, she sat fascinated by the fish tank in the lobby, watching the colorful creatures swim back and forth while I sat with Jay and we waited to see where Higgs stood.

"What was Detective Primrose talking about?

Higgs's tattoo? I don't get it. He has a bunch of them on both arms. What does that have to do with the murder of Fergus McDuff?"

Jay shrugged his shoulders, slinking down into one of the hard plastic chairs we sat on in the waiting area. "I don't know either, Trixie. She pointed at a tattoo he was forced to get when he was undercover in a gang in Minneapolis. I'm pretty sure he wouldn't want me to tell you that, but I don't see what it can hurt now. He had to do a lot of things—" He stopped short and grimaced. "That's his story to tell, I guess. But yeah. The tattoo she pointed to was part of an initiation and forced on him, and not by any stretch of the imagination the worst part of what he went through. I can't believe she'd arrest him. He's legendary all over the country in every precinct for his undercover work with gangs. This is insane."

"Forced... How awful for him," I murmured, unsure what else to say.

Oh, my great gracious, I'd heard about the horrible things gangs did when they initiated someone into the club, but actually knowing someone who'd suffered through it made it uglier somehow.

Jay nodded his sandy head, driving his hands into his hoodie pockets. "Yep."

I craned my neck in his direction and rubbed my arms, goose bumps running along their lengths. "And what's the tattoo of?"

The moment I spoke the words, it hit me like a bolt of lightning, but I let Jay say the words.

"It's stupid, actually, and I don't get at all what it has to do with Fergus, but it's a tic-tac-toe board—right on the inside of his wrist."

Bingo.

My stomach hit the floor hard.

Just like on Fergus's neck. Scratched out with a knife or something sharp. Now, the question was, did I tell Jay I'd seen that on Fergus's neck, as had Coop and Knuckles? Or shut my mouth because I was one of the few who'd seen it?

Was this all the evidence they had? And really, would he do something so obvious like carve a sign into Fergus's neck that matched a tattoo he had on his person?

Who's that careless a killer? The more I chewed on that, the less I believed an ex-undercover cop, one who'd dealt with gangs, would do something so stupid.

And I hoped his lawyer would say the same. But that small niggle in the back of my head, the one that said Detective Primrose didn't strike me as someone who would do something so rash as to arrest Higgs without cause, said they had something else. Something viable—something that would stick.

But I didn't have to worry about asking, because just as I was about to, Knuckles strolled in through the sliding glass door, his big body taking up the space with the grace of a panther.

He slipped into the waiting area, caught sight of us, lifted a big hand, a glint of concern in his eyes, and came to greet us.

"Knuckles," Coop said with almost a hint of excitement. Then she threw her arms around his wide waist, driving her hands into his leather vest.

At first he didn't look like he knew what to do with her affectionate greeting. Heck, neither did I. She didn't respond this way to many people, and so far today, she was oozing all manner of emotions.

But then he put his hands on her shoulders and patted them before setting her in front of him with a grin. "You okay, Coop? They treat ya right in there?"

She bounced her head, her gaze up at him blank, but I could tell she had an affinity for him she didn't know how to express. "I'm fine, Donald P. Ledbetter. Very fine. How are you?"

"Well, I came to check on you ladies and Higgs, that's how I am." He eyeballed me in the chair next to Jay then smiled, so I patted the seat next to me, and he wedged into it, putting an arm around the back of my chair as he reached over and shook hands with an eerily pale Jay. "You okay, man?" he asked.

"As okay as I can be. Thanks for coming."

I cocked my head. "Do you two know each other?"

Knuckles gave a sharp nod of his head and leaned back. "We've met once or twice in conjunction with the shelter."

"It's Knuckles, yeah? Last Christmas—the party at the shelter for the kids is where we met, right?" Jay asked.

"You bet," he responded. "I did the kids' tattoos."

"You gave *children* tattoos?"

Knuckles chuckled, his weathered face a welcome sight. "Not real ones, silly goose. Airbrushed. They love 'em. But forget about me. You okay, Trixie?"

"I'm fine. Really. But how did you know what happened?" I asked, giving his arm a squeeze to thank him for showing up. I didn't understand why he had, but seeing him brought a warmth to my heart I can't quite describe.

Running a hand over his beard, he settled in. "Well, I was headed to your place to talk to you two. I didn't like the way you left yesterday, Trixie. I was just so caught off guard... Still, it was wrong of me. I wanted to apologize and see if I could offer you girls some lunch so we could talk some more about Fergus's murder and opening the store. Delores told me what happened. Everyone was talking about it, in fact. So I came right over to see if you needed some support."

My heart fairly glowed. "That's so kind of you, Knuckles. You're a really good guy. Thank you, but so far, we have nothing. As much nothing as we did last night."

"So Higgs is in there being questioned right now?"

I sighed, raspy and annoyed at the very thought. "He is, and though it's only been a couple of hours, it feels like eternity."

"Tell me what I can do to make this better? You want me to make a lunch run? Take Coop with me and we'll grab something besides food from a dispenser, get her out of here to clear her head?"

I don't know how we'd gotten so lucky when we

found Knuckles, but I was ever so grateful today to whoever was in charge of the universe. Ever so. "You'd do that?"

His nod was brisk, his warm eyes crinkling at the corners. "I would. Of course, I would, kiddo."

"Let me give you some money." I began digging in my pockets, but he held up a hand.

"It's on me. I was coming by to see if you ladies wanted to have lunch with me anyway. Anything you absolutely won't eat? Allergies?"

Patting his arm, I smiled as my stomach grumbled. "I'll eat whatever if you're buying. How about you, Jay? Anything you're opposed to?"

His sigh was one of resignation. "I'm good with anything. Thanks, Knuckles."

Knuckles rose, his thick thighs lifting him from the chair as he called out to my demon, "Hey, Coop? You wanna ride on the back of a motorcycle?"

She hopped up from her chair in front of the fish tank about as fast as I'd ever seen her move unless she was preparing to slice someone's throat open. "You have a *motorcycle?*"

Knuckles laughed and offered her an arm. "I do. But you have to wear a helmet. I know some ladies don't like that because it messes up their hair. My daughter always gripes about it, but I insist."

She threaded her arm through his and said, "I'm not a lady. I'm a..."

I held my breath. *Please don't let her say demon. Pleasedon'tletthersaydemon!*

169

"I'm a Coop. And I like you so-so much, Knuckles."

Now he *really* laughed out loud, enough to turn heads in the waiting room, his eyes alight with amusement. "I like you, too, Coop. Let's get these people fed, okay?"

"Can I drive, Knuckles?" Coop asked, with a hint of eagerness in her tone. Yet another emotion she was picking up on, pleasing me to no end.

"Nope. You sure can't," Knuckles said with another laugh as they headed out the sliding doors.

And that left just me and Jay and my zillion questions, none of which I'm sure he wanted to answer if he was feeling anything like I had when Coop had been arrested. But I decided to do some research into this gang Jay had mentioned. I wasn't sure how to go about it. Did they just put gang sign information out on the Internet or was that unlikely?

Google and I had become good friends as of late, so I typed in tic-tac-toe plus Minneapolis plus gangs into my phone and let 'er rip.

My eyes widened as I scrolled. There were numerous articles to choose from about a rash of gang-related murders in a housing project in South Minneapolis, dubbed the tic-tac-toe murders due to the signs tattooed on the gang members' wrists. I looked for a reputable source, something Stevie said was very important due to the state of the Internet and shoddy reporting these days.

I guess I'd never considered Minnesota a place with gangs. I mean, New York and LA, yes, but Minnesota?

Where everyone said "you betcha" and it was as cold as Antarctica? But clearly, based on the number of articles, they did indeed exist there. I'd spent too many years in the convent, obviously. I was too sheltered.

I scrolled to the *Minneapolis Herald* and began to read about a night five years ago, in the winter of 2013, when multiple arrests were made after a two-year investigation into the gangs known as Young Money (or YM) and Blood Squad (or BS). Young Money being the bunch using the tic-tac-toe tattoo to represent their gang sign.

The charges against YM read like a laundry list of crimes. Narcotics distribution, narcotics conspiracy, arms dealing, racketeering, and the murder of nine people from the rival gang, Blood Squad, and one BS family member—a Diego Santino, the twelve-year-old brother of the leader of Blood Squad, Matias Santino.

As I read, still finding no mention of Higgs at all, my heart ached for Diego Santino, caught up in the crossfire during a turf war at a South Minneapolis housing project. The picture of this handsome young child with chocolate-brown hair and brown eyes made me close my own eyes and scrunch them tight.

He'd been so young...

And then I remembered, Higgs probably wouldn't be named, would he? Not if he'd been in deep cover with this gang.

As I read the retelling of that night from an innocent bystander who had hidden behind a pickup truck during the crossfire, my heart pounded. Apparently,

Diego had tried to stop his brother Matias from engaging with the rival gang and was recklessly gunned down.

Heaven in all its mercy, how awful.

Jay happened to glance over at my phone, his eyes boring holes into the side of my head. "I figured you'd look it up."

Holding up the phone, I ignored the tone that said "back off" and asked, "So is this what Higgs was involved in?"

"You really should ask him. He can tell you better than I can," he answered. Though, Jay didn't say it with any anger or even flippantly, he simply stated a fact with a tone that said, "respect my wish to stay out of this." But gone was the friendly demeanor, replaced by a terse glance.

So Higgs had a past, one I'm sure gave him night-mares. One that would give *me* nightmares, and I hadn't even experienced it. I can't imagine the pain he must have suffered seeing a twelve-year-old die.

But if he'd been undercover, and there was no mention of him in any of the articles—in fact, when I googled his name, he came up as the owner of the Peach Street shelter—then how had someone from the Blood Squad found him and possibly framed him? Because I was more certain than ever that's what this arrest was about. He was being framed. But why?

Did he have something to do with the death of Diego Santino? The article said the boy was caught in the crossfire. Maybe it was Higgs's bullet that had killed Diego? Surely an accident if that was the case, right?

But there was no definitive answer to my question. Ballistics determined the bullet came from a gun that remained unidentifiable due to the fact that every gang member carried the same gun. A cheap .38.

But then, wouldn't the Minneapolis police department protect their undercover officers by relocating them? Was that why Higgs had moved here to Portland? What was the protocol for something like this?

"Hey, Jay," I muttered. "How long has Higgs been here in Cobbler Cove?"

"Four years, I think. He opened the shelter, and I came to work with him about a year ago. So yeah. Four or so."

The timeline made sense. Maybe it had taken that long for the BS gang member to locate him?

Was it Matias Santino who'd killed Fergus to frame Higgs because he blamed him for his brother's death? How could he, if no one had determined who fired the shot?

But as I read more of the article, I saw Matias was doing life in federal prison for other related charges aside from the murders that night. There was no mention of any remaining members of BS still at large, and the only person left of Matias's family was his mother, Iris, who, at the time of the article, had been ill with cancer. Still, could there be someone else, someone who'd gotten away from the Blood Squad who wanted revenge?

I had to know. I don't know why, or what compelled me, but I had to know. This was no longer about the store being caught up in this, or the delay in getting in there to renovate.

My gut just said I needed to help Higgs. I'd felt nothing up until this point but skepticism for him, and a little fear, if I were honest. But now? Now something burned in the pit of my belly, and I needed to figure out what.

As I sat pressed arm to arm with Jay, I began to wonder how long he'd known Higgs and the background of their friendship.

"You know, how rude of me, but I never did ask what your role is at the shelter, Jay? Do you work with the men directly?"

But he shook his head. "Not as hands-on as Higgs, no. I do the books, hunt down charitable donations, fundraise. That kind of thing."

"Does Higgs rent from Fergus, too?"

"Nope. The shelter was bought and paid for by donations. Higgs owns it."

"Do you know anyone else who rented from him? Any of the other shops on our street, maybe?"

Crowley still hadn't sent me the names of the people he leased to, and I wondered if I wouldn't have to hoof it door to door in order to find out.

"I don't. My focus is mostly on the shelter and nothing else."

Admirable indeed. I didn't know what else to say to ease his worry, so I touched on a neutral topic. "Well, when things settle down, I'd like to get more involved in my free time and volunteer."

His smile was vague. "Higgs will be glad to hear it. You can never have enough volunteers."

"How long have you guys been friends?"

"Since college. How about you and Coop?"

Since my possession? No. I couldn't say that. "About a year now," I answered instead.

He looked at the door they'd led Higgs behind to question him, and sighed. "What could possibly be taking so long? It feels like hours. Doesn't it feel like hours?"

Waiting for something like this felt like an eternity. I could sympathize. But I was in for a penny, in for a pound. I wasn't going anywhere until we knew what was happening with Higgs.

But we didn't have to wait very long for our answer. Detective Primrose swished out into the waiting area, her eyes taking in both of us with a mixture of sympathy and something else I couldn't identify.

She came to stand before us, her arms crossing over her chest, her dark blue skirt and blazer covered in white lint. "Miss Lavender."

I gulped. Her tone sounded just like Sister Anne Margaret's. That tone meant I was in for a scolding. "Detective Primrose."

"Funny you and your friend should be in the middle of this, init?"

Uh-oh. I fisted my hands together. "Funny as in ha-ha. Or funny as in ironic?"

She eyeballed me from behind her owl-like glasses. "Maybe a little of both, love. I did some detecting, because I'm jolly good at it, and what do you suppose I discovered about you, Miss Lavender?"

I licked my lips. "That I like long walks on the beach, red wine over white, and foosball?"

"You like foosball?"

I sighed and rolled my eyes in mock irritation. "Well, yeah. But I suppose you consider that a sin, coming from England and all that rugby."

She fought a smirk. "I found out that not too long ago, you were embroiled in another murder with, and this ought to make you laugh, another one of your landlords. Funny that, eh?"

I winced. "Honest to goodness, we're a pox on landlords."

She rolled her tongue along the inside of her cheek. "Then I guess it's a good thing you both have such a solid alibi."

I wiped my palms on my thighs. "You know what they say about good things."

"What do they say, Miss Lavender?"

"They come in small packages?"

Detective Primrose sighed, indicating we were done sparring for today. "Listen up. You two might as well go on home," she said, her tone even and somber.

"What's happening, Tansy?" Jay asked, rising from the chair to run a hand through his sandy-blond locks, his eyes full of worry.

Her gaze pierced his. "You're not going to like it, mate."

My stomach took that nosedive again, but I stood up, too, my legs shaky. "What's happening?"

Just then, Higgs's lawyer shot out the door, his stout legs carrying him to where we stood. "Let's go," he ordered curtly, giving Detective Primrose a glance that was none too happy.

"Wait!" I ordered, making everyone turn around. "What's going on? What's happening and where's Higgs?"

Pensky's face, round and lightly tanned, went sour. "Hoping we can get him bail. He's officially been charged with the murder of Fergus McDuff."

rixie?"

"Yes, Coop?"

She put a hand on my arm and squeezed, something else she rarely does—touch people, that is. Yet, these last couple of days, she'd been hugging and shaking hands like there was no tomorrow.

I wondered where that was coming from. I wondered if it was genuine or she was doing it because it's what she saw other people do. But her hand on my arm meant something. It meant she wanted me to truly hear her.

"We can't let Higgs go to jail. He's innocent. I know he's telling the truth. *I. Know.*"

I pulled into a parking spot at the bank where only three days ago we'd opened an account, and turned to look at her.

She didn't look like she'd slept in a meat locker—unlike me. I had dark shadows under my eyes and my skin was pale from a long night of trying to make sense of this—all the while trying to comfort Coop, who was in knots about Higgs's arrest. But Coop looked as though she'd stepped off the pages of *Vogue* in her leggings and slim-fitting zippered jacket in hot pink and black.

The only good news we had was the store would be clear for us to move into in the next two days or so. But everything else was as horrible as horrible could get. Higgs was in jail, waiting on a hearing to see if he'd get bail, and Jay was in a tizzy trying to come up with the money, because Pensky had assured him bail wouldn't be cheap due to the severity of the charges.

Though, according to Jay, Higgs had property and a house in Minnesota he could use as collateral. I don't know how bail works, but that information had appeared to satisfy his lawyer who was, at this very minute, filing papers to expedite Higgs's bail hearing. If you listened to Pensky, with Higgs's squeaky-clean record and his former job as a police officer, making bail should be easier than the norm.

And I truly hoped that was the case. I'd even gone back to the scene of my dumpster attack, hoping to find a clue, but I'd come up dry.

I patted Coop's hand, making her let go of my arm. "I know you do, Coop."

"But do you *know*, Trixie Lavender? Do you know in your heart? Do you believe Cross Higglesworth is innocent?"

Sighing, I gripped the steering wheel. Did I?

Because it sure as heck wasn't looking good for Higgs. Not at all. After a second sweep of the store, they'd found a strand of what they believed was Higgs's hair.

That, combined with the argument he'd had with Fergus (which I'd blabbed to the police), the tic-tac-toe tattoo and the marks on Fergus's neck—and lastly, a damning voice mail Higgs had left Fergus about harassing the men from the shelter—convinced the Portland PD they had their man. At least, it was all enough to arrest him for murder and keep him in jail.

And all night long, as I'd scoured the Internet to see if anyone from the Blood Squad had been released from prison or escaped, or any little thing I could think of to help Higgs, the guilt of telling Detective Primrose about that tiff had eaten me from the inside out.

In a way, I'd helped land Higgs in jail, and I felt sick about it. What I couldn't come to terms with was the tic-tac-toe gang sign carved into Fergus's neck. I'd like to know how the police were going to explain the logic in that.

I'd asked this once before, but I had to ask myself again—what kind of killer leaves such an obvious clue? Especially seeing as Higgs had been a part of the gang and had its tattoo on his person?

That was just plain bananapants, and Higgs didn't strike me as the kind of guy who was at all stupid.

"Trixie!" Coop hissed my name. "Do you believe he's innocent?"

I swallowed hard, formulating the right words to soothe Coop. "I believe that *you* believe, Coop."

"That's not what she asked ya, sausage," Livingston chirped from the backseat.

"I know what she asked me, Livingston, and the best answer I can give is, I *think* so. I don't know Higgs. How can I possibly be sure he's innocent?" I snapped, and regretted it instantly.

But listen. I know yesterday I said I had to help him. That I felt it in my gut. Today? I wasn't so sure after hearing about the evidence they had against him. How had his hair gotten into our store and at the crime scene? If you listened to what Higgs said, according to Pensky, it had probably landed on Fergus when they'd argued. But Pensky told us it was found on the floor in the pool of Fergus's blood.

And the voice mail? That didn't bode well for Higgs, either.

Turning around, I reached into Livingston's cage and scratched his belly. "I'm sorry, Livingston. It's been a long night and I'm cranky. I didn't mean to snap at you."

"I know, love. But is it really your responsibility to clear this man of these charges? Don't ya have other tings you should be worryin' 'bout?"

"It's not like we have anything to do right now, Livingston. We can't get into the store for another couple of days. So we might as well try to solve a murder, right?"

Coop bounced her head up and down. "Right."

Gosh. She was so convinced Higgs was innocent, I didn't know what would happen if they found out he wasn't. Thus, I tried to brace her for the worst.

"Coop, you did hear what his lawyer said, didn't you? They have a voice mail from Higgs, threatening Fergus, and maybe even his hair at the crime scene. That's not good."

"I heard, but I don't believe them. I believe Higgs. I know I'm right. I feel it right here." She pointed to her non-existent gut. "And if you won't help me find out who murdered mean old Fergus McDuff, I'll do it alone. Just me and my sword." She looked at me with fire in her eyes.

Her conviction still left me astounded. "You don't have to do it alone. I'll help you. I promised I would last night, didn't I?"

"After six cups of coffee, two cheese Danish, and a bag of honey-roasted peanuts, ya did," Livingston reminded me.

"Danish helps me think. Don't judge. Now, let me grab some cash, and then we'll go look for Solomon, okay? I'm convinced he knows something about the night Fergus was killed. You two wait here."

I pushed the creaky door of our Caddy closed and headed for the ATM machine. As I slid my card in, I held my breath. We were about as low on cash as we'd ever been, but if we could hold on for another month, we just might make it.

Still, I hated seeing our balance—it was nothing to get excited about.

Punching in my pin number, I waited as the machine did its thing and looked inside the doors of the bank to see Jay at the counter. I would have waved, but his back was to me.

Golly, he'd been beside himself last night when we'd finally parted ways and he'd gone off with Pensky. Maybe he was here today in an effort to help Higgs with bail money?

I wondered that as I collected our cash and headed back to the car, the bright sun of the day burning a hole in the top of my head. The day felt especially bright because my eyes were grainy and tired, but it was warm, and the bustle of people on the sidewalk doing whatever it was they were doing made me smile.

Jumping back into the car, I settled in and put my seat belt on. "Okay, let's go and look under the Hawthorne, yes? We have to find Solomon. He's pretty much our only lead. Maybe he knows where the guy with the Gilligan hat is. You know, the one we saw after lunch the day Fergus was murdered? Maybe finding them will lead us to something else. Or maybe if we just ask around, we can find something— anything to help Higgs."

Coop folded her hands in her lap and nodded. "That would be helpful. I will help as hard as I can."

Yeah. That's what worried me. "Okay, but remember what I told you, Coop. No touching. Solomon is afraid, not to mention sick. He doesn't like to be touched, from what Higgs told me."

"That also means no threatenin' to lop off the man's ears, either, Coopie," Livingston reminded.

"I have never lopped off a man's ears."

"That's not true, lass. Not true at all. Don't ya remember about fifty years ago—"

"Not now, Livingston," I chastised. "As much as I'd love to hear what Coop was up to fifty years ago, we have more pressing matters. So, let's talk about where we are. We need to get our ducks in a row and make sure everyone's up to speed."

"It wasn't fifty years ago," Coop denied. "It was *fifty-seven*."

"Fifty-seven…two hundred and seven…what difference does it make, Coopie? A man has no ears because of you."

"That is not the truth, Quigley Livingston. I only nicked—"

"Guys!" I yelped as I pulled onto the road and out into traffic. Cobbler Cove was busy today, and if we hoped to get to the bridge before lunch, we needed to make haste. "Knock it off, would you, please? I'm tired. We need to be discussing a strategy or something, if we want to help Higgs, not bickering about lopping ears."

Wait.

I turned to Coop. "Did you *really* lop someone's ears off?" As quickly as I asked the question, I held up my hand to keep her from answering. "No! Don't tell me. Save it for later when I can handle hearing about an earless man. For now, what do we have to say about what we've learned so far? Do we think the murderer is an angry tenant or someone he loaned money to? Or do we think the person who killed Fergus is out for revenge against Higgs? Why not just kill Higgs and be done with it?"

Coop was the first to give her theory. "Where I come from, killing is a final act, but it isn't done in vain or without fanfare. The process before is slow and precise."

My heart pounded in my chest. The mere idea of killing someone—anyone—was so foreign to me. Yet, Coop knew all about it.

"I don't understand, Coop."

Livingston's feathers ruffled. "She means, torturing someone can be far worse than killin' 'em, lass. If Higgs were to rot in jail, especially in the way an ex-police officer likely would, his stay would be none too pleasant. Killing him is too easy. If this is an act of revenge, they want him to *suffer*."

I gulped, thankful we'd hit a red light so I could gather my wits. "But if that's the case, then who is it? Everyone from that gang is in federal prison and no one's escaped. That leaves us with a big dead end."

As I said those words, one light up, I spotted Jay again, crossing the crosswalk and, as my eyes followed to where he was headed, I noted he was entering another bank.

Huh. Good on him for having more than one bank account.

"How do we know all the gang members are in

prison? Maybe someone is still at large?" Coop reasoned, and I had to agree.

"Okay, so who from the Blood Squad is angry enough with Higgs to kill Fergus and frame him? Who has that kind of beef with him?"

"Maybe they're from Young Money," Livingston said—also a reasonable point. "Maybe their knickers are in a twist because your Higgs got them all arrested and they're out to make him pay. Someone who wasn't a part of the shootin'."

"Also fair." I pressed the heel of my hand to my head and rubbed, pulling into a shady area under the bridge where I'd seen many of the homeless gather. I turned the car off and sat, listening to the silence.

Most everyone was either off doing whatever they did to pass the time or they were ensconced in their tents. The rusty barrels typically lit at night for warmth were devoid of flames and only a few people gathered in clusters, but I didn't see Solomon or Gilligan, as I'd come to mentally call him, anywhere.

"Is your friend Solomon here, Trixie?"

I shook my head, dropping the keys into my purse, watching some boys on skateboards in the distance. "No. But it can't hurt to talk to other people about whether they've seen Solomon, can it? Or if they heard anything about what happened to Fergus."

"Then let's do this."

"Let's do this peacefully, yes?" I glanced at her with a question in my eyes.

I heard the thump of her sword, likely tucked next to the passenger seat. "Fine. No sword. Let's go."

Turning around, I caught Livingston's glassy eyes with mine. "Will you be all right for a few minutes if we leave you alone with the windows down? I'll never take my eyes off the car, okay?"

"Go on with ya, lass. Go save the handsome lad."

I gave him a crooked smile. "How do you know if he's handsome?"

"Coopie went on and on about him. Described him and everythin'. I'm sure he's a real looker. Now off with the two of ya. I'm needin' my mid-mornin' nap. But do me a favor, don't go adoptin' any more strays. The inn's full up with the crazies for now."

I barked a laugh as I jumped out of the car and shut the door, my feet sinking into the muddy terrain.

But once more, for the cheap seats, I tapped Coop on the arm. I didn't understand how or why this had become so important to her. "Coop? What suddenly made you decide Higgs and his arrest were so important that you had to interfere with police business? I don't get it. You've only met him once. Is it something more than your gut telling you he's innocent?"

She stopped and looked at me, that penetrating gaze she was so good at gluing me where I stood. "Because Higgs is important to our future, Trixie. He can't be important if he's in jail with the bad guys."

Her words stopped me cold. "Important? Important how?"

"Remember when I told you I feel his innocence in my gut?"

Crossing my arms over my chest, I rocked back on my feet. "I do. You said it was just like the way Stevie sometimes feels when she's trying to solve a murder."

"That's right. That's also how I feel about Higgs in our lives, in the future—and also about being a part of a community. He's an important part of it because he helps these people, and if what you say about community is true, how can we leave him to the wolves if we wish to be a part of this community? That's why it's so important to me. I'm preserving our community, and if someday we find ourselves in the same kind of trouble, I hope he'll help us, too. I don't have to be his best friend to care enough that he's not sentenced to life in prison, do I? I know what it is to be wrongfully accused of something I didn't do. It was an awful feeling, Trixie. I don't want to see that happen to him because I *know* he didn't do it."

Preserving our community, wrongfully accused... My sweet demon was learning. Every day. And her conviction in Higgs's innocence was admirable.

So I bobbed my head. "Okay then. That's good enough for me."

With that, we turned our attention to the encampments under the bridge.

Traffic on Hawthorne was light this midday, making for less noise. As I plodded through the encampment, trying not to disturb people sleeping, I weaved my way through shopping carts and endless amounts of plastic bottles and debris.

"Where do we start?" Coop whispered, her voice almost shaky, striking me as odd. Coop wasn't afraid of anything—ever.

I gripped her arm, keeping one eye on the car. "What's wrong, Coop?"

"This." She spread her lean arms wide, her face grimmer than usual. "This is truly Hell on Earth."

As I looked around, sadly, I had to agree. There was grief here, rife in the air. There was desolation, despair, isolation…and I wanted to make it better, or at least ease some of the suffering. But realistically, I knew some people simply didn't want any help. They'd been shunned by society, so they'd made their own place in the world together, and to encroach was invasive to them.

I smiled in sympathy. Once more wondering what Coop had seen in Hell, then I shut down that part of my brain. I'm not sure I'm ready to know how she suffered.

"Do you want to wait in the car, Coop?"

"And let you do this alone? Not on this day or any day hereafter."

I grinned at her and pinched her cheek. "Okay then. Let's poke around."

"Would ya look at the fancy ladies? More social workers, boys. Better hide 'em if you got 'em," a voice crowed, raspy and taunting.

Coop looked down at the ground about thirty feet

away and pointed to a spot by a concrete piling where a woman with wiry jet-black and silver hair and a fake purple fur coat sat, clutching a wide rectangular purse that had a picture of Hello Kitty on it.

She pulled it close as she rose, her knobby finger pointing at us in a manner that was anything but friendly as everyone around her scattered. "You go on and git!" she shouted, reeling toward us, the coat sliding off to reveal a bony shoulder.

I held my hands up in surrender fashion. "We mean no harm. We're just looking for a friend."

She popped her lips, her sunken mouth wrinkling in distaste. "You ain't got no friends here, fancy lady. Social workers and the cops ain't no friends o' mine!"

Instead of vehemently defending myself, I stayed as calm as I could and used my reasonable tone. The hope was to get these folks to trust me eventually. I planned on sticking around Cobbler Cove, and I wanted to be of service. But I fully expected to be met with skepticism.

Rolling up the sleeves of my thin pullover, I squared my shoulders. "Hi there. I'm Trixie Lavender, and this is my friend, Coop O'Shea. Nice to meet you. And we're not social workers. Not even close. We own a tattoo shop called Inkerbelle's—or we will once those nosy police are done with their investigation."

Now her narrow gray eyes expressed interest as her fingers clutched her purse tighter to her belly. "Ain't you the fancy pants who knew that Fergus McDuff? He's a bad man. So bad. He loans money to people and then he charges 'em crazy interest and if you don't pay up, he'll break your legs right off!" She mimicked a breaking motion with her two hands then laughed with glee.

But it wasn't anything we didn't already know at this point. Fergus was a loan shark, among other terrible things. If only we could find out who he'd loan-sharked to, we might have some suspects.

"Hey, didn't he get hisself killed over there at your place?"

I took a small step closer, keeping a serious face. "He did. Did you know Fergus?"

She screwed up her face and spat, "Yeah, I knew him all right. He stomped in a puddle once right next to where I was sleepin' 'cause he didn't like me camped out by the Thai place down the way." She ran a hand over her purple coat. "Got my beautiful coat all muddy and wet. It's all I got 'tween me an' the elements, you know."

"Look who's calling who fancy," I said, soft and low. "You with that beautiful coat and all.

She preened a little and curtsied. "I have a tiara, too."

"Oh! I'd love to see it sometime if you'll show me."

But her pride turned to suspicion. "You friends with Fergus?"

"I wasn't friends with Fergus. He was only our landlord for one short day."

"Until somebody whacked him," she cackled, then

straightened and narrowed her eyes. "He called me names sometimes."

"How rude of him," I replied, inching toward her. "Solomon told me he was mean to some of you. I'm sorry he was cruel to you and your friends."

Instantly her face went soft and dewy, made kinder by the shade of the bridge. "You know Saulie? My sweet, sweet Saulie?"

"I do. We met just the other night. I invited him to Inkerbelle's for some soup. We'd be honored if you dropped by, too."

She growled at us, making Coop stiffen. "I don't need your help, Fancy Lady. You stay away from me!"

I smiled and nodded my understanding, keeping Coop off to my side. "Oh, I'm not offering you help. You look like a lady who has it all together. You'd be helping *me*, in fact. I always make too much soup for just the two of us. I need someone to help us eat it all."

"Do you mean that icky soup with the chicken meatballs that aren't anything like spaghetti meatballs, Trixie?" Coop asked, pulling her hair away from her face and tying a rubber band around the width to fluff it into a messy bun.

I rasped a sigh of aggravation. It was good soup, for pity's sake. "That's the one," I said out of the side of my mouth.

She looked to the homeless woman and warned, "Don't do it, lady with no house. You'll regret it. It tastes like tires. Blech."

For a moment, the woman stared, bug-eyed at

Coop, and then she garbled a laugh. "I like you! What's your name again, girlie?"

Coop stuck her hand out. "My name is Coop O'Shea. What's yours?"

The woman drove her small hand into Coop's, and to my demon's credit, she didn't flinch at the dirt caked under her nails or the greasy streaks on the palm of her hand. "I'm Madge, and I don't think I want any of your stinkin' soup." Madge then took a step toward the both of us until I could smell the alcohol on her breath in the heat of the midday sun. "But I'd take a bottle of blackberry brandy if you got some for an old lady like me."

I held up both hands again before driving them into the pockets of my overalls and pulling out the material lining them. "I'm fresh out, Madge. Maybe next time? We need to get moving, but it was nice meeting you."

She latched onto my arm and Coop, always at the ready, moved in, but I waved her off and smiled in question at Madge.

"Where ya goin'?" she asked.

Clearly, I'd piqued her interest, which was what I'd hoped to do by behaving as though I wasn't interested in her.

I patted her hand, the skin rough and dry and spotted with age. "We need to find Solomon. He's sick. He needs medicine, Madge."

Madge scratched her head and nodded, her thin legs poking out beneath the ruffled nightgown she wore beneath her coat. "Aw, yeah. He always gets that bad cough. But he won't see no doctor. Guarantee it. He's scairt of 'em. Thinks they're gonna lock 'em up. I tried tellin' him the last time that looker Higgs was here, tryin' to help him, they was just gonna take a look at him and give him some medicine and send him on his crazy way. But Saulie don't believe nobody."

"You know Cross Higglesworth?"

Now she grinned, her smile revealing the loss of some teeth, and she giggled like a schoolgirl. "Who don't know him? He's dreamy-steamy, always down here bringin' food to everybody and checkin' on 'em."

Dreamy-steamy. I suppose that could describe Higgs... "Do you trust him, Madge? Is he kind to you?"

She shored up her shoulders and smiled wider. "We all like Higgs. Us girls, anyway. He's nice. Nicer than that Fergus McDuff."

"Was he nice to Solomon?" I know Coop was probably rolling her eyes at me right now because she thought Higgs invented the sun and the moon, but I had to be sure.

She looked at both of us. "Well, yeah. He's nice to everybody. Even Saulie, who isn't nice to *anybody.*"

"Have you seen Solomon lately, Madge? I'd be so grateful to you if you could tell me where he is."

She rolled her shoulders and shook her head. "Ain't seen him in a coupla days now. He's always wanderin' off to somewhere when he don't want to hear everybody chatterin'. Calls it too many voices at one time. Last time I saw him, he was talkin' about some guy he didn't like. But Saulie don't hardly like anybody."

Ah. The mad bad guy, likely. "Did he tell you who the guy was that he didn't like, Madge? Do you know who the guy is?"

"Nope. Saulie's always talkin' about somethin', though. He don't make a whole lotta sense most times with all his fancy old-time talk. But he gets the best day-old bread from Lettie's Bakery down on Sherman. They like him there. So nobody says nothin' to him about how nutso he sounds because everybody wants some of those high-falutin' sourdough rolls."

I sighed, my lips dry and my head pounding as I tried to think about what to do next. "Do you know if anyone else here knows anything? Do you think they'd talk to me, Madge? Solomon's very sick. I need to find him."

"Ya know," she said, planting a hand on her reed-thin hip. "He ain't never been gone this long before."

Worry stabbed at my heart and my stomach wobbled, my Danish spree from last night coming back with a vengeance. Where was Solomon?

"How about the man with the hat like Gilligan? Do you remember that show, Madge? You know, the Skipper and Mary Ann? Have you ever seen him?" I asked, putting a hand over my eyes to avoid the sun's sharp glare.

She kicked her torn sneakers around a little, scuffing the ripped soles against the ground, before she said, "Just saw him last night, ain't seen him today, though. Probably went to the bar to see if he can get some leftover beer cans with a couple'a drops a beer in 'em. He sure likes his beer. Lookit that pile over there."

I glanced in the direction of her finger, where a pile of old Busch beer cans sat in a crumpled heap. Okay, we were on a fast train to Nowheresville, and I had to pull the plug.

"Thank you, Madge, you've been very kind and very helpful. I won't forget that. If you ever want a hot meal, stop by the shop once we're up and running, okay?"

"Don't do it, Madge." Coop whisper-yelled the warning, making Madge giggle.

As we turned to leave, the boys who'd been skate-boarding zipped past us, skateboards tucked under their arms, their gazes aimed right at Madge, their feet thundering on the ground. Four of them, all mostly dressed alike in slouchy jeans and T-shirts, except for one, who also wore a knit cap.

In a split second, they grabbed her purse, something I suspected she treasured above all else, and began to toss it to one another, taunting her. "Look what we got, Madge! You want it back? Ya gotta pay the toll!" one of them crowed.

And Madge crumpled as some of her belongings fell to the ground, one of them a plastic tiara, like one a child would receive at a princess-themed birthday party. "Pleeease, give that back!" she cried, tears sliding down her gaunt face. "That's my favorite tiara in the whole world! Please don't do this again! Why won't you leave me alone?"

"Pay the toll, Madge! Pay the toll!" another boy with red hair and splotchy freckles teased.

They couldn't have been more than sixteen years old, tops, in my estimation. But as they lobbed Madge's bag around and somehow managed to knock her in the head with it, making her cry out in pain when the strap slapped her in the face, it was time to step in.

So here's the thing. I've mentioned before that I don't always know when whatever is living inside of me in some dark crevice, tucked away near an organ or something, is going to take over, right?

If I had an inkling, if I knew what it wanted or what encouraged it to possess me, I'd at least have something to go on. Maybe I'd recognize the signs it was going to happen, at the very least, and I could make strides to control this thing. And recently, with everything going on, I'd become complacent and had almost forgotten all about the evil lurking just beneath the surface of my skin.

But today, of all days, when I was trying desperately to placate Coop and find Solomon and help Higgs, while bumbling around this unfamiliar "find a murderer" territory the whole way, it happened.

Just like it always does—in a loud rush of rage and shenanigans.

And it was ugly, and maybe even a little messy.

Just ask the skateboarders.

CHAPTER 12

One minute, I remember being horrified these boys were treating Madge this way. If the word "bully" is overused via social media and the press by labeling anything and everything bullying, that wasn't the case here. These were bonified bullies. They were terrorizing her for the sheer pleasure of it, and I wouldn't have it.

Now, normally I'd try the nun's way. I'd attempt to talk it out with them. They were teenagers, and while rebellious, they likely wouldn't expect anyone to fight back.

And that was my intention. To attempt reason with them (my particular brand of fighting back)—and maybe send Coop in to grab Madge's bag before she collapsed in a panic. I also remember Madge's crumpled face and her words that they'd done this to her before. She looked defeated, and for all her bravado, she was afraid. I didn't like that one bit.

So I planned to say as much.

And then I don't remember anything—until Coop had me backed up into a corner under the bridge, her arm pressed to my chest, and she was yelling (yep. More yelling) in my face, "Trixie Lavender, you must stop this right now!"

When the evil left my body, it was often like a balloon deflating. My limbs turned into spaghetti noodles and my ears experienced this whooshing sound, rather like a tidal wave of water rushing in and out of my head.

The haze in my eyes would clear, and I'd be horrified at what was to come—because Coop was going to tell me, I'm sure.

As everything came back into focus, the sights and sounds under the bridge, the rush of traffic, the chirp of birds, I noted everything else remained silent. Jaws had unhinged, boys were cowering in the opposite corner, and Madge was looking at me as though I'd risen from the dead.

When my eyes met Coop's, I know she saw the panic in them. Licking my very dry lips, I asked, "What did I do?"

"You didn't do anything, Trixie. The thing inside you did it."

Breathing in and out, I looked past her shoulder and saw the terror on everyone's faces. The boys had abandoned Madge's purse in favor of pressing their bodies in a huddle of horror, eyes wide, breathing labored. Clusters of the homeless stood immobile and slack-jawed.

"Please tell me I still have clothes on." Instantly my hands went to my thighs to check.

"You still have clothes on. But you also have some bruises on your knuckles to match the ones on your knees, and your lip is going to be a little swollen. Okay, that's an understatement. It's going to be *a lot* swollen."

My hand went to my mouth, which was indeed sore. "Did I hit someone?" I squeaked, my pulse racing.

"You almost hit someone, but you missed and hit the concrete piling instead."

Putting my hands on Coop's shoulders, I gazed into her eyes, guilt flowing through my veins like ice water. "Tell me."

I didn't *want* to know, but I had to know who deserved an apology.

Coop's full lips went thin. "You became very angry when the boys wouldn't give Madge her purse. You demanded they do what you told them. They wouldn't do what you said, and then things tilted left. I swear on my guts, I didn't know it was the evil inside you taking over, Trixie, or I would have stopped you."

As my eyes finally caught up with my brain. I took in the scattered skateboards, broken in many, many, *many* pieces.

Oh, dear.

Inhale in, exhale out...

"I would have stopped you if I'd known it wasn't *you* running around like a mini-tornado."

"Have you seen a tornado, Coop?"

"I have. I created one once."

I gasped. "No way."

She nodded affirmatively with a bounce of her dusky red head. "Yes way. Not the point. The point is, I would have stopped you had I known."

"Stopped me from doing what, exactly, Coop?" I asked, my hesitance clear in the tone of my voice.

"From going into a rage. You went into one bigtime, Trixie. You screamed so loud when they wouldn't do what you demanded, and when they called you names, you shattered our windshield."

Eep. "Did I use my demon voice?" I whispered.

Coop puckered her lips, knowing how I felt about the demon voice. "You did."

"Was it scary?"

"Just like Jason Meets Michael scary."

Oh, heavens. "And then?" I winced as I asked.

"And then you ran after them when they tried to get away with Madge's bag. You tackled the one with the knit cap and the mean, beady eyes, and you dragged him to the wall here and told him Satan was going to eat his soul on a cracker."

Ooooh, that surely must have inspired faith and goodwill for all the homeless people under the bridge.

"And then?"

"And then when he said something very, very rude, something you told me I should never say, right in your face, you were going to punch him square in the nose—"

"Yep, right in his ugly ol' kisser!" Madge finally said, her voice trembling as she sort of hovered behind Coop, nervously bouncing from foot to foot.

"But I yelled at you and you missed and instead punched a hole in the concrete." Her eyes strayed upward and mine followed, my head aching as I did.

Ugh. "I cracked the piling." Sweet Moses and the Ten Commandments.

"You didn't just crack it, you made a hole in it. That made them all very afraid."

"Is there more? Did any of it involve taking my clothes off or swearing?" I've been known to say some awful things when under the influence—that and moon my superiors.

"There is more, but you did it with your clothes on and only a couple of bad words. By and large, as bad words go, that wasn't the worst I've ever heard."

Relief swept through me in a wave as I gripped her shoulders to steady myself. "Go ahead. Tell me the rest."

She removed her arm from my chest and stepped back a bit. "After you hit the piling and missed, you grew very angry. Almost angrier than I've ever seen you before, Trixie Lavender. You stomped over to the rest of the boys and grabbed all of their skateboards and broke them into little pieces, all the while screaming and howling."

Ah. That explained the shards of skateboard debris scattered everywhere, and my sore throat.

Breathing in, I closed my eyes, my body a blubbery

mess of nerves and twitches. And my hand hurt, but as I clenched my fist, fully expecting I'd need a hand surgeon and reconstructive surgery, it surprisingly didn't feel too bad.

I don't quite understand when I'm possessed why my physical body doesn't take as much of a beating as it should. If I'd literally punched a hole in some concrete, by all rights, my hand should at the very least be broken. I mean, holy juggernauts, I put a hole in *concrete*. But it was only very sore.

"And my lip?"

Coop reached out two fingers and tugged gently at the corner of my mouth. "A piece of shrapnel from the skateboard hit you. But it doesn't look like you need stitches."

My eyes went to the ground in shame. Poor Coop. If she could just barely handle my outbursts, and she was as strong as ten men, was there any hope? My deepest fear was I'd become so out of control someday, no one would be able to stop me.

"I'm sorry, Coop. I know this puts you in a bad spot. I feel dreadful that you have to babysit me like this. If not for you, who knows what kind of damage I would have done?"

But she shook her head. "I was going to put a stop to their shenanigans, too. You did the right thing. I think. I don't understand this evil entity, but instead of doing harm this time, it did some good, and I think we should roll with it," she whispered.

"Roll with it?" I was so exhausted and so confused

by what had just occurred, I didn't know what she meant.

"Follow my lead, Trixie Lavender," she ordered as she turned around, stray strands of hair falling out of her messy bun. "Madge. Please excuse me." She set Madge behind her and stalked toward the boys with me in tow, shaky-limbed and wide-eyed. "You!" she bellowed (yep. Even more yelling), the echo of it buzzing in my head as she pointed her finger at the four boys, still cowering. "Will never, *ever* assault Madge With No House again, understood!"

Oooh. Now I got what she meant by roll with it. So I sauntered up to them, bulging my eyes out.

One of them actually summoned the courage to speak, his voice high and quivering. "What is wrong with you, lady?" he squeaked, his eyes watery and red.

What was wrong with me? I'd like to know, too. But I decided to tell the truth—stranger than fiction as it was.

"I'm *possessed* by an ugly, soul-eating demon! And if you ever pick on *anyone* again, I'm going to know—and then I'm going to come find you. All of you," I whispered in my most sinister voice.

I'm pretty sure they already thought I was batty—why not keep up the pretense?

"Trixie…" Coop muttered in warning, her eyes flashing me signals.

"Too much?" I whispered back, grimacing.

The boys began to stir in discomfort and there was even a little whimpering.

But Coop reined them right back in. "Did you hear her?" she howled. "She'll find you and make mincemeat out of all of you!"

"Yeah! What she said!" I tried to yell some more, but my throat hurt—probably from my screaming like a banshee. "Now get on out of here and don't come back, you hear me? Or the next time, it'll be much, muuuch worse!"

Every last one of them was rooted to the spot, frozen in place, staring at me as though I'd ripped someone limb from limb. Which, listen, that option could still be on the table if they played their cards right.

"Did you hear me?" I screeched as loud as was possible with my scratchy throat. "Get out of here, and never bother Madge or anyone here again!"

With those words, four terrified boys skedaddled, running as though the hounds of Hell were chasing them, leaving nothing but the dust of the dirt and kicking up gravel.

And then it was eerily silent for a moment with nothing but the sounds of traffic on the Hawthorne.

I held my breath for a moment, my head pounding and my eyes grainy and tired.

Just as I thought this frightened-half-out-of-their-minds lot of people would never even look at me, much less talk to me again...they began to cheer.

Cheer.

And smile. And clap.

Then someone yelled, "Way to go! You sure showed 'em!"

Mind you, they didn't approach me—I think that might have been asking too much after using my demon voice and exhibiting the strength of Hercules, but it was a start.

Yet, it was Madge who touched my heart. She came straight up to me and put her arms around my waist and hugged me quickly before letting me go. "Thank you for saving Hello Kitty. I hope you find Solomon and Gilligan. You're nice. Even if you are possessed."

A tear stung my eye. We'd connected. That was the start I'd been looking for. "My pleasure, Madge. My pleasure."

$\sim$

"Slow down, Trixie! Land sakes, lass. I'm leavin' feathers all about the freeway!" Livingston griped.

I'd laugh if I didn't want to cry. I'd busted our windshield, all right, and now our usual route back to the motel was closed for construction, forcing us to take the highway, which was nearly blowing my skin off. That we hadn't been pulled over yet was a miracle.

The worst of this, though? We'd have to have a new windshield installed and our deductible was two hundred and fifty dollars. Another chunk of change we could ill afford to let leave our dwindling bank account.

But Coop turned around and gave Livingston the evil eye. "You hush, Quigley Livingston. Trixie's had a bad day. Stop complaining and be grateful."

"Grateful she almost blew my eardrums out, lass? I suppose I should be grateful for earthquakes and all manner of natural disasters, too?"

"Livingston! Hush or I'll leave you in that cage for eternity, and you'll never see another Tootsie Roll again," Coop chastised, turning back around with a huff.

Wow. She was chock full of the devil this afternoon, expressing herself left and right in the way of stern tones and harsh admonishments. Threatening Livingston with his beloved Tootsie Rolls was fightin' words in his book.

As for me? I was suffering from rage remorse. I'd almost hit someone. A child, no less. Well, okay, not a child, but a teenager who was still considered a child under the law. That was unacceptable. We had to find a way to harness this thing inside me or we were going to be in a real pickle.

"Don't ya tell me to hush when my ears are still ringin', Coopie! How can I listen to Yeezy if my ears are ringin'?"

Oh, and Livingston loved rap. I was less enthralled by it and more inclined to enjoy the classics of the seventies, like my parents used to listen to on Saturday nights when we all played board games, but to each his own.

"Livingston!"

I patted Coop's shoulder as I pulled off the highway, grateful for GPS. I wasn't familiar with this end of Cobbler Cove yet and with the rerouting of our trip home, I felt a little out of my element.

"It's okay, Coop. He has a right to be crabby."

"Darn roight, I do, lassie! I'm as close to deaf as I've ever been."

Coop growled, like she'd done in the early days after she'd escaped Hell and the only emotion she knew was anger. "She can't help it, Livingston. It's not her fault and you know it. Don't be such a complainer."

"Guys, I'm fine. A little roughed up, but fine. Let's get back to the motel and find some lunch and decide where to go from here. If we don't find Gilligan, Coop, I'm not sure what else is left. I mean, we can question all the people Crowley rented to, which might lead us to someone whose legs Fergus broke for not paying him back. But Crowley still, as of this morning, hasn't sent me the list of people he rents to. Aside from that, we don't have a whole lot in the way of solid leads."

Coop sighed as we passed another neighborhood I'd like to explore when we had time. There were tons of little shops and fun places to eat. "I know this, Trixie, and I know you're trying your hardest even though you don't really know how to be a detective like Stevie."

If I didn't love Stevie so much, I might be a little envious of the way Coop idolized her sleuthing skills.

"Have you heard anything from Knuckles today? He said he'd text us if he heard anything about Higgs's hearing. Mr. Pensky said he was going to try to get him an expedited hearing for bail," Coop asked, smoothing her hands down over her leggings.

I pulled my phone from my pocket and handed it to her. "I had my phone off while I was speaking with the people under the bridge. Turn it on and see, please."

After passing store after store, we came to a stop-light by a small outdoor market where I'd love to grab some fresh fruit if we had somewhere to store it.

When the light turned green and we crawled along, getting odd looks from people when they noticed our windshield was missing, that was the moment I saw Jay.

Again.

At another bank. Pacific Northwest Mutual, to be precise. I'm pretty sure he saw me, too, but he ducked into the bank before I could be sure.

"How peculiar," I muttered out loud before I real-ized I had.

Coop stretched her arms and rolled her head on her neck. "What's peculiar?"

"Everythin' about bein' in an owl's body," Livingston chirped.

"Everythin's not about you, Mr. Selfish," Coop chas-tised in her spot-on Irish accent. "Now, what's peculiar, Trixie?"

"Jay." I'd seen him at three separate banks in one morning. Different banks—not just different branches of the same bank. "I've seen him at three different banks today alone."

Coop frowned and sighed. "Maybe he has a lot of

money and they can't fit it all in one place?" She shrugged her slender shoulders. "I don't understand money here on Earth yet. After I finish the dictionary, I'm going to study *Math For Dummies* so I can understand your system of trade. In Hell, we traded things like days in the pit or soul reaping. These pieces of paper kept in a house with doors and windows, and tubes in boxes where you place your paper in them and press a button to send them to a lady who smiles at you and wishes you a good day before giving you another piece of paper, confounds me."

I laughed thinking about the times I'd taken Coop with me to the drive-thru at the bank and her amazement over the pneumatic tubes, then winced when my lip fought back. It looked far worse than it was, I suppose. It was swollen on the left side of my mouth, but I wasn't any worse for the wear.

"I promise to teach you everything you need to know about the economic system when things settle down, okay? For now, any word from Knuckles?"

She grimaced and tried to smile, leading me to believe her affection for Knuckles was growing. "He says to meet him at the motel and he'll buy us lunch."

I couldn't let him buy us lunch again. Yesterday, he'd brought us thick, delicious sandwiches from a place called Bunk Sandwiches. I'd had a pork belly Cubano that was to die for, and if I kept this up, my thighs would never be the same. What I needed was a salad and a fasting, or at the very least a treadmill —soon.

As we pulled away from the light, and I tried to catch another glimpse of Jay, I wondered once more who had three different bank accounts at three different banks?

But then I reasoned, maybe one was for the shelter and the rest were his? I'm not sure why the number of places he banked at troubled me so, but it just wasn't sitting right.

The wind began to blow warm and dry into the car again as we headed to the motel, and I was lost in my thoughts about Jay and where to look next for Gilligan and Solomon. I wasn't so sure this was going to work out the way Coop hoped it would.

"Trixie?" Coop interrupted my thoughts. "Lunch with Knuckles? He says he has a proposition for us."

I wondered what that was about, but I smiled in gratitude for the friendship we were building with such a kind man. "You tell Knuckles lunch is on us this time. How does pizza delivered to the motel sound? We can't leave the car without a windshield, but we can watch it from the picnic tables out in the courtyard."

"Almost as good as meatballs. Not your meatballs. Spaghetti meatballs," Coop emphasized, making me laugh out loud.

"Then pizza it is."

As we pulled into the parking lot of the motel and Knuckles waved to us from his motorcycle, he immediately frowned as he approached the car, a picnic basket in one hand and a colorful quilt in the other.

He pulled open my door and stuck his head inside,

his lined face full of concern. "What the hay-hay happened here, young lady? And what happened to your face? Are you okay?" he asked, eyeing my fat lip and the dried blood on my knuckles.

This was the part that got tricky. The explaining. "Long story. I'll tell you over some pizza. Our treat."

He held up the basket and shook it with a smile, his round face beaming and red from the heat. "Made some fried chicken and potato salad last night. Thought we could do leftovers and talk about where you gals are going to stay while the store gets a makeover."

I slid out while Coop covered Livingston and pulled his cage from the car. "Stay? We're staying here, and then we'll stay upstairs in the loft when the store's open."

He balked at that in a very fatherly sort of way, endearing himself to me more and more. I got the impression Knuckles missed his daughter and grand-daughter very much. Taking us under his wing gave him the chance to nurture, which he was robbed of living so far away from his family.

With a cluck of his tongue, he said, "You two can't live there, Trixie. It's not only unsafe, but it's no way to live. Who lives with just a single burner and a compact camping fridge?"

I flapped a hand at him as he handed me the bamboo basket with a colorful red gingham-checked napkin draped inside, then pulled his phone out of the pocket of his jeans and texted someone.

"We've lived in far worse, my friend. This is like a palace compared to some places we've been. Besides, it's just us, and we're not exactly gourmet chefs. Also, it won't be unsafe for long. We'll clean it up and it'll be like brand-new. We're going to be just fine, Knuckles."

I didn't want him worrying about us. It was sweet, but unnecessary. We'd learned to stand on our own two feet, and we'd keep doing that no matter what.

Knuckles looked up from his glossy phone to take a picture of our windshield, ignoring every word I spoke like all good potential surrogate fathers do.

I planted my hands on my hips, ignoring the stabbing pain in my fingers. "What are you doing?"

"Showing my guy your windshield. Said he'd be right over."

Of course, Knuckles knew "a guy." I couldn't help but smile. "You're so awesome. Thank you. Let me get my insurance card and I'll give them a call."

He tucked his phone back into his jeans. "No need. Fifty dollars and some of my chicken and we're square."

His need to take care of us would border encroaching on our independence if we didn't like him so much. But worse, we didn't want to appear as thought we were taking advantage. Something I'd never allow.

"Knuckles, I can't let you do that! We're happy to pay."

"I'm not doing it. My *guy* is. Now, let's go sit under that tree where we can see the car and we'll have some lunch and talk about what's fit for living in and what's not."

He didn't wait for my answer, instead, he plodded over to a big maple in the small square between the motel and the store and spread out a blanket, setting the basket on it.

Coop and I trudged behind him with Livingston and we dropped down, sitting cross-legged. I leaned back and let the warm breeze waft over me. It was a lovely afternoon in the seventies and as exhausted as I was, I just wanted to sit a moment and reflect. I wanted to watch the cars drive by, listen to the sounds of children playing in the park across the way, see people walking their dogs.

But Knuckles wasn't having that. He set a red paper plate in front of me filled with lusciously cold, golden fried chicken and a heaping spoonful of creamy potato salad. "Eat. While you eat, listen to me, please?"

I chuckled, pulling a napkin to my lap. "No, no, Knuckles! Please don't make me eat homemade fried chicken! I can't bear the torture!"

Now he laughed as he set a plate in front of Coop while she fiddled with Livingston's cage, pulling the garbage bag off and drawing curious stares from people passing by.

Settling down, Knuckles handed us each a bottle of water then leaned back on the palms of his hands. "So let's talk about living at the store and how it's not a good idea for two young women such as yourselves."

I cocked my head at him as I took a bite of the

chicken, my eyes widening. Even cold, it was delicious, still a bit crisp around the edges and tender. "This is amazing, Knuckles. Who taught you to cook?"

"My mother and my nana Nettie, and don't change the subject. Hear me out."

I had no choice but to hear him out because my mouth was full of delicious food. So I nodded, as did Coop, who also clearly enjoyed the mouthful of potato salad she was chewing because her eyes were closed and her face was serene.

He smiled, obviously pleased at how much we were enjoying his cooking. "The guesthouse out back at my place. Two bedrooms, two bathrooms, a decent enough kitchen if not all that big, still all brand-new. I was going to rent it out anyway. Why not rent it out to you two girls? It's five minutes from the store and it's a heck of a lot nicer than that upstairs deathtrap. Whaddya say?"

I stopped gnawing on my succulent chicken and wiped my mouth, reluctant to stop eating. But I had to protest. We couldn't afford a place as nice as Knuckles's house—not even his guesthouse. We hadn't made a dime yet either, and we didn't even know if we'd make anything at all. To lock ourselves into another lease would be foolish.

I regretted not being able to take the offer. Who wouldn't want to live in a house so beautiful? But right now, that wasn't an option.

So I smiled to soften the blow and said, "Oh, Knuckles, you're so sweet. But we can't afford rent on top of the rent for the store. That was part of the beauty of leasing a space with living quarters upstairs. Though, I'm sure it's a beautiful guesthouse if *your* house is any indication. Your place is amazing."

But he shook his head, his piercings glinting in the patchy sunlight, poking through the leaves on the tree. "I'm not talking *rent*-rent, Trixie girl. I'm talking you give me the space for free at the store, I bring in my clientele, you stay at the guesthouse rent-free. It really benefits me more than it does you girls. I need a place to bring my clients, and you need clients."

Setting my plate aside, I couldn't find the words to speak my appreciation, but I tried. "I feel like we're getting the better end of the deal here, Knuckles. You're moving into a dump and in return, handing over the keys to paradise. How's that a fair trade?"

But he only winked, that Santa Claus-ish twinkle in his eyes. "Trust me when I tell you, I'll be doing a *lot* of tattooing, and some of my clients are going to want Coop's brand of magic on their skin once they get a load of her talent. We're helping each other, Trixie. What's the world if we can't at least do that?"

A breath shuddered out of my lungs and tears stung my eyes. Cobbler Cove was looking more and more like the best decision we'd made so far.

"I don't know what to say, so I'll just say this. I'm not sure what I believe in anymore since leaving the convent. I don't know if there's a higher power or something else at work here, and I'll leave it at that. But I do believe there are people placed in our lives at exactly the time they're supposed to show up. You're one of those people, Knuckles, and I don't know how I'll ever be able to thank you for everything you've done for us."

He reached out and chucked me under the chin. "Don't go getting all sappy now, young lady. You just work on getting things moving, and I'll put the word out on social media we'll be opening soon."

"*You* have a Facebook page?"

"And an Instagram, and Twitter, and even Snapchat. It's what all the hip grandpas who never really grew up do."

That made me laugh and laugh. I grabbed his hand and squeezed it. "Then you, Mr. Donald P. Ledbetter, have a deal."

Now *he* laughed, a deep rumble from way down in his belly. "Now that we've handled that, where are you on this investigation thing? Any more leads?"

"Yeah, Trixie. Where are *you* on this investigation thing?"

I looked upward at the tall, looming figure standing over me.

Looks like somebody made bail.

CHAPTER 13

"*They call Portland the City of Roses. A thorn disguised in a deceptively pretty package, if you ask me. Wander the rain-soaked streets and you'll find a hundred stories just like the one I'm about to tell you. A story of betrayal and greed mingled with the scent of desperation, and thick with despair—*"

"Trixie?"

I turned to look at Higgs from the passenger side of his very nice car, an older BMW, I think he said—a classic, according to him. One he's had for fifteen years.

I unrolled the piece of sketch pad paper I'd been using as my microphone. "Yes, Higgs."

He peered at me, his eyes narrowed but amused. "What are you doing over there?"

I rolled my eyes. "A voiceover, silly. You know, like Kolchak on *The Night Stalker*? All good detective shows from the '70s had them."

He pursed his lips. "Kolchak?"

I gasped, outraged he didn't know who I was talking about. "You don't know Kolchak? I watched every episode on YouTube. As a former police officer, I'd think you'd know who he is. A brilliant, if not unconventional detective."

He shrugged, looking back into the binoculars he'd brought to watch the homeless under the Hawthorne in order to locate Gilligan, our only true lead in this mess so far aside from Solomon.

"I guess I was more an *NYPD Blue* kind of kid."

He kept looking through the binoculars without missing a beat. I think he was still a little perturbed with us for sticking our noses in where they didn't belong—or at least he said something to that effect, sugar-coated with the fact that we could get hurt if we weren't careful.

Really what he meant was, stay out of it. But I was in too deep—I was in for Coop. So here we were, on an official not-so-official stakeout, looking for Solomon or Gilligan.

I rearranged myself in my seat, enjoying the comfort of the cushiony passenger side and the excitement of a stakeout. "Oh, I didn't watch it as a kid. That was long before my time. How old do you think I am, anyway?"

"Thirty?" he answered, his hard jaw nothing more than a sharply angled shadow in the dark car.

"Close enough. Thirty-two. How old are you?"

"Thirty-six."

"And how long did you do undercover work with the gang?"

His hands tightened on the binoculars, enough that I saw the veins in them pop out, but his answer was easy. "Long enough."

I wondered his reasoning behind keeping the tic-tac-toe tattoo. Jay had said it was forced on him. Why would you want to keep something like that? Something symbolic of the pain you'd suffered.

So I asked, "And the tattoo? Why didn't you have it removed, Higgs? You have a bunch. It could very easily be blended into one of your other tats."

His jaw went hard. "Because it meant something to me. It was a reminder of what happened that night."

I wanted to delve deeper, but his body language said Do Not Pass Go.

So I sighed, tucking a leg beneath me. "Listen, I came here to help you find this Gilligan guy. I'm not asking questions to pry. I'm only making conversation. If I wanted to know any other way, I'd just google you."

He scoffed. "You wouldn't have much luck. The Minneapolis PD removed all traces of me and my work with them when I left the force after the bust."

His words were quick and efficient, but underneath them, darkness lurked in his tone. Sorrow over Diego Santino's death, I'd wager. And it confirmed why he wasn't mentioned in any of the articles I read.

"But you kept your real name?" That was either brave or crazy. I'm not sure which.

"They wanted me to change it. I didn't want to

change it. I'm not hiding. No way was I going to lose the last bit I have left of my family by changing my name for WITSEC."

Oooo. More acronyms. "WITSEC?"

"Witness protection. I knew I was taking a chance someone would come after me because of my undercover work, but they'd taken enough of my life. Not a chance I was going to give them everything else."

Okay. I guess the word brave fit his scenario. "You don't have any family?"

"Both of my parents are gone. Cancer and a massive heart attack. No siblings. Just me. Which is why keeping my last name means so much. I was really close to my father. I want his name to live on."

My heart ached. I knew that kind of loss. I missed my mom and dad every day. "I'm so sorry. Mine are gone, too." Tucking my chin under my hand, I tried to find a way to relate to someone who didn't appear to want to relate to me at all. "So here we are, two parentless, sibling-less people, trying to solve a murder you were wrongly accused of. What's next?"

Higgs set the binoculars on the dashboard and turned to look at me, a half smile on his face. "You seem pretty certain I didn't kill Fergus, but I distinctly remember a woman who called me a murderer a mere two days ago."

Was it only two days? It felt like a lifetime. Yet, how was I going to explain Coop's gut to him? I'd sound nuttier than a can of macadamias. Or the fact that she wanted to help him because she'd been where he was before. Definitely something he could find out on his own, but if he knew Coop, the demon Coop, he'd understand how important this was to her, and by proxy, to me.

"Things can change…" I mumbled vaguely.

Now he chuckled, stretching his arms, the muscles flexing. "Obviously. So tell me again what you *think* you've found?"

Said the ex-undercover cop to the detective-show-binge-watching ex-nun. I squirmed a little in my seat. "Well, like I told you, it might not be a lot, but I think someone from one of the two gangs, either Young Money or the Blood Squad, killed Fergus and framed you."

He nodded his dark head slowly, the light from the fire in a barrel off in the distance dancing in his eyes. "And you think that why, Sister Trixie?"

I'd already explained this twice, for Pete's sake. But what was one more time? "Because of that dang mark on Fergus's neck. It's just like your tattoo from Young Money. You already know that, I'm sure, Higgs. Your lawyer probably already told you all this. But I've known about it since day one because Fergus was found in my store. I saw everything. Well, except the hair or whatever. I didn't see a strand of hair. Er…and the voice mail…"

I didn't tell him I'd taken pictures of Fergus's body, or that we'd scoured them endlessly for clues, and if I'd seen his tattoo before Coop had had all these gut instincts, there's no way I'd have stored my things at the shelter. I'd have gone directly to Tansy Primrose and reported it.

"They have some pretty compelling evidence against me, Trixie."

"Whose side are you on, Higgs?"

"I'm just stating a fact. That I managed to get bail is a miracle."

And after the story he told us about how hard his lawyer, Mr. Pensky, had fought for him, and the exorbitant amount of money to do it, I couldn't agree more. He was lucky in that he was an ex-cop and had no criminal record, but that would only go so far.

"Did jail suck?"

"Does sleeping with thirty other inmates who don't have any problem with nudity and gen-pop potty time sound like a party?"

I winced and jammed my knuckle in my mouth. There was nothing tactful about me today. "Okay, so it sucked. I'm sorry. But you're out now, and that means we can look for the killer together."

"No, Trixie. It means you're going to identify this Gilligan guy from a safe distance and go home to your safe motel room—"

"Guesthouse. We're renting Knuckles's guesthouse, and it's gorgeous," I replied on a sigh.

After Higgs had shown up and we'd parted ways while he handled some things, and our windshield was fixed, we'd followed Knuckles to his house and he'd shown us our new home.

I cried, it was so beautiful. I'd have my own room, a

room I still can't quite define in words, it's so amazing. I'd have my own bathroom and even a small patio off my bedroom. It was paradise, and Coop was there right now, unloading the boxes of inventory we'd gathered from Higgs. And I was grateful. Gosh, was I ever.

"Guesthouse, cabana, townhouse, whatever you want to call it, you're not looking for anything *with* me, Trixie. This isn't one of your detective shows. This is my life. This right here," he spread his arm in an arc to encompass the car, "is as far as it goes."

I made a duck's bill with my fingers and stuck them under his nose. "Quack, quack, quack. I can't hear you."

He chuckled, despite his obvious irritation. "Don't sass me, Trixie, and get that twinkle right out of your eyes. You're not getting involved. I only agreed to let you come with me tonight because you're the one who got the best look at this guy and Solomon seems to like you. This is dangerous, and on top of worrying about whether I'm going to be able to prove my innocence, I don't want to have to look out for your welfare, too."

I made a face at him. "I'll look out for my own welfare, thank you very much. I'm an adult. If I want to investigate a murder, I'm going to investigate a murder."

"Do you want to investigate death, too? Because that could be the end result."

I winced, leaning my head against the car's window and looking over Higgs's shoulder into the deep, velvety darkness of the night, and decided to change the subject. He was right. It could be dangerous if someone was following him around, and I was nothing if not mostly sensible.

But this mystery bug had bitten me, and I wanted to see this to the end.

"Speaking of bail, I'm going to get super personal here, and you're going to hate it. But that's too bad because you have a good friend, and you should know it. He deserves some praise."

Higgs cocked his head, his eyes glittering. "Do you mean Jay?"

"I do. Earlier today, I saw him at three different banks, probably draining his savings to help you make bail."

At least that's the conclusion I came to after giving it some thought while we moved boxes out of the shelter and to Knuckles's guesthouse—it was my latest theory.

Now I had Higgs's attention. He swiveled in his seat and looked at me hard. Gone was the "whatever" attitude replaced by a hawk-eyed gaze. "Jay didn't make bail for me, Trixie. *I* made bail for me with some properties I own as collateral."

"Oh," I murmured. Now with my theory—my one and only theory—blown to smithereens, I didn't know what else to say. But I was pretty sure there was a reasonable explanation for his odd banking habits.

Or was there? This whole murder business made me suspicious of everyone and everything. But that was silly. What did Fergus's murder have to do with Jay's banking?

Higgs cut off my train of thought when he asked, "Did he tell you he'd made bail for me?"

"No. No, no. I incorrectly assumed, I guess." Licking my lips, I tried to keep his gaze, but jeepers his stare was intense. Everything about his face changed as he looked at me.

"And what made you do that, Trixie?"

"I told you. Today when we were out and about, we saw him three separate times."

Suddenly, he relaxed. "That's not unusual in Cobbler Cove. It's a small-ish community."

"It wasn't that we saw him on three different occasions. It was *where* we saw him."

"I'll bite. Where did you see him, Trixie?"

The tone of the question sounded a little, I'm the pro, you're the novice, okay, give me what you've got, yawn-yawn-yawn-ish. But I told him anyway.

"At the bank. Three different banks, in fact. None of the branches related to each other."

If my confession affected Higgs, he didn't show it in his facial expressions. He still had that amused look on his face as though I was the bumbling amateur sleuth and he was the expert.

Oh, wait. That was kind of true.

"Interesting," was all he said. "Anything else I should know?"

Thinking back, there was one thing. I didn't know if it connected to Fergus, but it might be worth mentioning.

"The other night…just before I saw you when you helped me with the boxes, remember?"

"You mean when you thought I was a serial killer?"

"Stahp! I mean, c'mon. I didn't know you. I don't really know you *now*. For all I know, you could *still* be a serial killer, Higgs. I'm out on a limb here, taking a risk, sitting in this car with you just waiting to be murdered, so gimme a break."

He laughed, deep and husky, before he prompted, "Okay. Sorry. Go on. The other night when I saw you and you thought I was a serial killer…"

I flicked his arm. This joke was never going to die. "I had an incident by the dumpster in the alleyway. Someone jumped out of it and dropped down on my head. I tried to grab them, that's why my finger was bleeding, but they got away. The dumpster is right under the window of my store. Now, I don't know if it was someone homeless, rooting around for treasures or whatever, but I figure it's worth a mention. I didn't see them clearly at all. The only thing I remember is the distinct smell of garlic and their shoes—boots, to be precise—but absolutely nothing else."

"Also interesting."

My eyes bulged and my mouth dropped open. "That's all you have to say? No theory?"

He shrugged and cracked his knuckles. "No theory. But this conversation you had with Solomon and didn't tell me about? Talk to me about that."

"I didn't tell you because at the time, I still thought you might be the murderer. How was I to know whether he ran away that night because he was afraid of you?"

The corners of his mouth lifted ever so slightly. "But now that I've been arrested for murder and released on bail, you don't think I'm the murderer? Explain your logic again?"

Rolling my eyes at him, I wrinkled my nose. "I already told you why I don't think that anymore. I feel it in my gut." Or Coop's...

He leaned back in the seat and grabbed his cup of coffee from the holder between our arms. "Yeah. Coop said that, too. Why do I feel like there's more to the story?"

"Like?"

"Like Coop was accused of a murder she didn't commit not too far back in your past? I can google, too, you know," he teased, smoothing his hand down his red T-shirt.

Man, for someone who'd spent the night in jail and could possibly go to prison for murder, he looked pretty relaxed.

I felt self-conscious in my dirty jeans and holey shirt compared to Higgs, who didn't look any worse for the wear after spending twenty-four hours in the pen.

"Fine. I'll tell you if you really want to know. So it was more Coop's gut than mine. She knows what this must feel like for you, and it upset her enough to want to help. But I trust her, and she thinks you're innocent, and that's why I'm sitting in this car with you, looking for this ghost we've called Gilligan."

His eyebrow arched in a cocky fashion and he smiled. "So *you* didn't really want to help me, Trixie? It was just Coop?"

When he'd found out we'd been asking questions of the homeless folks under the bridge, and that I'd waited with Jay at the police station, he'd warned us in his ex-police officer's voice that we shouldn't be poking around in something as risky as a murder investigation. But then Coop told him how much she believed in him, and he'd softened.

"Do you want honesty?"

"Always," he said, his husky voice deep and resonant.

Confession time. "At first I just wanted to find out who'd done it because it would let us get back into the store sooner, and we need to get into the store and start earning some money. We need a reason to get up in the morning. We need purpose. But when Coop did what she did at Betty's—you know, trying to stop them from arresting you—it sort of cemented your innocence. Coop doesn't sway easily. She doesn't trust easily. Yet since we came to Cobbler Cove, she's all in trust's face, shaking her fist at it. That's what changed my mind, and that's why I want to help you find Gilligan. I'm the only one who's seen him who doesn't need a bottle of blackberry brandy to bribe me into indentifying him," I joked, referring to Madge.

"Speaking of Madge—"

"Who thinks you're 'dreamy-steamy,' by the by."

He grinned, but he didn't address my mention of his steaminess. "I hear through the homeless grapevine you saved Madge's Hello Kitty bag."

Now, I looked away. The embarrassment of that moment still stung. I'd been ugly, and even though I knew rationally it wasn't my fault, that didn't make it any more digestible.

"If you mean I got it back from some ruffians for her, then yes. I guess that's true."

I wouldn't apologize for that. They were cruel. Someone had to stop the bullying. Maybe they didn't have to break skateboards while screaming in their demon voice to do it, but it is what it is.

"I hear you broke some things—including a concrete pillar under the bridge while you chased them off. That can't be right, can it? Anyway, word is, you're a hero."

"I'm pretty sure my heroics are greatly exaggerated. I did scare them off, but that's mostly it." Not a total lie, but there were simply some things I couldn't be entirely truthful about or I was bound for, at the very least, a psych eval.

Afterward, when we'd had time to reflect, I prayed no one had used their camera on their phone to record my outburst. We couldn't afford to end up on YouTube tagged with things like "crazy woman possessed by Satan."

Higgs paused, taking a long look at me, his handsome face unreadable. Reaching out, he grabbed my hand and inspected it. "And this? Not from a concrete pillar, I suppose?"

I pulled my hand back and dropped it into my lap, embarrassed at the condition of my nails and my beet-red knuckles. "It's just a scratch. No big deal."

"And your lip? That's no big deal, too?"

Oh. That. Yeah, that still stung a bit and made putting on lip gloss impossible. "Look, with every great battle comes great sacrifice. Madge shouldn't be taunted that way. I made sure she wouldn't be taunted anymore. Those boys were dreadful."

Higgs's voice was soft when he said, "Her Hello Kitty bag is her most prized possession, Trixie. I don't think you know how much that means to her."

"You know a lot about these people, don't you?" I said, and I didn't bother to keep the admiration out of my voice. He knew all their idiosyncrasies, their deficits, their quirks. I liked that—a lot.

"I love my work at the shelter. It's the most fulfilled I've been in a very long time. And don't change the subject, Trixie. You really helped Madge out."

My cheeks turned red. "I'm just glad she got it back. But as I said, and the reason we're here to begin with, she wasn't much help in locating Solomon and Gilligan."

He scratched his head. "I wish I knew who this guy you keep calling Gilligan is. I know most every person under that bridge, Trixie, and I don't know anyone like that. I've established relationships with almost all of them, and no one's ever talked about him, either. But Madge said she saw Solomon with him?"

I shook my head, running my hands over my beloved sketch pad. We'd dug it out of the backseat of my car, and I'd hoped to pass the time on this stakeout sketching—my head was filled with ideas and images since this afternoon. I'm sure in part because I was less stressed about where we were going to stay. But Higgs wouldn't let me use the light in the car—which made sense, seeing as we were staking things out.

"No. She said she'd seen him, though. She knew exactly who I meant."

"And you think Solomon knows who killed Fergus, why?"

I clapped my hands on my thighs. "Because of what he said to me, Higgs. He said there was a bad mad guy with special powers. I don't know what the heck that means, but a bad mad guy sounds like someone who's a killer, no? He saw him the night Fergus was killed."

"You do know, as much as I like Solomon, he's not exactly a reliable source of information, Trixie. He's mostly sweet and unassuming, if a little standoffish sometimes. But as a source of reality-based informa-tion, I don't think I have to remind you, he takes talk-like-King-Arthur-day to a new extreme."

"And that's a fair assessment, but if we don't at least try to find him, how will we know? You said he responded well to me. So I'm here to help. If my theory is too kooky for your super-special undercover skills, what can I say? I'm new at this."

He barked a laugh. "I don't have a super-special undercover skill. And your theory is a sound one, mostly. I mean, about someone looking for revenge against me anyway."

A chill ran along my arms and up my spine. "So you think it could be a gang member?"

He huffed a breath and ran a hand over his hair. "I think it's very possible."

"Well, okay then. *Who*, is the question? If they're all locked up, who wants you framed for murder? The why goes without saying."

He sighed and it sounded a little ragged to my ears. "Yeah, I suppose it does."

There was no denying Higgs experienced great guilt when I even mentioned his undercover work, but I didn't know how to approach it without making him angry. I mean, in truth, we hardly knew each other. Why would he want to talk to me about anything deeper, like his innermost feelings on the death of an innocent child?

Still, I found myself asking, "Do you want to talk about it?"

Running a hand over the stubble on his chin, he rasped another sigh. "It seems like a long time ago, when in reality, it was only five years. But I was in deep cover for a year, which felt like an eternity. The cold hard facts are, a young kid was killed in the mess of our bust. If I could change that, I would. If I'd just…"

As he stopped, his words fading, I wondered what

he'd been about to say. But I didn't want to press when our focus had to be on finding who was framing him.

"Okay. So how do we do this? Is there a checklist we go over? Do we write things down? Tell me and I'll do it."

"There's no method, really. Sometimes it's just gut instinct and looking at everything with suspicious eyes."

Well, I had that part mastered. Sighing, I folded my hands in my lap, my head pounding, my hand sore. "How long do we sit here until this stakeout's considered a bust?"

"Do you have something to do? I don't want to keep you, Trixie. I really appreciate the help, but I don't want you in any danger if someone's looking for me."

I shrugged. "I don't really have anything to do. We don't have much to unpack at this point. I do need to do some laundry…"

Gasping, I sat up straight.

"What? What's wrong? Are you all right? Is it your hand? Your lip?" Higgs asked, concern riddling his voice.

Without thinking, I reached out and grabbed his arm. *"Laundry!"* I shouted. Holy dirty underwear —*laundry!*

Higgs put both of his broad hands on my shoulders, turning me to face him as he searched my eyes. *"What are you talking about?"*

I almost laughed out loud, but I had to force myself to calm down and voice my thoughts.

"Solomon! Solomon said the mad guy doesn't like laundry!"

Higgs's brow furrowed, deep lines forming in his forehead. "I don't get it."

"What don't you get it? *Laundry*. Fergus was an infamous loan shark, according to Crowley. Surely you knew that?"

He let me go, leaning back, surprise in his eyes. "No. No, I didn't know that. I knew he was a jerk. I knew he was cruel to the homeless, but I didn't know anything about loan-sharking. I had very little to do with Fergus McDuff, Trixie, and I've made it my mission to stay out of anything remotely investigative or police-ish. My life is different now, and I want it to stay that way."

Gosh, the horrors he must have seen. Sympathy for him swelled in me, but I was on to something. I knew I was.

"I get it. I mean, I don't know what you've been through, but I understand why you'd want to avoid anything that has to do with your old life. But don't you see what I mean?" I bounced enthusiastically in my seat.

"I see a big fat nothing. Maybe I'm too close to this, but I don't get where you're going."

"*Laundry*, Higgs! Solomon must have heard someone talking to Fergus about laundering money! I mean, he was a loan shark, for heaven's sake. Is laundering money that much of a stretch? He did time for armed robbery. He hiked up rent prices his brother Crowley wasn't aware of and likely pocketed the extra cash. Of *course* he'd launder money. Maybe through his brother's buildings? Solomon said—and I repeat—*the mad guy doesn't like laundry*! I'd bet my arm he heard Fergus threatening someone, and he's gotten the information mixed up in his head somehow. I'm telling you, Higgs, I'm right. I *feel* it! Maybe our murderer is someone Fergus had laundering money for him! Maybe they got fed up. Maybe he went one threat too far?"

Suddenly, Higgs grew very quiet. Eerily quiet. So much so, I almost wanted to check and see if he still had a pulse—and then he was pulling his phone out and texting someone, and I sat silently, trying to figure out what I'd said wrong.

Now, I was beginning to panic. "Higgs?" I reached a hand out and placed it on his arm. "What's wrong?"

When he looked at me, his face was grim. "I think I know who murdered Fergus."

CHAPTER 14

*H*iggs took off so fast, I had to hold on to the divider between our seats, and I had no idea what his intent was.

Were we on our way to catch a murderer? I mean, he was an ex-police officer. He wouldn't be afraid. I, on the other hand, was scared silly. My heart was beating so fast, I felt sure it would plop right out onto the floorboards of the car.

He drove down side streets to get to the shelter in what felt like two seconds flat. I'm sure it was more, but if G-force were a thing you could create in a car just by driving fast, he was doing it, and my face would never have another wrinkle.

Everything on the way flew by in a blur as we passed the lights of Cobbler Cove and swerved into a parking spot directly across the street from the shelter.

And then the sounds of sirens, bleating out their howl, followed right behind.

Higgs threw open the drivers-side door and turned only briefly to tell me to stay in the car. "Don't move, Trixie!" he ordered, slamming the door shut and running toward the shelter.

Don't move. Sure. As if that had ever stopped me. As two police cars pulled up and one unmarked screeched to a halt, I popped the door open in time to see Higgs hauling Jay out of the shelter, Jay's feet scuffing and dragging across the pavement.

My heart crashed in my chest until I slowed to a halt as I heard Higgs bellow, "It was you! *You* killed Fergus!"

And then it became clear. Jay was the launderer.

He'd told me he did all the financials and fundraisers for the shelter, which meant he had access to donations and all manner of things. So he'd been laundering money for Fergus? He was the mad guy?

Every last ounce of energy drained from my body right then and there. I didn't understand entirely how he'd done it—or even what laundering entailed in the long run, but murder?

Jay?

"It wasn't me, Higgs!" he yelled, tears flowing from his face as Detective Primrose shot from her car and ran to pull Higgs from Jay.

"Higgs! Stop messin' about!" she cried, pushing her way between the two men, giving Higgs a shove—a hard one, which I had to admire. Higgs was no slouch in the fit department. "Higgs! *Let him go!*"

Higgs finally saw something other than the color

red, I suppose, because he let Jay go, hurling him toward one of the officers who caught him, but not before he almost took him out like a bowling pin.

My feet were finally able to move and they carried me to the cluster of people gathered on the sidewalk in front of the shelter.

I heard Jay's cries, his words of denial, and my stomach turned. "It wasn't me, Higgs! I didn't do it!"

"You stole from me!" Higgs thundered over Detective Primrose's shoulders. "You stole from helpless people—people who *trusted* you—and then you framed me to cover your sorry hide!"

"Higgs!" Detective Primrose shouted once more, putting her hand on his chest. "If I have to tell you one more time to back off, mate, I'm going to cuff you and throw you in the cage!"

Higgs's nostrils flared, but he took a step back, and that's when I approached. Cautiously, mind you, and Higgs was so rigid, so tense, every muscle in his body thrumming a palpable vibe, I was almost afraid, but I needed to understand what just happened.

As the officers kept the two men separate, and they began to question them, I eavesdropped while my knees wobbled and my breathing came in short huffs of air.

Jay was, in a word, hysterical as he pleaded with Higgs to listen to him from behind the officers who'd cornered him. "I swear to you, man, it wasn't me! I didn't kill Fergus!"

"Higgs," Detective Primrose ordered, using two

fingers to point at her eyes. "Look at me and tell me what you know. Don't look at *him*, or in the paddy you go. Now talk. Explain this text."

Higgs rolled his head on his neck, but he appeared to have calmed enough to speak his thoughts rather them spit them in anger. "Okay, I don't know if he took Fergus out for sure, but he was using the shelter to launder money for Fergus. I *know* he was."

Detective Primrose, her lipstick faded, likely from a long day, squared her shoulders. "And you know this how, Higgs? Give me something to work with here. Give me something solid."

Running a hand over his chin, his eyes said it best. He was in pain—and that left me very sad. "I know because of Trixie. I know for *certain* because of Trixie."

"And where is our lovely ex-nun?" Tansy asked, her eyes scanning the crowd forming.

"Here," I squeaked from behind a tall onlooker, trying to summon some bravado and not sound like a total chicken. I wanted to see justice done, but I somehow couldn't wrap my head around Jay being a murderer. "How can I help?"

Higgs pointed a finger at me, his lips a grim line. "Tell her how you saw Jay at three different banks today. That's what tipped me off, Tans. Remember that money-laundering ring we worked eight years or so ago?"

Tansy nodded her blonde head, her eyes sharp and clear. "You mean with Bulldog Joe?" she asked.

"That's the one," he confirmed, his jaw so tight, I

thought it might snap. "Remember how he'd make deposits in a bunch of different banks to keep the IRS off his back? Trixie saw him today at three separate banks. He was dumping the money for whomever Fergus works for. That's classic laundering behavior, Tans."

Ahhh. Now I understood. Almost. Not entirely. I didn't understand why he used three banks, but I understood certain amounts of deposits one made could flag the IRS. I knew very little about this sort of thing, but then, I hadn't planned to launder money through Inkerbelle's.

Detective Primrose looked down at me, her glasses at the tip of her nose. "Is that true, Trixie?"

I nodded my head slowly as I attempted to parse the hows and whys of money laundering. "Yes. It's absolutely true. I saw him at three different banks, all unaffiliated with one another, just today."

Higgs's nod was sharp, his expression tight. "And do you remember how Bulldog cooked the books? I'd bet my kidney if you get a search warrant, you'll find two sets of books for the shelter. The one I have and the one Jay has."

Jay had become quite silent as he watched with frantic eyes from the other side of the shelter. In fact, he looked quite miserable and haggard. His clothes askew from his scuffle with Higgs, his hair, usually brushed neatly, mussed.

Detective Primrose chewed on her lip, dragging a hand through her hair. "Then we'll haul him in for questioning. But that doesn't mean he's guilty of murder, Higgs," she said, but it sounded so pleasant with her British accent, it almost didn't seem like such a bad thing.

Higgs's eyes went hard. "I think it at least warrants an investigation, don't you? It's pretty suspicious, all those bank runs, don't you think? If Fergus was a loan shark, it's not a stretch to think he'd launder money, Tansy. If Jay got caught up in this somehow, and he wanted out, what better way to *get* out?"

Tansy looked doubtful. "And frame you with something as obvious as leaving a mark on Fergus's neck like your tattoo?"

"Well, why not? You guys sure don't have a problem thinking *I'd* do something as stupid as carve a sign in his neck that matches my tattoo, now do you?"

"Higgs," Tansy said, her tone full of warning. "You know it's not just that, mate. You know."

Higgs lifted his chin, his eyes hardening. "Yeah. I know. My hair and a phone call. You don't suppose my hair could have been planted there by Jay? He's in my apartment all the time, Tansy," he said with disgust.

Clearly, she wasn't going to elaborate or theorize anymore with her onetime colleague and friend. "Gentleman, let's take him in," she ordered with a wave of her hand.

"Nooo!" Jay howled, so loud it reverberated around the street. "I swear, I didn't kill him! Higgs, you have to listen to me! I didn't kill him! Please listen!"

I'm pretty sure my eyes were bulging out of my

head as he begged and pleaded with Higgs and Tansy, but I found myself rooted to the spot, unable to process all of this. How did you process this kind of betrayal?

Detective Primrose tapped Higgs on the shoulder. "Hear me now, Higgs. You do know you're still our prime suspect. Don't you dare think about going anywhere or it's *my* backside, understood?"

"Aw, Tansy, would I leave you high and dry without anyone to wrongfully convict of murder?" His words weren't malicious at all. In fact, they were pretty light on the sarcasm.

Man. I'm glad *someone* could joke about this. I wasn't quite ready. I was emotionally invested now, and I wanted to understand. "Do you really think he killed Fergus, Higgs?"

Now his face looked raw under the streetlamp, his eyes dull and glassy, probably from lack of sleep. "I don't know, but it's likely, don't you think?"

As I thought about that for a moment, I waffled. Something just didn't feel right.

"It makes sense. If Fergus was threatening him, and let's say he wanted out. Which also makes sense because of what Solomon said about him being mad about the laundry. And I'm convinced that's what Solomon meant. Sure…he could have been angry enough to kill him. But to plant *your* hair at the crime scene and carve that gang sign in his neck—does that sound like Jay?"

Higgs rocked back on his heels, driving his hands into his pockets. "Money laundering didn't sound like

Jay either, but the more I think about it, the more I realize I had an inkling all along—for at least the last six months or so. I didn't want to believe there was the problem. He's my best friend. My judgment is pretty cloudy these days—and especially since I left the force. I let my attempt to detach from my old life keep me from paying attention to what was going on right under my nose, Trixie. All the 'charitable donations,' all the times he had to go take care of 'business,'" he spat. "And no, that's not murder. But *could* he have murdered Fergus? Sure."

"And that's just it?" I asked, throwing my hands up in the air, feeling this odd sense of unfinished business. An emptiness of sorts. I definitely didn't feel the way Stevie said she felt after she'd solved a crime. "You just decide your best friend is a murderer? That he framed *you* for murder? No ifs, ands or buts? I mean, money laundering is one thing, Higgs. It's bad. Yes. Very bad. A broken law, for sure. But it's not murder. *Murder*."

He crossed his arms over his chest and looked down at me as a cool breeze blew and the bustle of commerce on our street slowed. There was so much hidden behind his eyes, I didn't know where to begin, and he wasn't sharing how much this hurt him, I can tell you that much.

"After what I've seen, anything is possible, Trixie. I realize you've been cloistered a good deal of your life, and I'm sorry if that sounds unfair or I sound jaded, but I've seen brothers kill brothers over minor infractions like changing the position of the driver's seat of their car. It's not a stretch to think Jay might have killed Fergus and framed me if he was panicked enough."

Well, okay then. What was left to say? And he was correct. I hadn't seen a lot of the outside world. I *did* live in a semi-bubble of love and understanding, at least until my untimely demise as a nun. But I wasn't completely ignorant to the goings on of the world.

Detective Primrose didn't say anything about her feelings on who'd killed Fergus, but she did nod her head as we spoke. I imagine she was right there with Higgs in terms of seeing the horrors of the world.

Finally, she turned to me, a smile on her face. "So, I see you're knickers deep in this Fergus's murder, aren't you, Miss Lavender?" she said, but she didn't say it with malice. Her tone was more teasing.

I shrugged my shoulders and sighed. "I didn't mean to be. Not really, anyway. I was just in the right place at the right time, I guess."

"That's not what I've been hearing around the station, love," she said with a wink. "I hear you had yourself a jolly brawl with some tossers who were picking on one of the homeless."

Suddenly, I was very tired. I fought a yawn and tried to downplay my role in that particular incident. I didn't need any more trouble. "I scared them off. Nothing more, nothing less. So is there anything else you need from me, Detective Primrose?"

"I'll need you to come down to the station and make a formal statement about what you witnessed today."

"Can't it wait, Tansy?" Higgs asked as people began to shuffle in impatience now that Jay was being loaded into a police car and the drama had passed. "She looks exhausted. Trixie needs to go home and get some rest."

My cheeks warmed a little at the thought Higgs had noticed I was dead on my feet, but I forced myself to ignore his concern. I was, after all, his best witness at this point. Certainly he'd want to see after me until I gave a formal statement.

"It can. But I have your word you'll come to see me directly tomorrow morn, Miss Lavender?"

I saluted her with a smile, my eyes grainy and tired. "Are you kidding? Miss the chance to be grilled by Portland's finest while I drink burnt coffee and eat food from a machine that costs as much as a steak dinner? I wouldn't miss it."

She smirked at me, but her eyes twinkled. "Good enough then. On the morrow. For now, I have work to do. Higgs? I meant what I said, bloke. No trouble from you."

"Not a chance. Let me know when you get that search warrant to Jay's place, would you? I'm dying to know what you find."

"I most certainly will not," she said on a chuckle as she stepped off the curb and moved toward her car. "You're a murder suspect, and don't you forget it."

Now Higgs chuckled, thought I still couldn't find the funny in this. "Night, Tans." He held up a hand and waved as Detective Primrose left us standing there together.

"So that's that then, huh?" I asked, pushing my hands into the pocket of my jeans, feeling deflated, though I couldn't say why. For now, I wanted to go home, crawl into that amazing bed in my new bedroom, and sleep for a year.

"Maybe. I don't know. I guess we'll see when they question him."

He shook his dark head, his eyes changing from dark to light. He didn't want to talk about this accusation against Jay, and I sort of understood that. It hurt to find out you'd been betrayed by someone so close to you.

I put a hand on his arm, noting just how intricate his sleeve tattoos were. I wanted to see them in the light, but for tonight, we both needed some rest. "Will you be okay, Higgs?"

"I will." He sounded determined to be okay, but no one was okay after finding out their best friend had been using something as important to them as their life's passion to siphon dirty money.

"Listen, I know we don't know each other very well, Higgs, but if you ever want to talk, call me—anytime, day or night. Or stop by the store. I'll always have an ear."

Suddenly, he smiled, warm and bright. "I'll do that. But first, are you okay, too?"

I flapped a hand upward, my cheeks red. "Aside from the impact of that G-force-worthy ride over here? I'm fine. Just tired and thirsty. I'm ready to go home and sleep this murder-mystery hangover off."

Higgs laughed and pointed inside the shelter. "I knew he was here at the shelter. I didn't want him to get wind of this and run before we could confront him."

I coughed, my throat still scratchy. "Fair enough."

"You want a bottle of water for the ride?"

"That would be awesome. Hey, can I have your keys? I left my sketch pad in your car."

He dug them out of his jeans and tossed them to me. "Back in a sec."

I zipped across the road as fast as I could, my legs sluggish and achy, still pondering the idea Jay was potentially a killer. Maybe I was being naive, but it still felt wrong.

As I popped the lock on Higgs's car door and reached in to grab my sketch pad, I heard something faint. Stopping, I tilted my head and listened again.

"Fair maiden!" someone cried, hoarse and deep, making me whip around and peer into the dark spots where there were no streetlamps. We needed more streetlamps on this dang street. I don't know who I'd have to contact to make that happen, but I was sure going to try.

"Fair maiden, helllpp me!"

And then I heard a cough. A phlegm-filled cough, and someone gasping for breath.

Solomon?

Adrenaline rushed through me as I lunged across the street. Naturally now, it was virtually empty of all the rubberneckers.

"Solomon?" I yelled.

"Help me, please! Stop! Solomon says *stop!*"

Gosh, now he sounded kind of far away. But his words had chills racing along my arms. So I stopped cold in my tracks and listened, my pulse beating in my ears. "Solomon! Answer me—*where are you?*"

But all I heard was the sound of traffic on the bridge and the quiet of the night now that most of the shops had closed.

"Solomon!" I hissed into the night, clinging to my sketch pad.

And then that dreadful, awful hacking cough—only curiously muffled this time—sounded again.

My heart began to race as I ran toward the dark alleyway , stopping only to call his name and listen for a response. "Solomon! Where are you?"

Just as I rounded the corner of the building to the alleyway four doors down from the shelter and Inker-belle's, I saw someone ,and relief flooded my veins.

"Oh, Solomon! Thank goodness you're okay! Where have you been, my liege?" I asked as I ran blindly into the dark alley.

Note to self: In future, when doing a good deed, do it where there's a lot of light.

CHAPTER 15

*A*s I ran toward Solomon's voice, two things happened at once. I tripped (go me), and dropped my sketch pad, and someone with strong hands grabbed me and shoved me to the ground.

I fell with a small yelp of surprise, the force of the shove leaving me breathless as I hit the ground—which was pretty hard and slimy, by the way—and scraping the palms of my hands.

"What the…?" I cried out, rolling to my back to find someone standing above me with a shaking and stiff-as-a-board Solomon in front of them.

My first thought was, he didn't like to be touched. Whoever was holding on to Solomon had a fierce grip on him.

I attempted to rise without using my hands (I vow to work on my core and lay off the Voodoo Donuts, if I live), but a foot came down hard on my abdomen.

"Don't move!" the voice above me shouted, stomping the heel of their foot into my gut.

I gagged and sputtered, the searing pain in my belly shooting upward to lodge in my throat. "Stop!" was all I managed to cry out before I attempted to roll away again.

"Get up!" someone hissed into the dark with a raspy, husky voice—a voice I couldn't distinguish as male or female. "Get up, and keep your mouth shut, lady, or I swear, I'll shoot this blabbering idiot!"

Those words forced me to push myself to my knees and rise, leaning back against the side of a building for support.

Also note to self: Don't let yourself get backed into a corner—ever.

"Solomon's not an idiot—not an idiot! No idiots!" he cried, making my stomach turn and my heart ache for him.

And that was when everything became clear, and it wasn't just my eyes adjusting to the dark. I mean, I fully understood what was going on.

A terrified, shaking, cringing Solomon, still in his Viking hat, was held captive by none other than Gilligan. Who'd said the word *shoot*, and as I glanced at the hand he had driven into Solomon's ribs, I saw what he'd shoot him with.

Sweet heaven and a candy striper, he had a gun. *Gilligan had a gun.* What was going on?

"Put your hands up in the air where I can see them

and do it *now!*" he hissed, showing me the gun, a shiny revolver, glinting under the bright moon.

I threw my hands upward, trembling as they were, and gasped for more air in my lungs, still stinging from my fall and the foot to my gut.

Swallowing hard, I licked my dry lips and, for the first time, really took a good look at my attacker. It was Gilligan all right. He wore his white hat and the navy pea coat, just like he had when I'd first met him outside the store.

But why in all of damnation was he holding a gun to Solomon's head? For that matter, where had he gotten a gun? Was he going to rob me?

So what to do next? What would Stevie do?

Then suddenly, in my whir of thoughts, I knew what she'd do. She'd find a way to distract him away from Solomon, who literally quaked with terror, his eyes pleading with me to help him as his hands fluttered and flapped.

So I made a point of backing away, and somehow I managed to speak. "Solomon, where have you been? I've been looking everywhere for you!"

Gilligan gave Solomon a hard nudge, as though they were buddies. "He's been with me, haven't ya, pal? But you slipped away when I wasn't looking. Best friends don't do that, do they, Saulie? They don't run away from their friends. Silly Saulie!"

But he shook his head violently. "Not my friend. Not Saulie's friend. You are not my friend!" Solomon cried on a hacking cough, trying to get away, but he was too weak.

My eyes went wide and my head throbbed, but I pushed forward and began to bargain because I didn't know what else to do.

I looked directly into Gilligan's eyes, pleading with mine. "Just tell me what you want and I'll give it to you. I have money tucked into the back pocket of my jeans. Take it and I'll never tell anyone about this. I swear. Just let Solomon go. *Please*."

But he shook his head as though I were madder than a hatter. "I don't want your money, you idiot!"

Well, what the flibbetyjib kind of robbery was this then? "Then what do you want?" I squeaked in confusion, my arms beginning to ache and tingle.

"I want you to shut up while I think!" he yelled at me, hugging Solomon closer to him and pressing the gun tighter to his side—and that was when I saw the tattoo on his arm. A very slender arm, I might add.

"Sorry! Sorrysorrysorry," I muttered, as I remembered the words he'd said when he was talking about the mad bad guy. He'd said he had a tattoo...

Solomon shifted and shuddered, and I said a silent prayer he'd stay still. But he couldn't stop his hands from fluttering, meaning he was beyond distressed and had no other outlet to express his fear. Worse, his eyes flitted from place to place, his body swaying against Gilligan's.

"My liege," I said, forcing my voice to remain steady.

"Pay heed. Stay the course and all will be well. You are strong. You are wise. *Stay the course.*"

Instantly, he caught my gaze and whispered, "Please, please, please, please, pleeease make him let me go! I want to go. King Solomon wants to go!"

But Gilligan leaned into Solomon's ear and whispered, sinister and low, "Shut up, you halfwit! You got away from me before, but you're not getting away now!"

As my mind raced and I sought the best way to understand what Gilligan wanted, I remembered Stevie telling me when she was in a particularly sticky situation, she stalled by getting to know her attacker—by personalizing herself to him.

So personalize I did. "Listen, let's make a deal, okay?" I offered in a shaky voice. "You let him go and you can have me, right? I'm easygoing. I don't eat much, I travel light. Oh, and I'm an ex-nun. Maybe I can pray for your absolution? I do sort of have an in with the people upstairs, if you know what I mean. Plus, come on. I'm super nice. Ask anyone—"

"I can't let him go, you stupid, stupid fool! He *saw* me! He saw me through the window that night, and now he has to die—and you have to die, too!"

I blurted the words out before I really thought about them, my arms aching so much, I thought I'd have to have them amputated if I got out of this alive. "He saw you *what?*"

"You're bad. Mad and bad!" Solomon cried.

But Gilligan's eyes narrowed to tiny slits in his

head, glinting with malice from beneath his white hat. He tightened his grip on Solomon, making him whimper. "Shut up, you yapping fool!"

"Solomon told you!" Solomon crowed like a parrot. "Solomon told you he was mad. Mad and bad, mad and bad!" And then he coughed, his thin shoulders racked with violent shudders.

"Shut up!" Gilligan ordered, this time driving the gun against Solomon's temple and knocking his Viking hat off.

Mad and bad. Mad and bad. Those words kept running through my brain.

As though I'd been struck by a thunderbolt, I suddenly saw everything very clearly. I wasn't sure about the whys and wherefores, but I was sure of one thing. "*You* killed Fergus?" This homeless man had killed Fergus McDuff?

And that was when he cackled, sort of long and really evil. Just like in the movies—which is crazy. Who knew that really happened?

He gripped Solomon's arm, keeping him close to his body by twisting it behind his back. "You bet I did— and I'm going to watch that pig traitor Cross Higglesworth take the fall for it!"

Pig traitor? *Pigtraitorpigtraitorpigtraitor.* The words whooshed through my mind—and then it hit me, for all the good knowing would do me. This had to be someone from the Blood Squad. Who else would call an ex-police officer a pig?

Of course, because I'd only just put this together in

my mind, and in my excitement that I'd finally gotten one daggone thing right, I had to open my big mouth and share my revelation.

"You're from the Blood Squad!" I all but yelped loud enough to wake the dead, then just as quickly realized I was consorting with the enemy like we were playing a game of Trivial Pursuit.

Now he smiled, wide and dripping menace. He wanted to share, too, I suppose. Gloat. Brag. Stevie said some killers liked to do that, in order to take credit for their crimes.

"You betcha, I am," he sneered, the spit forming at the corner of his mouth glistening under the full moon. "And I'm going to make that undercover rat-pig pay! It took me a little while to find him, but when I did, all I needed was somebody to take out. Somebody he knew. The fact he argued with that ugly old dinosaur made him a perfect victim. The rest was easy."

Oh, sweet heaven. His words made me gulp my fear as my legs shook and my heart throbbed against my ribs. But I had to keep him talking because he had a gun. A. Gun. People. I didn't have an inkling how I was going to keep not just Solomon but myself from, at the very least, losing an eyeball.

And what would I defend myself with? As I tried to keep it together, I realized the alleyway had nothing to hide behind, nothing that would be of any help to me in aiding an escape. We were surrounded by brick and nothing else.

Still, I forced myself to ask from trembling lips, "So why didn't you just kill Higgs? Why kill Fergus?"

He lifted his chin defiantly, and there was something about the way he did it that struck me as peculiar. It didn't seem true to his character...or something like that. I can't explain it; there was just something out of place.

Gilligan clucked his tongue. "Because I want Higgs to *suffer*," he drew the word out on a raspy breath in a sob of agony. "Do you know what they do to ex-cops in the pen? Do you have any idea how long he'll go away for murder in the first degree? That kind of hell will go on and on. If I killed him, it'd be over too soon. He needs to pay over and over for what he did to my Matias and Diego! Day after day after day!"

My Matias and Diego? Who was this? Dear heaven, *who*?

At those words, my entire body went cold and clammy for a moment, my pulse pounded in my ears—and then something odd happened. It was as though an entity other than the evil inside me took hold. Something calm. Something purposeful, and for whatever reason, real or imagined, I wasn't afraid.

Then I heard Stevie's voice in my head. I heard all her words of wisdom rush through my brain in a wave of sentences, and I felt resolve.

If Gilligan was going to kill me, I'd go down fighting—but not without some answers to all my questions.

"It was you who planted Higgs's hair at the crime

scene, didn't you? You framed him," I said, all the while searching every nook and cranny of the dark alleyway for something to help me get us out of this mess.

Gilligan rocked back on his heels, taking Solomon with him, his smile full of devilish glee. "Yeah. Nice touch, right? I needed to cement the deal. What better way than physical evidence? Gets 'em every time."

"So it was you in the dumpster? It was you who jumped on top of me?"

His grin grew into an ugly sneer. "Yep. I had to get in there somehow, didn't I? So I climbed the fire escape, broke in the window, and dumped some of Higgs's hair there. That was easy enough to get from his brush. I knew forensics would do another sweep. Those idiots always do. Clever, don't you think?"

Golly, my arms were surely going to fall off if I didn't think of something to save us soon.

Thus, I stalled some more, trying to keep my eyes on this madman and Solomon, who whimpered and groaned each time Gilligan snarled.

"And the tic-tac-toe mark on Fergus's neck? Why? To what purpose? You do realize even the police wouldn't fall for him doing something as stupid as carving a gang sign on a victim when he has an identical sign on his arm, don't you?"

He flashed the gun again, pulling it away from Solomon's temple and pointing it at me. "So Higgs would know somebody from Blood Squad had been there. It was my special calling card just for him. Just for that lying, traitorous pig! I wanted him to know someone was coming for him."

Ahhh. Okay. Point for the bad guy.

He sounded so pleased with himself, I wanted to retch, but that wouldn't get Solomon away from him. So I inhaled and continued to ride this feeling of deep calm.

What I said next wasn't going to endear me to Solomon, but it would endear me to Gilligan, and that would have to do. I'd apologize a million times—later— if we lived. Stepping forward (a bold, crazy move, I know), I turned my back to the opening of the alley-way, looking Gilligan dead in the eyes while my chest heaved and my lip throbbed.

"And Solomon? Why can't you let him go? You've heard him babbling. He's a fool," I said, though my heart ached at my cruel words. "No one pays attention to him. No one cares what he says. No one *believes* what he says. He talks like a pirate some days. Let him go. Shoot me instead."

Yep. I said that, and I don't know where the courage to say it came from, but I meant it. I don't even know what Gilligan would gain from shooting me instead of Solomon. But if he had to take someone out to assuage his rage, I wanted it to be me.

Gilligan shook his head with a hard twist of his neck. "But don't you see? I can't let either of you go! You both know too much. He has to go just like you do, *Sister Trixie Lavender*!"

My eyes went wide. He knew me?

"What? You look surprised. I know all about you, Trixie Lavender, and your friend Coop, too! All your little homeless friends couldn't stop talking about you, especially that crazier than a bedbug Madge. If you'd have just kept your nose out of it, if you'd just stopped poking around—"

"Trixie?" I heard a man call out.

Higgs. The person he most wanted dead in all this. I couldn't let Higgs get to the alleyway.

I don't know what made me do so, knowing I was likely going to lose my life because of it, but I yelled back, "Go back, Higgs! *Call for help!*"

Yes. I told an ex-undercover police officer to call for help as though that wouldn't incite him to come see what was going on.

"What's going on, Trixie?" he yelled again, this time closer, and in that second, in that very tiny, minute, heaven-sent second, Gilligan became distracted—and I took my shot.

My only shot.

I dropped my head low and used my feet to propel me, aiming for the middle of Gilligan like a bull aims for a red flag.

I roared, "Duck, Solomon!" just before I crashed into Gilligan, who, in the moment, I oddly thought wasn't nearly as heavy or muscled as I'd anticipated, and knocked him to the ground.

We crashed to the ground in a tangle of limbs and grunts. I heard his enraged scream whistle through my ears as we landed, but if nothing else, Solomon heeded my words and fell to the left of us before all hell broke loose.

Then I did the only thing I knew to do—the only thing I thought might come close to saving us. I straddled him and grabbed for his hand—the hand with the gun.

And listen, I'm not an exerciser by nature. In that, I don't do it willingly. So I don't have a kung-fu grip, and I'm certainly not winning any contests for most fit, but I clung to that man with my thighs like I was riding a bucking bronco.

And that worked for a hot minute.

But I'll be darned if he didn't buck me right off him, catching me off guard and hurling me to the ground, where my head flopped backward with such force, I cracked it on the slimy ground.

With a groan, I rolled to my side and willed myself to a sitting position to see Solomon cowering in a corner, coughing up a storm.

And then Higgs was there, launching himself on top of Gilligan with a howl of rage so loud, it rattled my bones, but he, too, missed the hand that held the gun, and I knew I had to do something. But *what*?

Oh, divine intervention, don't fail me now!

Just as Gilligan yanked his arm upward, just as he rolled with Higgs over the alleyway's hard surface, his hat fell off and I realized, this wasn't a Gilligan at all— this was more like a Ginger or a Mary Ann.

Her hair, dark and thick, fell to just past her neck, gleaming under the moon.

That was when I heard Higgs bellow, *"Iris?"* His voice was full of surprise—and a bit of anguish, if I heard correctly.

Iris? Why did I know that name? *Iris, Iris, Iris...* Her name rang through my mind on an endless loop, and then like a slap to my head, I remembered.

She was Matias and Diego's mother!

"You killed my baby!" she screamed up at him with a ragged sob, bringing the gun down hard on his temple with a crack so hard, so loud, I cringed. "As sure as you're here in front of me! I hope you rot in Hell!" She railed against him, grabbing him by the hair and driving the gun into his chest.

That was when I saw Higgs clearly, just as the streetlamp hit his face. He was bleeding, disoriented and I knew I had to do something.

Maybe some of that divine intervention came into play, maybe it was just pure luck, but when I screamed Higgs's name in warning, as loud and with as much force as I could, Iris somehow got lost in her rage and I got lucky, because that was the moment I lunged for her arm.

A shot rang out, booming and harsh in my ears, seconds before, there but for the grace of something, I landed on Iris's arm, knocking the gun out of her hand, the clack of it hitting the ground sharp and resonant in the alley.

I scrambled to find it, to ensure she wouldn't get her hands on it once more, but Higgs had Iris covered when he hauled her upward, dragging her to the brick wall and pressing her against it with the fiercest look I've ever seen on anyone's face, bar none.

As I scrambled, I realized my foot hurt something fierce—and that's when I saw I'd been shot, clean through my sneaker. Oddly, there wasn't a lot of blood, but sweet fancy Moses in pajamas, it hurt. Yet, I couldn't think about that. Solomon was huddled in a corner, terrified and I had to get to him.

"Trixie? Trixie Lavender? Where are you? What's happened?" I heard Coop call out.

Thank all that was good and mighty, Coop was here.

"Call 9-1-1, Coop—now!" I yelled, crawling to where Solomon sat rocking, his whimpers tearing at my soul. I spotted the gun, too, just before I reached out a hesitant hand and placed it on his knee, while I used my good foot to kick the gun out of the way.

He jerked in response to my touch, but I calmly spoke to him in the way I hoped would best reach him. "My liege," I whispered. "'Tis a brave man you are. Come, we must gather our spoils and cheer your victory! Take my hand, I shall lead you to Castle Hawthorne!"

He curled into a tighter ball, but he did look at me, and in his eyes, I saw sheer terror. "He was a bad, mad man. A bad, mad, mad man! Make him go away!"

I smiled in sympathy, keeping my eyes focused on him even as my foot throbbed, among just one of the many places on my body. "Yes, my liege. But look yonder," I suggested, pointing to where Higgs had Iris pressed tight against the brick. "The enemy has been captured and all is well in the kingdom. Peace reigns. Come, take my hand. We'll travel together to safety."

And miracle of miracles, he took my hand in his clammy grip, his skin so warm, I knew I had to talk him into seeing a doctor. His eyes, so frightened, so glassy, darted to mine briefly, desperately searching, before he looked away and began to rock again.

But he was still holding my hand.

By now, Coop was at my side, with Knuckles right behind her, his eyes wide, his face full of concern. "Trixie girl, what happened?" Then he looked down. "Jumpin' Jehoshaphat!" he almost shouted when he saw my foot, lifting me from the ground with strong arms while Coop helped Solomon, who still clung to my fingers.

"Oh, Coop! Can I tell you how glad I am to see you?" I crowed, my voice hoarse as I wrapped my free arm around her neck.

She gave me an awkward thump on the back as I craned my neck to see where Higgs was. "The police officers are coming, Trixie. When you didn't answer my text after you were done with the stakeout, I grew worried. I made Knuckles bring me to you straight away. He brought me on his motorcycle. I love his motorcycle. Can I have a motorcycle?"

I smiled up at them both in gratitude. "How about we talk about that later? Until then, you did good, Coop. You did so good."

"What happened here, Trixie?" Knuckles asked as he

looked to where Higgs held a sobbing Iris captive, his face a hard mask.

I still wasn't exactly sure how she fit, seeing as how the article I'd read said she had cancer. But this had to be the Matias and Diego's mother, Iris. She'd said, *you killed my baby.*

"I'll tell you all about it later. Okay?"

As sirens sounded, I had Coop and Knuckles help get me to Higgs, who held onto Iris with such force, I thought he'd crack her in half. As sirens blared, now a familiar tune to my ears, I stood to the side of them.

When I heard him say he should kill her from teeth clenched tight, I knew I had to intervene.

With Coop, Knuckles and Solomon surrounding me, I spoke to him. "Higgs, take it easy. The police are coming. Hear that? Tansy's surely on her way. We have Fergus's killer. She confessed to me. Don't do anything you'll regret. You love the shelter. You said so yourself. I can't volunteer at a shelter if there *is* no shelter. Don't throw it all away. Ease up. *Please, please*, listen to me."

Next, I heard the thunder of footsteps and the welcome sound of Tansy's British accent. "Higgs!"

Oh, thank goodness Detective Primrose was here! As she pushed her way through us to get to Higgs, she cried out in surprise, too, when she saw who he held captive. "Iris Santino?"

But Iris didn't acknowledge Detective Primrose. Her eyes were searing holes into Higgs's face as she struggled and strained against him. "I *hate* you! I hate you and one day, you're gonna get yours, you pig! For my Diego!" she spat.

"All right, that's enough!" Detective Primrose, who looked like she'd been through the ringer, intervened. "Higgs, step aside." She gave his shoulder a yank and, as if by magic, his face relaxed and he took a step back and she took over Iris.

He pushed his knuckles against his temple where Iris had whacked him with the gun and wiped at the blood with a wince, his chest pumping up and down. An officer approached him with a wad of tissues, and he acknowledged him by nodding as he appeared to gather himself and dab at his wound.

When the haze of his anger cleared, Higgs suddenly saw me. When he assessed me with a scan of his eyes up and down my body, his handsome face instantly became riddled with concern. "Someone call an ambulance!"

"Don't be silly. I don't need an ambulance, Higgs. That's a waste of a good paramedic. I can catch a ride to the hospital. I'm not bleeding out. Also, they cost the earth. I can't afford to pay for a ride to the hospital *plus* pay for the hospital," I joked.

Higgs put his hands on his hips and frowned, but there was amusement in his eyes. "How did you get mixed up in this?"

"Well, how do you think?" I asked as we all began moving out of the now-crowded alley. "I thought to myself, Trixie Lavender, what would you like to do more than anything else in the world tonight? How about get shot in the foot? Yeah, I said. Let the good times roll."

He laughed out of the blue, a bark of a laugh that had him throwing his head back. "I think you're the funniest ex-nun I know, and probably the coolest. You took a hit for me, Trixie. I'm never going to forget that."

My face went hot and my throat tight. "I'm probably the *only* ex-nun you know. As for cool, that's up for debate. Now, no more talk, Cross Higglesworth. We need to get both King Solomon and myself to the hospital. He needs meds and a good night's rest and I need a foot replacement." As I hobbled to the cracked curb, with Coop and Knuckles helping me and Solomon still clinging to my hand, I handed Knuckles the keys to the Caddy. "Would you mind driving me, and Solomon, too?"

He chuckled his hearty Santa Claus laugh, chucking me under the chin. "Would I mind? Be back in two shakes, and then I want to hear all about how my favorite ex-nun took a bullet. You're a hero, Trixie girl!"

Now I laughed as I watched him cross the street, his big body lumbering toward our car.

But Higgs grabbed my arm and turned me to face him as Coop stood with Solomon, just close enough to his side for his comfort level—something I was so proud of her for gauging.

"Seriously, Trixie," he said, his eyes dark and

somber. "Iris would have killed me if not for you. If you hadn't screamed, she would have shot me."

I smiled warmly at him, uncomfortable with the intensity of his gratitude. "But she didn't, Higgs. She didn't. And I'm okay. And you're okay. We're all okay."

But his eyes held mine, gripping them until I couldn't look away, as though he wanted me to see the words he wanted to say, but didn't have. "I owe you, Sister Trixie. I owe you *big*."

And even though a tear stung my eye, even though I was just glad we all had our faces still attached to our heads, I didn't feel like Higgs owed me a darn thing. Rather, I felt as though we'd finally connected on some level.

But then the moment passed, and I grew embarrassed by the force of his appreciation and overwhelmed by the events of the night.

Now I planted a hand on my hip, looking up at him and grinning. "Oh yeah, Higgs? How big is *big*? Is it drywall-and-drills big? Paint-a-room big? Fix-the-plumbing big?"

He smirked at me, but his eyes danced with amusement. "It's at least grab-a-cold-beer-and-supervise big," he joked.

And then the three of us laughed—even Coop, who did her best imitation of Joan Collins yet as she tipped her long neck back and let out the fakest, loudest giggle she's ever attempted.

And she was right. Laughter does make me happy.

Even if it's only Coop's attempt at fitting in. That she was trying so hard made me even happier.

But all of us laughing together after what we'd been through as of late?

That was the best sound ever.

EPILOGUE

Two weeks later...

"Are you serious, Knuckles? *Really?*" I squealed.

He pointed to the paper and nodded, smiling his huge grin down at me with the twinkle in his eye I'd come to love after spending so much time with him these last weeks. "This paper says I'm purty serious."

My mouth fell open and my heart flooded with all manner of emotions I didn't know how to express.

He nudged me and winked. "So no more worrying, okay?"

I threw my arms around his wide waist and gave him a hug, burying my face in his T-shirt—a T-shirt that matched mine and read Inkerbelle's Tattoos and Piercings. "I can't believe you did this," I said, my voice muffled by his barrel chest as tears threatened to escape my eyes.

He put his hands on my arms and set me in front of

him, his cheeks red with what I suspect was embarrassment. "Well, I did. Now, don't we have some spaghetti to eat? I'm starving after all that hard labor you've been forcing me to endure. Let's get outta here."

My head fell back on my shoulders and I laughed. "How will I ever thank you?"

"By making this shop the best tattoo parlor in Cobbler Cove—maybe even in all of Portland. That's how. Now, spaghetti?"

Knuckles had bought the building from Crowley, and he was renting the space to us for even less than Coop had pressured Fergus into. It was such a kind gesture; I almost couldn't speak.

So instead, I grinned, something I'd found myself doing a lot these last two weeks since we'd begun to transform Inkerbelle's. "Yes! Yes, I have an enormous batch of spaghetti and meatballs. Higgs loaned us a big table and chairs, and earlier, he hung up some lights in the square across the street. It's beautiful."

And it was. I pointed across the street, where everyone had gathered at the long table. Twinkling lights hung from the big maple, a line of lanterns sat at the center of the table, where wine glasses were filled, music played, and the low hum of chatter resonated in my ears.

Coop, our new friend Delores, and ten or so of our fellow business owners were all present to enjoy this day—with us—together. All the people who had dropped by to lend us a hand with the store clinked glasses, laughed, smiled.

Even if the store wasn't perfect just yet, it was coming around, and that was what made it so beautiful —everyone in the neighborhood had chipped in and helped. At different times each day, one shop owner or another had shown up and grabbed a paintbrush or a hammer, and as a result, things were really looking up. I gazed around the space proudly.

The walls were funky multi-colors of purple, orange and blue. Framed originals of some of my black-and-white sketches hung on one wall, and of course, Knuckles's pictures with a zillion celebrities right alongside them.

There was a puffy sectional sofa in royal blue Delores had so generously given us, packed with an array of throw pillows, where clients could sit and wait for their appointments. Cool, geometrically shaped tables in glass scattered about, holding tattoo magazines.

The bathroom now worked, thanks to Fester Little, who owned the vacuum cleaner repair shop called Suck It Up down the way. Turned out, his father had been a plumber by trade, and not only did he fix the toilet, but he'd sold us some of the inventory his father had left behind after his death. That meant we had an old-school pedestal sink made of dark blue porcelain with gold fixtures.

And lastly, we had our tattoo stations almost complete and, as word got around about our grand opening next week, we'd had several applicants, including a guy named Goose, who wasn't just a character, but a close friend of Knuckles.

Things were really looking up. Gone was the frustration of standing still, replaced by the thrill of seeing our hard work pay off.

And now, tonight, as a way to not only celebrate and honor the people of our community who'd helped us, we were having a celebration for Higgs being cleared of all charges.

It was in fact true, Jay had been laundering money for Fergus through the shelter, and it was in the quiet times when Higgs and I worked side by side, as he made good on his promise, that I felt his sadness over the devastating loss of his best friend. We hadn't talked about it much, but he'd opened up a little, and that was enough for now.

Iris, on the other hand, was in far worse shape than Jay could ever be. That everyone had thought she was still ill with cancer worked to her advantage in framing Higgs. Not even Higgs had thought her capable. In fact, he'd told me while he'd sat in jail that night, he'd dismissed the idea she could be a suspect entirely.

But after several rounds of chemo and radiation, she'd beat her disease, and then set about getting her revenge. Posing as a homeless man was clever indeed, I'll admit. Her voice was just deep and raspy enough for me to believe she was a man that night. Somehow, that she was a mother—even a murderous one—still left me with a tiny bit of sympathy for her. What I didn't sympathize for her over, was what she'd done to

Solomon. Though, she'd admitted to framing Higgs for the murder of Fergus McDuff to avenge her son Diego's death without much pressure.

There was still a trial to come—one I'd have to testify at. Higgs, too. But that was a little ways down the road. For now, Iris Santino was in jail awaiting trial, the last of the Blood Squad, family members or otherwise. And that made me breathe a sigh of relief.

"Aw, look. It's Solomon," Knuckles said, pointing out the window to our friends across the street, putting an arm around my shoulder and giving me a squeeze. "He looks good, eh? How's the nightmares?"

I smiled even as I sighed. Solomon was better now, dressed in a pair of jeans that clearly weren't his size and a button-up shirt I'd bought for him. The jeans sagged and wrinkled at his ankles, and the shirt wasn't a perfect fit by a long shot. But he was clean and healthy, and at the shelter with Higgs for now.

However, he'd gone through a really tough week after we'd caught Iris, where he'd spent a great deal of time lost in his own medieval world while he recuperated from pneumonia in the hospital. But he was coming around.

Leaning into Knuckles, I said, "I think the nightmares are better, if his doctor is telling me the truth. But I also think he's still coming to grips with the fact that he saw Iris kill Fergus through the window. He saw her hit Fergus with a hammer. That had to be awful."

From the bits and pieces I'd been able to gather

from Solomon when I visited him in the hospital, he'd hidden from Iris, and was still hiding from her when he met me. But she'd found him the night she'd tried to kill us—he'd managed to get away from her momentarily, and that's when he'd called out to me, but she caught back up to him moments before I found them.

"Man, I'm sorry, kiddo. But he's got you and Higgs. I have every faith you'll help him mend, physically and mentally."

I patted his hand and smiled. I hoped for that, too.

"And the tattoo? I see it's healing nicely."

"It is! Didn't Coop do an amazing job?" I held up my forearm for him to see the tattoo Coop had inked for me. Words I plan to do a better job of living by. *Walk by faith. Not by sight*, in a beautiful script with a cross I'd sketched myself.

Sometimes, when everything is at its bleakest, when you couldn't see the light all around you, you had to give faith a chance, and that's what we'd done.

"My girl sure has a way with ink." Then Knuckles nodded to my foot and the black brace I wore. "How's the foot today?"

I grinned. Thankfully, it had been a clean shot through and through, with no residual damage. I'd heal up just fine, according to my doctor. "It's good. Sort of awkward on a ladder, you know, but the boot will be off in two weeks. I'll manage until then. So whaddya say we go have some spaghetti?"

"Question?"

"Shoot."

"Did *you* make the spaghetti?" Knuckles asked as he looked around at the work we'd done.

I gave him the old eyeball of death. "Why ever do you ask, Donald P. Ledbetter?"

"I ask, Sister Trixie Lavender, because I hear from Coop you can't *give* that chicken noodle meatball soup away—not even to the stray cats. I'm just protecting my innards," he teased, patting his belly.

I held the door to the shop open for him and pointed across the street. "I can't even believe the disrespect I get from you bunch. Get over there, mister, or you'll get no supper at all!" I teased.

He held out his beefy arm with a laugh and I threaded mine through it as we made our way across the street.

Coop rushed up to me, her Inkerbelle's T-shirt hugging her in all the right places, her standard happy grimace in place. "Did you hear? Knuckles bought the building! We don't have to worry about our landlord anymore, Trixie Lavender. I love Knuckles. So-so much. I love our new house. I love our new store."

I smiled at her and squeezed her hand. "Me too, Coop. Aren't we lucky?"

She nodded rapidly, a new expression she'd been practicing while she worked on her smile. "The luckiest. And look," she waved her arms upward at the lights, and then at all the people sitting at the table. "Everyone's here and they're lit."

I covered my mouth with my hand to keep from laughing out loud at her newest slang word. She'd found YouTube with a vengeance, and she'd peppered every conversation with a new word she'd learned since.

"It's definitely lit, Coop. Are you having a good time getting to know everyone?" The people of our community had welcomed Coop and her strange nature with open arms, and for that, I'd always be grateful.

"Oh, I am. They're on fleek. I love them, too. Not like Knuckles and Stevie. It's different love. But I love them just the same. But you know what I love most?"

"What's that, Coop?" I asked, as I saw Detective Primrose and Higgs approaching us.

Her eyes were bright, despite her expressionless gaze. "Spaghetti. I love that more than I even love my sword."

Wow. Big words from my demon. I grinned at her. "Then you'd better go get some, huh?"

With that, she took off to grab a seat at the table next to Livingston, who had somehow managed to become the community mascot without saying a word —thankfully. He sat on the back of a chair, holding court while everyone ooed and ahhed over how beautiful his feathers were.

Of course, we'd never hear the end of it, but if he wasn't complaining about something, he wouldn't be our Livingston.

"Hey, Trixie," Higgs said with a wave of his hand and a warm smile. "I invited Tansy, too. Hope you don't mind."

I smiled at the detective, so casual in her floral

sundress and flat ballet slippers compared to her typical stoic black suits. "The more the merrier. She's a part of our community, too," I said with a smile. And I meant it.

She gave me a skeptical look, her blonde hair lifting in the warm evening breeze. "Not everyone always feels that way, love, you know."

I gave her a confused look, as if I didn't have a clue what she was talking about. "Is that so, Detective Primrose? Well, you're always welcome at Inkerbelle's. Unless you've come to put me in the paddy. Then there's no more spaghetti and wine for you."

She threw her head back and laughed, mouthing the words *thank you* before patting me on the shoulder and heading off to join the rest of our new friends, leaving just Higgs and me.

As I looked at everyone laughing and chatting, and the Eagles played on some speakers Delores had brought, I sighed in contentment. "So how does it feel to be cleared of all charges, Cross Higglesworth?" I asked.

"Better than being called a serial killer, Trixie Lavender." And then he grinned, tucking his hands into the pockets of his jeans.

And I laughed before I sobered. "How are you feeling, Higgs?"

He turned to me then, his eyes warm, and gave my shoulder the lightest of squeezes before letting go. "I feel pretty good, Trixie. Promise."

"And the tat Coop did for you?"

He held up his arm with a grin to show me how she'd turned that tic-tac-doe sign into an extension of the rest of his tattoos. I don't know how she did it, but it blended beautifully. Like mine, she'd done it with her special ink so Higgs would never be troubled with a demon at his doorstep.

"All I have to say is Coop's brilliant."

"You bet she is."

"How about you? Any nightmares?"

If he only knew the kind of nightmares I had living inside me, Iris's attempt to kill us—him—was almost like cake. "I'm okay, too. But let's talk sometime. Okay?"

Higgs didn't readily commit, instead he said, "I almost forgot. Let me introduce you to Jeff." He turned toward the far side of the patio area and whistled. "Hey, Jeff! C'mere, guy!"

Out of the dusk, a spry, four-legged creature shot toward us. Higgs knelt down and greeted him with a grin, scruffing his head with and affectionate palm. "Trixie, this is Jeff. Found him yesterday, rooting around the alleyway, looking for food. Decided I needed a new best friend."

I looked into Higgs's eyes. He'd been back to the alleyway again, which meant he was still reliving that night. But looking down at this tan and white terrier mix, with ears that stood at attention, sprigs of white and tan hair for eyebrows, and a tongue that hung out of the side of his mouth, I thought maybe—just maybe —a good memory would replace the bad.

I reached down and scratched his ears, loving the soft feel of his wiry fur. "Well, hello, Jeff. Do you like spaghetti?"

He panted up at me, his chocolate-brown eyes following mine, making me smile wider. "Aren't you the cutest ever?"

Higgs rose and pointed to the table. "I'm gonna grab a glass of wine. You want?"

Jeff pushed his compact body against my leg as I nodded. "Do I want wine? Does the Pope wear a funny hat?" I teased, listening to Higgs's laughter as he sauntered over to the table where endless bottles of wine sat.

As the dusky purple sky began to turn dark and bruised blue, I watched everyone talking and laughing. I listened to the music play, I saw Coop's head bounce enthusiastically as she chatted with our guests. I grinned as Detective Primrose and Knuckles clinked glasses, and twirled spaghetti on their forks, and my heart filled to bursting.

This was what I'd hoped for all along. It's what I'd hoped for in Ebenezer Falls. What I'd hoped for when we'd first chosen Cobbler Cove as our new home.

This.

"Pssst, Trixie?"

I looked around, unsure where the voice had come from.

"Hey, Trixie! Down here! Down here!" a light, squeaky voice said.

Frowning, I looked down at my feet.

"Yeah, yeah, it's me. I'm talkin' to you."

My mouth fell open and I blinked—but I managed to say, "*Jeff?*"

"Yes! Good human! Hey, listen. I got a message for you."

So look, I know I should be all manner of freaked out, but you have to consider Livingston. He's a talking owl, for Gabriel's sake. And I'm possessed by an evil entity. And Coop's a real, live demon. Not much surprised me anymore.

Instead of giving any thought to the idea that a *dog* was talking to me, I asked, "A message from whom?"

"From Hell, Trixie. From Hell…"

The End

Thank you for joining Trixie, Coop, and myself on our first journey together! I hope you'll come back for more at Inkerbelle's in *Hit and Nun*, book 2 of the Nun of Your Business Mysteries—coming soon!

Chapter 1

"Jeeeff, Jeff-Jeff-Jeff-Jeff, slow down, little buddy," I urged his adorable puppy face, giving him a quick scratch between his spry ears. "You're talking a mile a minute. Take deep breaths."

"Ooooh, yeah," he cooed a groan followed by a happy sigh. "That's nice, Trixie. So nice."

Yes. That's the dog talking. With a Boston accent, by the way. He sounds a lot like Peter Griffin from *Family Guy*. No. I'm not off my rocker. Jeff really is a talking dog. He sort of makes a nice pairing with our talking owl, Livingston. Rather like mac and cheese or eggs and bacon. Except the bacon's a little tough and the eggs are a bit runny.

Jeff sat for a moment at my feet, looking up at me with his soft brown eyes, his white and tan tufted eyebrows so expressive. "Sorry, Trixie. I can't seem to control myself. My words just pour outta me like water from a fountain. I try to slow them down, but my mouth works wicked faster than my brain in this body. I always feel like I'm going to explode."

I reached down and stroked his tan and white head. "I get it. On the inside you're a strong, silent pitbull, but on the outside, you're a yippy, excitable Yorkie who wants to lift his leg on everything, right?"

"Winner-winner-chicken-dinner!" he crowed before letting out a howl he clearly couldn't contain.

I leaned back in my white Adirondack chair and nodded with a smile. "So we'll take it slow. Let's go over this one more time, okay?"

"Alrighty-do, but I'm telling you, Trixie, it's like a block. A big block in this pea brain I ended up with."

I tried not to show my discouragement, but we'd

been doing this off and on for a few weeks now since we'd first met, and I didn't hold out much hope we'd ever find out what the message he was supposed to bring me, courtesy of Hell was. Or if there really even was a message.

Our friend Higgs, who owns the men only Peach Street Shelter or what we lovingly and jokingly call the GUY-MCA, found Jeff rooting around in the alleyway by the shelter, starving and homeless. So because Higgs had recently lost someone very close to him in a way that was nothing short of a painful betrayal of trust, he'd scooped Jeff up and the rest was history. He never went anywhere without him if he could avoid it.

Higgs doted on Jeff like a new father dotes on a newborn—and it was adorable—if not a little disturbing to see a big, tough, tattooed ex-undercover cop like Higgs use baby-talk to coerce Jeff into taking his heartworm pills.

I met Jeff shortly after Higgs found him a few weeks ago at a party we had to get to know our fellow shop owners and neighbors and celebrate Higgs's official release from a murder charge, which is where Jeff first approached me with an alleged message from Hell.

A message he couldn't remember.

Now, after weeks of trying to get him to remember what that message was, I was beginning to think we'd never know, and I'd have to chalk it up to yet another unanswered question in my topsy-turvy world since being possessed by an evil spirit.

If Hell really was trying to reach out to me, and I

can assure you, the evil thing inside me has reached out plenty, then it's crucial I make every effort to leave no stone unturned. I had to know I'd done everything I could to help Jeff remember if I hoped to protect myself from the forces of evil working to consume me.

I don't ever want to suffer another time in my life like I did when I was booted from the convent aka, the great "mooning incident of 2017."

Not to mention, there's video of the incident—in case my shenanigans weren't properly cemented in history by the gossiping all the nuns did when this occurred. I've seen it, making the number two spot on my list of things I hope to never experience again.

I often wondered what it be like for me, for *us*, if Knuckles or Higgs saw me possessed and found out Coop was a demon? Worse, what if a client at Inkerbelle's witnessed me in full on possession? The very thought made me shudder.

Thus, as we sat outside on this warm day in late August, on my tiny deck located right off my bedroom in the guesthouse we rented from our friend Knuckles —a fellow tattoo artist and probably one of the best things to happen to myself and my demon friend Coop since I'd left the convent—I inhaled the scents of his luscious garden and tried to set aside all the bad things that could happen if we didn't check every box and instead focus on this mystery message from Hell.

My eyes zoomed in on the last of the season's beautiful blue and purple hydrangeas, Knuckles so lovingly tended, lining the cedar fencing and thought pleasant thoughts.

Since we'd moved into the guesthouse behind Knuckles main house, and we'd opened Inkerbelle's Tattoo's and Piercings, things had become exponentially better.

We'd found our home here in Cobbler Cove, Oregon. We had a semblance of normalcy these days. We had friends. We had a very small profit in just under a month (mostly thanks to Knuckles and his grizzled tattoo artist friend, Goose).

We were thriving both mentally and physically—all of us—even Livingston, as much as he hated to admit it. We did normal things like have dinner at seven every night unless the shop was open late. We watched television with Knuckles and sometimes Higgs and Jeff —all piled together on the couch here in the guesthouse with popcorn or the snack du jour.

We went for long walks with Jeff and Higgs when the sun began to set and it was cool enough. We laughed. We talked. We joked. And then we got back up and we did it all over again the next day.

And it was bliss. We'd grown so used to merely getting through each day after I'd been booted from the convent; we'd forgotten the simple pleasures of a routine.

Now, if we could just rid me of this thing inside me —release me from its greasy black clutches—everything would be perfect.

Which brings me back to my current dilemma. How to get Jeff to remember the message from Hell?

Clapping my hands on my thighs, I clenched my fists and inhaled, exhaling with determination. "So from the beginning, Jeff. You escaped through the portal that Coop and Livingston escaped from, correct?"

He panted, running in a circle as he tried to catch his tail and said, "Um-hmm." Then he stopped and looked up at me, the morning glare of sunlight making his sweet face particularly adorable. "Why the heck do I do that? Rationally I know, I'm never gonna catch my tail, but I can't stop," he complained in his squeaky voice as he made another dizzying circle.

I scooped him up and sat him in my lap, stroking his spine to relax him. There was nothing Jeff liked more than a good massage.

Instantly, his body became less rigid as he leaned into me. "Better?" I asked as Coop plopped down in the chair next to mine, Livingston my favorite sassy owl on her arm.

"Muuuch," he crooned with a rippling shudder that ran from his head to his hind legs.

"So from the beginning—"

"Aye, lass. Not again," Livingston scoffed his disapproval in his light Irish accent. "I don't think I can do it one more time without losin' my ever-lovin'."

Coop put a finger on Livingston's beak to quiet his complaining—something he does often, by the way.

"You're being rude, Quigley Livingston. It's important we let Jeff share his journey."

Livingston flapped his gray and white feathers, letting the warm breeze catch them. "His *journey*? This isn't Oprah, for the love of leprechauns. Let's not romanticize it as though he found himself at the infamous fork in the road, Coopie. He made a mess of everyting when he escaped Hell. That's no journey, lass. That's a bloody road trip gone sideways. And now, he's somebody's pet. What's left to go on about?"

I poked Livingston in his round belly, filled with far too many Swedish Fish, using a gentle finger. "Technically, *you're* somebody's pet, buddy. Glass houses and all," I teased, trailing my finger over his beak.

"Yes, yes, and I have the gilded cage to prove it. But I don't spend every wakin' hour tellin' ya 'bout my *journey*. Besides that, the poor lad says the same ting every blinkin' time. Nothin' changes. I don't know how much more I can stand."

I leaned over and dropped an indulgent kiss on Livingston's round head. "Then close your ears, Mouthy McMouth."

"Would that I could," he mumbled before giving his head a swivel and closing his glassy eyes—meaning, he was done with us mere mortals and we were dismissed.

Jeff moaned as I stroked his fur, holding his face up to the sun. "So, tell me again how it happened, Jeff. And be careful. We almost got caught the last time you were trying to remember and Higgs walked in on us. I had to pretend I was playing sock puppet with you—with a

Boston accent to boot. Just keep in mind, Higgs is going to be here any minute to pick you up. We can't afford to have him catch you talking."

"But you're wicked good at it, Trix," Jeff said.

I sort of am pretty good at it, if I do say so myself. "How about we err on the side of safety and just not get caught. Higgs would have a heart attack if he knew you could talk."

Higgs didn't like to leave Jeff alone in his apartment for fear he'd get lonely. So he brought him to work with him every day—which was terrific for the shelter. The guys staying there loved him and doted on him as much as Higgs did, much to Jeff's dismay.

But today he'd had a dentist appointment, and he asked us to watch Jeff—which we were pleased to do because we'd come to love him, too—even if he talked at warp speed.

"Hiiiggs," Jeff mumbled. "I like Higgs. He's nice to me. He gives me good dog food. The expensive kind. He gives me scraps, too. Lots of scraps. Yummy scraps. The other day he was talking about getting me certified to become a therapy dog. He talks to me all the time. I don't know how I feel about being a therapy dog, Trixie. I mean, look at what happened to me. How can I help other people when I can't help myself? And then there's my bed. It's awesome. It has a special temperpedic mattress and a heating pad—"

"Jeff…" I said, raising my voice an octave. I didn't want to chastise him, but my patience had begun to wear thinner than thin. I offered to leave things be almost every time we went over how he'd managed to find his way to us, but Jeff is the kind of guy... Er, canine who fits the expression "like a dog with a bone" to a T. He claimed trying to remember this infernal message kept him up at night.

Jeff leaned back against my chest and looked up at me with his big, brown puppy dog eyes. "Sorry. I told you, I don't know how to stop it. Every thought in my fool head just comes out of my mouth."

I took a sip of my coffee and sighed as the warm breeze blew, ruffling Jeff's wiry fur. "I totally understand. So one more time for the cheap seats, okay?"

He let out a soft moan, scratching at his hindquarters with his back leg. "Okay, so here goes. When Coop and Livingston escaped, they opened a portal to Hell that none of us minions knew about until I happened upon it one day. I mean, it was right there—all open and a black hole. I don't even remember how I found it."

I still don't understand how a portal is created or how one from Hell, of all places, ended up in our convent. I mean, a portal to Hell via a convent? I'd always been taught good would win over evil. Wasn't the convent filled with nothing but good? How much gooder did it get than nuns and priests?

I'd always felt protected at the convent from the outside forces working toward the world's demise. But after the tussle that went down that night, if I didn't already have a million doubtful questions about scripture and what I'd learned in my time as a nun, I had a whole lot more since.

One of those questions had to do with the idea that a demon could actually walk on sacred ground. Coop wandered around the convent after saving me as though she'd been baptized in Holy Water and sworn in as the Second Coming. In other words, she didn't have a single problem—which meant we weren't safe from anything if we weren't safe from the occupants of Hell—in a *convent*. Evil exists and it doesn't stop existing merely because a bunch of women wear habits, crosses and denounce the devil on the reg.

Don't get me wrong; no one is more grateful than I am that Coop didn't burn to a crisp upon entering sacred ground. If Coop hadn't come through that portal at the exact moment I was in the midst of being possessed by this evil spirit, it would have eaten my soul. But hello—she's a demon, for pity's sake—foot-loose and fancy free in, I repeat, a *convent*.

I nodded for the umpteenth time at the same exact spot in the story where I always nod. "Right. The portal that led to the inside of my convent, and it doesn't matter how you found it, Jeff. That part of the story is inconsequential."

"Maybe it's not? Maybe the portal means something we don't understand."

Maybe it did. And I said as much. "Maybe it does. But we can't get bogged down with that detail right now."

"Okay," Jeff said. "So yeah, a portal. I didn't know

that's what they called it. It just looked like a big, black hole. Being adventurous in nature, I decided to see what was on the other side. I'm tellin' you, Trixie, the second I stepped through that thing, it closed up tighter than a clamshell. Just poof—gone."

I continued to massage his back, feeling the tension in his muscles as he retold the story. "Right. So you escaped, but you don't know if anyone followed behind you the way you followed Coop and Quigley—or if you all even escaped through the portal at the same time, correct?"

Which scared the ever-lovin' stuffin' out of me. What if Jeff wasn't the only demon to escape Hell? What if far more malevolent forces had escaped along with him and they inhabited the bodies of more road kill like Livingston had—or worse, innocent people like me?

Not everyone has a Coop to save them the way I did.

And what if Jeff didn't really escape at the exact time Coop and Livingston had? His puppy age of around a year says it's feasible. That's how long it's been since I was booted out of the convent, but what if that portal is some sort of time warp—or what if Jeff's confused about when he arrived—and does it even matter? What if I've been watching too many sci-fi related shows on Netflix and they're all in my head, swirling around with crazy conspiracy theories that don't really exist?

"Righty-O. You are correct. After I landed in your

convent, it all gets kinda blurry—sort of like a dream, you know? Bits and pieces all broken up in weird fragments is all I remember. I don't know if I had a body during that time. I don't even know how the heck I got to where I got. I do remember following Coop's scent, and trying to keep track of her and Livingston. But then I don't remember anything else until I woke up next to something warm and fuzzy—something that felt like home," he said on a wistful sigh.

"That would have been you're mother, Jeff. You managed to find your way to a newborn litter of puppies. Likely, one of them didn't survive and you used the opportunity to hop inside its body. You're mother must have been a stray."

"Are you saying my mother was a dog?" he asked on his infectious high-pitched giggle.

Sometimes, Jeff was like a twelve-year old boy right before their voices change and they begin the long hard road to manhood. Which begged the question, what was Jeff before he was a dog and how did he end up in Hell? But alas, he couldn't remember that either.

I laughed, too, because Jeff's laugh was nothing if not contagious. "That's exactly what I'm saying. So what happened next?"

"Well, then I couldn't see much because my eyes were still closed and I wasn't weaned yet." He paused and sighed again. "Ahhh, the good old days when I didn't have a worry in the world…"

"But then you realized where you came from and…?" I coaxed as I looked at the time on my phone.

Higgs was going to be here very soon—we had to get to the point.

"Yeah," Jeff drawled. "I don't know what happened or why I remembered everything that happened that night I got to the convent all of a sudden. I think it was a dream or something... Or maybe I got a whiff of something that smelled like Coop. Yes! That was it. It was the scent of her hair—smells like honeysuckle. There was a whole patch of it by the barn where we were all born. We used to play by it all the time. Musta jarred my memory or something... You know, like déjà vu?"

This was the part of his tale that always made me sad. Jeff had brothers and sisters. Okay, not technically, but in this life anyway—all scooped up by a rescue and taken off to find loving families to adopt them—except Jeff. He'd managed to escape.

However, the scent of honeysuckle was a new memory. Maybe this might actually pan out. It just might take a long time.

Dropping a kiss on his head, I decided maybe it was time to let this story be for a while. "How about we stop for today, Jeff? I don't want you upset when Higgs gets here. You know how he is when he thinks something's wrong with you... You'll be at the vet with a thermometer up your watoosie lickety-split."

His head hung from his shoulders for a moment before he lifted it, his eyes looking off into the distance. "It's okay, Trixie. They were nice rescue ladies. I bet the gang got great homes—my mom, too."

I lifted my face to the warm breeze and nodded. "I'm sure they did. I'd lay bets on it and if you knew where the barn was located, I'd find them somehow and prove it to you."

"And I'd help," Coop offered, sipping the last of her orange juice.

"But I couldn't read back then," Jeff replied. "So I have no idea where the barn was and BTW, Oregon's a pretty big state."

I nodded my head in sympathy. "There is that. So what happened next?"

"After they all got caught by the rescue, I decided to follow the scent because it was so familiar. Little by little, things started coming back to me, like my memories of Coop's escape. So I tracked her for days, lived off the land, took some handouts along the way, somehow avoided getting caught until I got to Cobbler Cove. By then I could read and Coop's scent kept getting stronger and stronger. But the whole time I was hoofin' it across Oregon, something kept nagging at me. One night, just before I got to Portland, I was sleeping in a Christmas tree field and I had a dream, and the dream reminded me somebody saw me escape. It was like they knew I was going to come looking for Coop. Like they knew I'd see you, Trixie. Like they knew you guys were all together. And that's when they told me to give you a message..."

And this was the part that sent shivers up along my spine and down over my arms. "But you don't remember who it was? You don't remember if it was a demon or maybe even the devil himself?"

I gulped nervously, trying to keep my voice calm. The very idea it might have been Satan had me up at night.

He exhaled long and slow, his shoulders slumping in defeat. "Nope."

"Maybe it really was just a dream, Jeff the Dog?" Coop asked as she pulled her dusky red hair up into a bun, her slender fingers twisting the elastic band around her thick rope of hair. "Maybe you didn't really get a message at all?"

"Ya know…" he started then stopped and gave his head a shake, making his ears flap. "Nope. I'm pretty sure that happened, but every time I get to the part where the person is about to tell me what the message is, I wake up. That dream is what helped me remember what happened just before I stepped through that portal, Coop. I know I'm right. That part really did happen. Swear."

Coop reached over and ran a hand over his head, giving him an odd look. This week, she was working on her sympathetic expressions. They still came off a little pained, but she was getting there—and it was better than her grimace of smile by a long shot. That still looked like she'd eaten something bad.

"You're a good boy, Jeff the Dog. A very good boy. Would you like a cookie?" she asked, driving a hand into the pocket of her black leather pants and pulling out a bone-shaped treat.

"I'd rather have a steak."

"But they're the soft ones," she enticed, waving it under his nose.

He scoffed. "Made out of oats and dandelion shoots."

"Higgs just doesn't want you to get fat. You heard what the vet said," I reminded him with a smile, chucking him under the chin.

"Yeah, yeah," he groused. "More exercise, less hot dogs. Does Higgs have listen to everything that crazy old coot tells him? I might look like a dog, but I still have the taste buds of a man, and this man wants a steak. A big, juicy, rare steak."

Coop tapped his paw. "You be grateful, Jeff. Higgs just wants you to live a long, healthy, enriched life. He takes very good care of you. Everyone should be so lucky to have a Higgs."

Coop had fallen in deep like not only with Knuckles but with Higgs. As she watched the way he cared for the men who inhabited his facility, as she watched his dedication to helping feed the homeless, saw him help them with rehabilitation and finding jobs and purpose within the community, her admiration grew.

And I had to admit, mine had, too. We'd come a long way since I'd accused him of murdering our last landlord, Fergus McDuff. We'd definitely become friends in the short time since we'd arrived in Cobbler Cove, and that was really nice.

"Coop's right, Jeff. Higgs only wants what's best for you, bud," I reminded.

"What does Higgs want?" His voice, now not only welcome but familiar, sounded through Knuckles' small backyard.

"Higgs wants to feed Jeff a big steak," Jeff called out, making me lightly pinch him.

"Knock it off, troublemaker!" I whisper-yelled.

As Higgs came around the corner of the main house, he smiled at us. Tall and powerful, his strides ate up the small area from the main house to our little haven. His bulky, tattooed arm swung at his side while the other one held a cup carrier from our favorite coffee place, Betty's, his dark hair trimmed just above his ears, gleamed in the sun.

"Morning, ladies. I brought coffee as a thank you for watching my little buddy."

I gave Jeff a small nudge so he'd remember to greet Higgs the way most dogs would greet the owners they were supposed to love. As a dog, he had some things down pat—others? Not so much. We were a work in progress much like all of us.

Jeff grunted before hopping off my lap and standing on his hind legs, jumping excitedly on Higgs who reached down to give his head an affectionate scruff. "How are you, buddy? Didja miss me?" he asked in that weird voice meant specifically for Jeff.

"You brought the nectar of the gods for us?" I asked, batting my eyelashes at him as I twirled my hair in my comical bid to be flirtatious.

Of course, I was jokingly being flirty. We were just friends, but it was fun to try out some of the feminine behaviors I'd never been able to utilize when I was a nun. I looked ridiculous, of course, but whatever.

He grinned, driving a hand into his pocket as Jeff settled by his feet, winding his tail around Higgs's leg. "It is. I got your favorite, Sister Trixie, and some ice cold OJ for Coop."

Coop peered up at him, her green eyes glittering as she took the orange juice. "You're very nice, Higgs. I like you more every day."

Coop was also working on expressing her emotions to everyone around her—we were still working on what was appropriate and what was a little too Terminator, but we were getting there. Though, I had to give it to my demon. She lived every day like she wouldn't see another, and she spoke her heart in the same vein.

Higgs gave her a pat on the back with his infamous smile, the vivid sleeve tattoo on his forearm of skulls with red bandannas and a colorful eagle taking flight stood out under the morning sun. "I like you, too, Coop. So, you girls ready for World Naked Bike Ride day?"

Every year, Portland hosts a World Naked Bike ride where bikers from all over participate. The route is typically undisclosed until the last minute to avoid gawkers, but we'd heard a rumor, it might pass right by our shop, and we wanted to be ready on the off chance someone might want a tattoo to commemorate their experience.

Plus, Knuckles had some celebrity clients flying in from LA today, and we wanted to put our best foot forward in his honor. I'd been up sketching late into the night so I'd have something new to show his friends.

Coop frowned. "Tell me again why everyone rides bikes with no clothes on, Higgs. Seems to me, your tender bits would get all scraped up."

Higgs threw his head back and laughed, the exposed length of his bronzed throat strong and supple. "I imagine one's tender bits take a beating. However, the ride is sort of a protest against the use of oil and what it does to the planet—and it's also about body positivity. About being comfortable in your skin. Both good causes, right?"

She frowned harder, the lines in her forehead going deep in her tanned skin. "I don't understand being uncomfortable in your skin. I like my skin." To emphasize her statement, she tugged at the flawless flesh of her face.

I patted her on the arm, her long, slender, perfect arm. "That's because your skin is perfect, Coop. Not everyone is as lucky or as comfortable, and we have to try and be sensitive about their feelings," I reminded her, sitting up straighter when I thought about the oozing flesh of my thighs encased in my Bermuda shorts.

Coop cocked her head at me, the length of her neck swan-like. "Everyone should just be happy to have skin. I know people in Hell who don't have any—"

I interrupted her by coughing really hard,

pretending I had something caught in my throat—a clear signal to Coop she was about to spill the beans.

"You know people in Hell, Coop?" Higgs asked, though his face clearly said he was teasing her.

Immediately she sat up straight, recognizing her goof. "Doesn't everyone?"

Higgs laughed his husky laugh and I followed suit.

We couldn't afford to be found out. Not when our relationships here in Cobbler Cove were all so new. I mean seriously, how do you tell your new friends you're possessed by an evil spirit, your owl has reincarnated himself in the body of some random road kill, your best friend's an escapee from Hell and a demon, and the dog your new friend loves so much can talk?

You don't.

That's how.

NOTE FROM DAKOTA

I do hope you enjoyed this book, I'd so appreciate it if you'd help others enjoy it too.

Recommend it. Please help other readers find this book by recommending it.

Review it. Please tell other readers why you liked this book by reviewing it at online retailers or your blog. Reader reviews help my books continue to be valued by distributors/resellers. I adore each and every reader who takes the time to write one!

If you love the book or leave a review, please email **dakota@dakotacassidy.com** so I can thank you with a personal email. Your support means more than you'll ever know! Thank you!"

ABOUT THE AUTHOR

Dakota Cassidy is a USA Today bestselling author with over thirty books. She writes laugh-out-loud cozy mysteries, romantic comedy, grab-some-ice erotic romance, hot and sexy alpha males, paranormal shifters, contemporary kick-ass women, and more.

Dakota was invited by Bravo TV to be the Bravo-holic for a week, wherein she snarked the hell out of all the Bravo shows. She received a starred review from Publishers Weekly for Talk Dirty to Me, won a Romantic Times Reviewers' Choice Award for Kiss and Hell, along with many review site recommended reads and reviewer top pick awards.

Dakota lives in the gorgeous state of Oregon with her real-life hero and her dogs, and she loves hearing from readers!

Visit Dakota's website at
http://www.dakotacassidy.com for more information.

A Lemon Layne Mystery, a Contemporary Cozy Mystery Series

1. Prawn of the Dead
2. Play That Funky Music White Koi

Witchless In Seattle Mysteries, a Paranormal Cozy Mystery series

1. Witch Slapped
2. Quit Your Witchin'
3. Dewitched
4. The Old Witcheroo
5. How the Witch Stole Christmas
6. Ain't Love a Witch
7. Good Witch Hunting
8. Witch Way Did He Go?

Nun of Your Business Mysteries, a Paranormal Cozy Mystery series

1. Then There Were Nun
2. Hit and Nun

Wolf Mates, a Paranormal Romantic Comedy series

1. An American Werewolf In Hoboken
2. What's New, Pussycat?
3. Gotta Have Faith
4. Moves Like Jagger
5. Bad Case of Loving You

A Paris, Texas Romance, a Paranormal Romantic Comedy series

1. Witched At Birth
2. What Not to Were
3. Witch Is the New Black
4. White Witchmas

Non-Series

Whose Bride Is She Anyway?
Polanski Brothers: Home of Eternal Rest
Sexy Lips 66

Accidentally Paranormal, a Paranormal Romantic Comedy series

Interview With an Accidental—a free introductory guide to the girls of the Accidentals!

1. The Accidental Werewolf
2. Accidentally Dead
3. The Accidental Human
4. Accidentally Demonic
5. Accidentally Catty
6. Accidentally Dead, Again

7. The Accidental Genie

8. The Accidental Werewolf 2: Something About Harry

9. The Accidental Dragon

10. Accidentally Aphrodite

11. Accidentally Ever After

12. Bearly Accidental

13. How Nina Got Her Fang Back

14. The Accidental Familiar

15. Then Came Wanda

16. The Accidental Mermaid

The Hell, a Paranormal Romantic Comedy series

1. Kiss and Hell

2. My Way to Hell

The Plum Orchard, a Contemporary Romantic Comedy series

1. Talk This Way

2. Talk Dirty to Me

3. Something to Talk About

4. Talking After Midnight

The Ex-Trophy Wives, a Contemporary Romantic Comedy series

1. You Dropped a Blonde On Me

2. Burning Down the Spouse

3. Waltz This Way

Fangs of Anarchy, a Paranormal Urban Fantasy series

1. Forbidden Alpha

2. Outlaw Alpha

Made in the
USA
Monee, IL

14127125R10185